ICE COLD MALICE

A DCI EVAN WARLOW CRIME THRILLER

RHYS DYLAN

WYRMWOOD
BOOKS

COPYRIGHT

ISBN 978-1-915185-05-1
eBook ISBN 978-1-915185-04-4

Published by Wyrmwood Books.
An imprint of Wyrmwood Media.

EXCLUSIVE OFFER

Please look out for the link near the end of the book for your chance to sign up to the no-spam guaranteed VIP Reader's Club and receive a FREE DCI Warlow novella as well as news of upcoming releases.

Or you can go direct to my website: https://rhysdylan.com and sign up now.

Remember, you can unsubscribe at any time and I promise won't send you any spam. Ever.

OTHER BOOKS by RHYS DYLAN

The Engine House
Caution Death At Work
Suffer The Dead
Gravely Concerned
A Mark Of Imperfection
Burnt Echo
A Body of Water
Lines of Inquiry

No One Near
The light Remains
A Matter of Evidence
The last Throw

CHAPTER ONE

ALEX MAITLAND RAN his bike down the concrete slipway onto the beach with glee. He turned and beckoned to his younger brother, James.

'Come on, Jam.'

James, ten, younger by a year and a half, looked red in the face from the two-mile ride through the marshland to the shore. He stood astride his bike, gulping down water from a plastic bottle.

'Wait for me, Al.' He screwed the cap back on and fought against the buffeting wind as he dismounted.

But Alex was in no mood to linger. They'd made it to the beach. He'd checked yesterday on the *QuinetiQ* website to make sure the firing range was shut and the beach was open. When he'd woken up that morning and found the sun gleaming in a cloudless sky, he knew there'd be no excuses. He'd told their parents they were following the track next to the stream known as Railsgate Pill, towards one of the estuary inlets. A muddy path on a wet day, a glorious bike ride in the dry. One they'd done many times with their dad. But this time, like the big boys they were, they had the entire afternoon to do it alone.

Supposedly.

Alex, however, had other plans.

Once out of the caravan park, instead of taking a left over the cattle grid, they'd kept going, straight down the wetlands and through the gate onto Ministry of Defence land.

Ginst Point drew Alex like a moth to a flame. Remote and wild, accessible only when they weren't testing munitions. Mr and Mrs Maitland had taken them on a blustery *let's-go-for-a-drive* day the year before. James and his mum had been happy to stay in the car rather than get blown away. Only Alex and his dad had braved the August squalls and walked the few yards to the public beach.

It had been deserted, and they hadn't lingered. A five-minute stroll to stretch the legs, his dad had promised. But then Alex saw the signs. Read them in awe. This wasn't just any beach. This beach had secrets. Alex, smitten, dreamt about going back there ever since.

Today was the day.

'Hurry up, Jam,' he urged his brother once again. James arrived, and they put their bikes flat against the pebbles. Alex turned to survey the vast expanse of sand that stretched away in front of them. The tide was halfway in, but still waves lapped a hundred yards away from where they stood.

'There it is,' Alex said, and sprinted towards a yellow sign on a metal board. James joined him a minute later, and the boys stood in wonder beneath it. The sun on their backs, wind whipping their hair while Alex read aloud the information that had thrilled and inspired him the first time he'd read it.

MINISTRY OF DEFENCE

When the beach beyond this point is open to the public,
you must proceed with caution.
Observe the speed limit and comply with the Road Traffic
Act. Do not pick up any object.
It may kill. Report the presence of any bomb or missile to
the *QinetiQ Security Service.*
The use of metal detectors on the MOD beach is
prohibited.

'Wow,' James said. 'Are there really bombs and bullets and
stuff on this beach?'

'There's tons,' Alex replied, his eyes alight. 'They fire
missiles all the time. They'll get duff ones that land unex-
ploded. Must do.'

James stared at his brother. 'A whole one?'

'Yeah. Course.'

'But we don't want a whole one, Al, do we?' James
asked, anxiety angling down the edges of his eyebrows.

'No, just a bit of one. A bit of shell casing or a detona-
tor. We could sell that for shitloads on *eBay.*'

The boys hailed from the outskirts of Bristol, and
Narrowmoor Farm Caravan Park was their regular Easter
and summer holiday destination. With Carmarthen Bay on
their doorstep and the Southern Pembrokeshire coast next
door, so long as the weather was good, there was enough to
do. But Ginst Point remained the jewel in the West Wales
crown for Alex.

'Keep your eyes peeled, Jam. If you see anything, don't
touch it,' Alex ordered, designating himself a munitions
expert. 'Let me see it first. But grab some ammo to throw
at anything we find. That way, we'll see if it's safe. If it
blows up, we run for it.'

The boys ran to the pebbles that spanned an area in

front of the dunes and stuffed their pockets with small, smooth stones.

'Let's go down to the water and work our way back.' Alex started off, pockets bulging.

James didn't move. He'd turned his eyes west to where Laugharne Sands became Pendine Sands for some seven miles.

'It's massive,' James muttered, awestruck.

'That's where they do the land speed thing. Rocket cars and that.'

'Wow.'

'But we're not going over that way. We'll stay this side. Come on.'

The boys started walking with the wind at their backs. The beach was deserted except for some fishermen far off to their right with rods set up vertically in the sand, tips bent with lines deep in the surf. But they were a long way off. Stick men on the far horizon.

'What's that?' James asked, pointing towards a spot at the water's edge where seagulls congregated above a dark unmoving shape.

'Dunno.' Alex put a hand over his eyes to shield them.

The birds kept up a constant racket, wheeling above, and landing on the shapeless blob.

'Could be a whale, or a dolphin.' Alex's voice rose at this suggestion. 'Sometimes they get beached.'

'Is it dead, then?'

'Duh. If it's not in the water then yeah, it's dead. Let's have a look.'

Alex started running. James called after him, 'No, Al. I don't want to see a dead dolphin.'

Alex stopped and turned. 'That's mad. It can't do nothing to you.'

'But it'll probably stink.'

'So? Hold your nose you minger.' Alex pinched his nose in demonstration.

'Let's stick to missiles,' James argued, knowing this battle was already lost.

'Come on. Maybe there'll be a harpoon.' Alex started jogging backwards, his face animated. 'We can stick that on eBay, too.'

James kicked at the sand and reluctantly followed.

The shapeless mass remained formless but got bigger the nearer they got. Shells crunched underfoot and patches of sand were firmer than others. Where it was damp, the boys' footsteps appeared and then faded to nothing as they ran, ghostly and untraceable. James struggled to keep up with his older brother. And all the while the gulls kept up their noisy performance until the boys were within thirty yards. Then the birds finally took flight, squealing out their objections.

James pulled up, hands on his knees, heaving in breaths, but his eyes glued to the object of their quest. 'What's that brown stuff?'

'It's seaweed,' Alex explained.

Tendrils of brown-stalked kelp reached out like the arms of some sea monster from the main mass.

'I expect it got wrapped around the dolphin when the sea brought it in,' Alex added.

He delivered this with a surprising confidence. He found it best to provide explanations when he was with James. His younger brother got nervous, let his imagination run away with him.

'What if that thing moves, though?' James said. 'What if there's something alive in there?'

'Seagulls wouldn't be landing on something alive. No way.'

James wrinkled his nose. 'It stinks, though.'

'It's the rotten seaweed. I told you.'

'Let's leave it, Al. Let's search for bombs instead.'

'We're here now,' Alex insisted. 'We'll take one look and then go back up the beach. Do a sweep. Look' – he pointed – 'there's a big piece of driftwood we can use to poke a bit of seaweed off.'

James retrieved the bleached curved branch and handed it to his brother.

They inched onward towards the clump of seaweed. It was dense and thick, with no sign of anything obvious underneath. James clamped a hand over his nose when they were within poking distance.

'Wow, that's so manky,' he said.

Alex held the stick in both hands and began peeling away the seaweed with clumsy strokes. 'Na, nothing...' He replaced the sweeps with a poke. As the stick hit the centre of the mass, the whole mess moved in response. Alex grinned. 'See that? There's something solid in there.'

'I don't like it,' James said in a voice that made him sound two years younger than he was.

'Here, you take pictures on my phone.' Alex held out the iPhone.

'I don't want to.'

'Come on, Jam. This is part of it. This is our adventure. You said you wanted to come.'

'I wanted to look for missiles.' James dropped his head, his voice petulant.

Alex gritted his teeth. He hated that whining voice his brother used when he couldn't get his own way. 'We will. Honest. But let's get a snap of this dolphin first. We could stick it on *Insta*. We'll get a million likes.'

James sighed, but took the phone from his brother.

With exaggerated sweeps, like waving a cricket bat, Alex slashed at the kelp. After half a dozen strokes, strands of the rotting brown stuff flailed away. He kept at it, providing a constant stream of encouraging words to keep his brother happy.

'Yay, slash the dolphin. Slash the dolphin.'

Despite his misgivings, James laughed and joined in. 'Slash the dolphin. Slash the dolphin. Slash the dolph—'

When his brother stopped talking, Alex was laughing out loud mid slash. He turned to stare at James.

'What?' he asked, expecting him to come back with something rude. But he wasn't saying anything. He was staring, mouth slack, his face as white as the shells beneath their feet.

'Wha-at?' Alex demanded, expecting a silly reply.

'It's not a dolphin,' whispered James. There was something in his voice that made Alex frown. Though he kept a smile on his face, the laughter drained away. James was shaking. He'd dropped the phone but kept his eyes on the point where Alex had last slashed the seaweed. 'Don't look, Al. Don't look,' he whispered.

But Alex, still thinking his brother had suddenly found great acting skills, turned to stare at what James's eyes were glued on.

Through a tangled net of brown leaves, something pale and round was now visible. A moon shaped ball against the streaky brown. Alex leant in to stare, but then froze as his stomach lurched. Not a football, as he'd first thought. Because footballs didn't have mouths with grey lips, or noses with black choked nostrils, or eyes. Or at least something that once might have been eyes.

Memory of the seagulls swooping and pecking with their big sharp beaks, calling to others to join the feast, flooded his mind. But only for a moment before horror gripped him and he reared up and back, legs wheeling until he fell bum-first onto the sand with a thud, unable to drag his eyes away from what he'd seen.

Above, the gulls bugled their objections. The water

lapped as it crept in. It was only a few seconds, but later Alex would admit how it seemed like he sat forever staring as the thing in the kelp looked back with unseeing eyes. He scrambled to his feet, words tumbling from his mouth in a panicked rush. 'Come on, James. We can't stay here.'

He got no reply because James was already tearing up the beach to the bikes, not daring to look back even when Alex called his name.

A slight movement drew Alex's focus back to the thing in the seaweed. A crab scuttled out from under a broad brown frond over the face's forehead, above the point where it stared out with those ruined eyes.

Alex felt the wind gust, pushing him with one faltering step towards the tangled mess. He regained his balance, let out a low shuddering moan, turned, and ran into the breeze after his brother.

CHAPTER TWO

At about the same time that Alex and James Maitland desperately waved down a car in the car park at Ginst Point to report their horrific findings, DCI Evan Warlow sat in the waiting room of Neath Railway Station staring at his bought coffee. He took a sip and grimaced. Whatever it tasted of it was not the 'exotically fresh, heavy and rich' Brazilian blend the glossy posters on the wall advertised.

Not even close.

Next to the cup on the table were his phone and the Sunday paper he'd bought to read on the train back from London where he'd visited Tom, his youngest son. He'd gone up the day before and stayed the night, caught the 11am back from Paddington and should, by now, be on the way to pick up Cadi, his black Lab, from his neighbours. He drove to Neath because it was a mainline station on the Great Western South Wales to London line. A quick two and three quarter hours for the 180miles. The follow-on journey for the remaining 75miles from Neath to Fishguard took two hours on a Transport for Wales trundler.

Bugger that. Much quicker and more convenient to take the car and park it.

And under normal circumstances, he would have walked off the platform into his Jeep Renegade and been on the M4 within minutes.

But not today. Not this trip. Not since his son took the call from Warlow's ex-wife, Denise.

Jeez, Denise, as Warlow had called her. To start with affectionately. By the end, anything but.

It had all gone well the day before. Warlow met Tom in town, and they'd wandered around Oxford Street and Regent Street. Tom needed to do a bit of shopping, and Warlow never minded visiting some of his old Met haunts further east. They ended up in a Hipsterised Shoreditch pub. Warlow laughed when Tom suggested it but had gone along to humour him. The Duck Shoot was the last place Warlow expected to have sat down and eaten in. He remembered it as a place you visited with the genuine fear of someone stabbing you in the eye if you looked at them the wrong way.

It had pleased Tom greatly to see Warlow's genuine surprise at its transformation into a trendy hotspot. After that, they'd found a sports bar and watched a premiership rugby game before heading to Tom's flat in Willesden. Tom's partner Jodie, a nursing sister in Northwick Park where Tom was doing a surgical rotation, greeted Warlow with a hug and the two of them treated him to an expensive dinner in an Asian fusion restaurant. He'd enjoyed the food. Enjoyed the fact that he wasn't paying for once even more. Tom and Jodie were doing well.

'So, Evan, how are you coping being back at work?' Jodie asked when they were on desserts.

'I'm coping well, thank you.'

'Have you finished everything on the cottage?'

'I don't think it'll ever be truly finished. But it suits the dog and me.'

At the mention of the dog, Jodie melted. 'Oooh, Cadi. How is she?'

'She's good. Still wants to lick everyone to death when she meets them, but otherwise she's fine.'

'She looks fit in all the photos, Dad,' Tom added.

'We do a lot of walking.'

'What will you do with her when you go out to see Alun?' Jodie asked.

Warlow didn't answer because he didn't have one. Alun, Tom's brother, lived in Perth. Not the one in Scotland, the one on the other side of the world. Had done for nigh on four years. Warlow had never been for a variety of reasons, each one of them becoming less and less acceptable as time wore on. Initially, it had been his and Denise's separation. Then there'd been the cottage to renovate. Then there'd been the return to work.

'I don't know,' Warlow said after too long a silence. 'How do you two fancy house-sitting?'

'Love to, Dad,' Tom said. 'So long as you give us enough notice. Like a year.' Tom looked at Jodie with an expression that said more about unmanageable rotas than any number of words.

'Right, well, we'll cross that bridge—'

'Just before it collapses,' Tom cut him off. An old joke, but one that earned Tom a smile from his dad.

There was more talk, more smiles, the odd laugh. And Warlow relaxed into it because they didn't talk about Denise. He guessed that Tom and Jodie must have decided this beforehand. Whether to spare Tom's feelings or his, he didn't know. They needn't have bothered from his point of view. Warlow had Teflon-coated his emotions regarding his ex-wife.

But Tom was her son. And he and Warlow had talked about Denise many times and at length without ever quite reaching a satisfactory exit point. So much so that there was little left to say. They'd both witnessed at first hand her drunken temper and manipulative lies. She was an alcoholic in denial. In Warlow's experience, the worst kind.

He felt sorry for Tom because, unlike Warlow, he was emotionally invested enough to keep in touch with his mother. Warlow had no such qualms. He'd been bitten too many times to be shy about it. He'd cut the cord and had no intention of ever trying to splice the bloody thing back together.

On Sunday, Warlow, Jodie and Tom brunched, and he'd taken a Tube to Paddington for the train to Swansea. He'd got as far as Bristol when Tom had rung. Warlow had chosen a quiet carriage and so took the phone to the space between carriages to speak.

'Okay, Tom?'

'Dad, it's Mum.'

Warlow's body tensed. He recognised the loaded mix of panic and desperation in Tom's voice. 'What has she done?'

'Martin phoned. They've arrested her for driving under the influence ...'

The sentence broke off . Warlow wanted to add another word. *Again*. Martin was his ex's current partner and generally the bearer of bad news. 'Jesus Christ. She doesn't even have a licence.'

Tom explained, his words tinged with reticence. 'Martin went with some friends to a shoot. Someone picked him up. When he got back, the car was gone and so was Mum. The police rang him half an hour ago. She was passed out in the car on the side of the road. Dad, I'm sorry to drag you in to this. I don't know what to do. I'm at work at five.'

Warlow grunted. Largely because his brain put up so much resistance to his mouth forming any coherent words.

'Sorry, Dad.'

Warlow's heart stuttered. Here was his son apologising for his own mother's failings. Tom was an adult, but family dynamics never changed. He was still Warlow's boy, even if he was a good couple of inches taller. And you did whatever it took to protect your kids, no matter how much pain it caused.

'You shouldn't have to put up with this bullshit, Tom. We both know that.'

'It's hard, Dad.'

'I know. And I will not mollycoddle her, Tom. That ship has sailed.'

'I know, Dad.'

'Where is she?'

'She's at home now.'

'Let me find out what I can. If she rings you again, don't answer.' Harsh words. But there were no niceties when it came to Denise. In Warlow's mind, it was a simple decision. Black and white. Like a skunk. And you needed to avoid too many conversations with skunks because spraying you with the contents of its anal glands was a reflex. A defence mechanism. And, like a skunk, Denise couldn't help herself. Except that her spray was all emotional.

All Warlow knew was that talking with her left him with an equally bad smell.

They were in Newport by the time the call ended. Warlow went back to his seat and sat as they pulled into Cardiff, then Bridgend, and finally Neath. He justified not calling her from the train because he didn't want anyone else to hear. But now, here he was. Not on the train anymore. No more excuses.

He took a sip of the crap coffee, stood up, threw what was left in the bin, grabbed his overnight case and paper, and walked out into the huge car park. He found her number in his contacts and thumbed the call button, holding the phone to his ear as he walked. She answered in her best, quivery, *I-am-a-damaged-individual-that-needs-everyone's-sympathy* voice.

'Hello?'

'Denise, it's Evan. What the hell have you done?'

'Oh, great,' she sobbed. Her voice was ragged, either from crying or the fags and booze she couldn't help consuming. 'That's all I bloody well need. Evan the policeman on his big high horse.'

A quote from one of his DC's sprang to mind. A response to Warlow suggesting that the best thing to do when you failed at something was to get back in the stirrups. 'I can't ride a horse, sir,' he'd said. Hilarious, but highly inappropriate here.

Warlow huffed out a sigh. 'Is it worth me even asking what the hell you thought you were doing driving somewhere to get shit-faced and then driving home?'

'I wasn't shit-faced. I went to the wine bar for a quick drink. It's the drugs. I'm on some new ones and they don't mix. I only had a couple, Evan, I swear. I had a reaction to the antidepressants.'

'Ding-a-ling, Denise. That's my other leg, in case you're wondering. The one with the bells on.'

That did it. Pierced her I'm-a-victim balloon like a steel lance. When she spat out the reply, the old Denise was back. The vicious one that had somehow crept in like a shapeshifter to replace the girl and woman he had once loved. 'Is that why you're calling, Evan, to gloat? Is that it?'

Warlow ignored her. 'Did you give a breath sample?'

'No. I refused.'

'Blood sample at the station?'

'I told them to get stuffed.'

Warlow stuttered to a halt. This was worse than he'd thought. 'Christ, Denise. Did you get a solicitor?'

'I told them to piss off. It's the drugs. I can prove I'm on medication.'

'You can't prove anything without a blood test.'

'I wasn't even driving the damned car,' Denise barked.

Other people from the train walked past him, hurrying to their vehicles, heads down, sensing the vitriol in the exchange. 'Makes no difference. If you were in the driving seat and the keys were in the ignition, you were in charge of that vehicle.'

'That can't be right—'

'It is. Believe me. And what does it matter if the car was moving or not? You don't have a bloody licence.'

'Yes, but…'

Yes, but. Warlow let silence speak for the rest. He said nothing, allowing enough time to pass for the gravity of her situation to sink in. At least, that was his hope. But in the end, he said, 'Did they charge you?'

'I can't remember—'

'Stop the crap, Denise. Did they charge you?' Warlow snapped.

'They said something about failing to provide a sample for analysis.' The words blurted out. 'I wasn't listening properly. I told you. I'm on medication.'

He squeezed his eyes shut. Charged and without a solicitor. If she'd been within his grasp, he'd have wanted to shake her. One reason he walked away before that temptation got the better of him.

His pulse thrummed in his throat. But he didn't give in to the anger. Way too late for that. 'I'm ringing to beg you not to involve Tom or Alun in this, Denise. This is your problem, not theirs.'

'Tom understands. He's a doctor. He's sympathetic.' She defaulted to pathetic victim mode again.

'He's our son. He's embarrassed and humiliated. He won't ever tell you that, but I can. Christ knows I can…'

He eased off on the anger throttle before it got out of control. Before he crashed and burnt.

Again.

When he spoke next, it was more measured. 'I can't stop what's coming, Denise. Not this time. And I can tell you it won't be good.'

'What do you mean?'

'Driving without a licence or insurance. Drunk in charge of a vehicle. That's bad enough, especially when it's happened Christ knows how many times before. But failure to supply a sample is a different ball game.'

'They can't prove anything. They haven't tested my blood.' Her defiance was still there, but half-hearted now.

'They don't have to.'

'That's not fair.'

A little bomb of frustration exploded in Warlow. 'Fair? You are a liability, Denise. Wake up. Get some help before it's too late. You could have killed someone.'

Denise snivelled. Warlow's words were striking home. Good. They were meant to.

'You hate me. You always have.'

'That's not true, and you know it. If I hated you, why would I be calling?'

She flipped in an instant. 'I'm like this because of you and that sodding job.'

Warlow's smile was rueful. There she was: *When-there-is-no-chance-of sympathy-go-for-the-jugular-Denise.*

'Nice try. But they bounce off now. I've grown armour. Evan the Armadillo.'

'You bastard. You bloody bastard.'

'I'll speak to the CPS and find out what's likely when you go to court. At least you can be prepared. I'm asking you nicely not to burden Tom or Alun with this crap. You made your bed, lie in it alone.'

'Martin says—'

'Martin needs a bloody medal. But he also needs a kick up the arse for leaving you alone with his car keys.' Warlow cut her off.

Silence. Warlow took it and ran with it.

'I'll be in touch, Denise.'

He killed the call and let his pulse subside. A family of four hurried past on the way to catch a train. A couple with their kids: a boy and a girl of seven or eight. Warlow let them pass with a smile and a nod and then stopped to follow their progress. That had been him once. A long time ago, admittedly. And Denise had been that woman. That laughing, healthy, good woman. What the hell happened?

Life happened. Work happened. Vodka happened.

Warlow turned away, pressed a button on the key fob, and the Jeep's indicators flashed once. He slid in and gunned the engine but just sat there, forehead on the steering wheel. It had been a wonderful weekend.

Had been.

Time to go home.

CHAPTER THREE

He waited until the Bluetooth on the phone linked up with the Jeep's sound system and found a number in his contacts conveniently displayed on the dash. A colleague. One that would give him a straight answer.

'Mr Warlow, what can I do for you?' The mock formality of the reply triggered a flicker of a smile in Warlow. He and Bob Callan were on first-name terms. But as a CPS solicitor, a call from a DCI on a Sunday afternoon hardly ever meant good news.

'Bob, I know it's a Sunday. Apologies all round.'

'Evan, if it's you, it's necessary. What can I do?' Bob Callan was an unusual beast. An ex-copper turned solicitor who'd worked for the CPS ever since qualifying. A terrier who had never yielded to the temptation of straying over to the dark side of defending the crap sacks he prosecuted in court.

'Advice only,' Warlow said.

'I see. Phoning for a friend, eh? Spurs are losing two nil. I'm glad of the distraction. Let me leave this house of pain and go into the kitchen.'

Muffled noises of movement and the diminishing clamour of a televised match followed. 'Go ahead, Evan.'

'Refusal to give a sample. Implications?'

'Are we talking at the roadside or in custody?'

'Both.'

'Hmm.' Warlow visualised the man going into solicitor mode. He'd seen it enough times in court. 'Failure to participate in the prelim test at the roadside is four points, or a disqualification and a thousand quid fine. Failure to provide an evidential specimen in connection with a drink-driving offence is an unlimited fine, disqualification, or a custodial sentence. Up to six months.'

Warlow stayed quiet, busy thinking.

'Is that what you needed?' Callan prompted.

'Are aggravating circumstances likely to result in imprisonment?' Warlow asked.

'Such as?'

'Such as having been already disqualified for the same offence and no insurance.'

'Ah, a recidivist.'

'Yep.'

Bob sighed. 'The CPS would probably bring the hammer down. If he, or she, is a danger, then three months inside might drive the message home.'

'Yeah. It might,' Warlow agreed.

'I have a list of defence lawyers who specialise in this sort of thing if you need it?' Callan offered. 'Not something I broadcast, mind you.'

'No, you're alright. I don't need it. As I say, sounding out the nitty gritty.'

'Okay, but as I say, if there's anything I can do.'

'Get back to Spurs. Sounds like they need all the support they can get. I owe you one, Bob.'

'Any time.'

Warlow hung up. He should have taken up Bob's offer

of numbers for the specialist lawyers. Passed them over to
Denise or even Martin. See what might be done to limit
the damage. But so help him, he didn't want to. Because a
part of him thought three months in prison might be
exactly what she needed. There'd be no vodka hiding in a
plastic Evian bottle there.

He headed up the slip road that would take him
through some suburbs and past the CCTA campus, past
the old Abbey on the A465, and on to the motorway.

But he took little or no notice of these landmarks. All
he could think about was sodding Denise. 'Christ,' he
muttered. 'That it's come to bloody this.' The sigh that
followed contained a lifetime of regrets.

———

HE FOUND a radio station and turned the music up, hoping
it might distract him. It didn't. But traffic was light, and he
made good time with no snarl ups on the motorway and its
continuation on the A48 west.

There was no quick way to Nevern, where he lived in a
cottage called Ffau'r Blaidd that had once been a shep-
herd's hut and named for the wolves that hunted the sheep
in those bygone days. So he drove north from St Clears
across the open countryside towards Crymych. He wasn't
one for country drives, but it was a spectacular run through
a sparsely populated area along lanes lined with hedgerows
and views of the Preseli Mountains. He let the journey
take him, a balm for his troubled soul.

'You're going soft in your old age, Warlow,' he grumbled, as he turned off the radio and embraced the silence.

One hour and thirty-five minutes after driving out of
Neath station, Warlow pulled into the well-kempt driveway
of a whitewashed cottage a mile from his own house. The
stone sign on the gatepost read: *Cuddfan*. The literal trans-

lation was a hiding place. And, he supposed, if you didn't know it was here, it might take some finding since it shared a common entry-lane with a couple of other properties much closer to the B road he'd driven along.

The neat garden was surrounded by strong fencing. The kind designed to keep animals out and in. A glossy-black front door opened as he exited the car and a furry black missile raced towards him. He knelt and allowed his black Lab Cadi to do her greeting thing. All out, no holds barred adoration full of wagging, wiggling, and licking.

Warlow didn't object.

'She missed you,' said a voice from the doorway. Maggie Dawes had a good fifteen years on Warlow and the man peering out from over her shoulder, her husband Bruce, had a couple more. But they were fit and weather-beaten from the daily walks they took along the lanes and hills. Two seconds later, a yellow version of Cadi bounded from between Bruce's legs. Bouncer, their golden Lab gave Warlow an equivalent welcome.

When they'd finished, Warlow stood while the dogs took the opportunity of being outside to relieve themselves.

'Has she behaved? Been any trouble?' Warlow asked.

'Of course not,' Maggie replied. 'They've had a whale of a time. As always.'

Warlow had met the Dawes on one of his walks. Kept meeting them as creatures of habit. Cadi and Bouncer were immediate buddies and, when Maggie and Bruce learnt that Warlow sometimes had to go away for work or to see Tom, they insisted on taking Cadi in. Warlow had offered to pay and had been shot down in flames. All he had to do was pick up the phone and drop her off. Cadi never objected. In fact, one mention of Bouncer sent her into a mad dance of delighted expectation. And the Dawes genuinely seemed to love having her.

'How was Tom?' asked Bruce.

'Fit and well.'

'Did he feed you? We have Sunday roast leftovers if you'd like some?' Maggie offered.

'No, I can't. I've been royally entertained.' Warlow tapped his stomach. 'No more room.'

'Cup of tea?' Bruce asked.

The journey had tired him. Talking to Denise and then Bob had depressed him. Tea sounded good. 'Why not?'

Warlow walked across the swept drive into a neat little kitchen with exposed stone walls and a range with a black stove pipe disappearing into the ceiling. A Sunday paper folded open on the crossword page lay on the table. Bruce put the kettle on and Maggie, despite Warlow's protestations, brought out the cake tin.

Lemon drizzle.

He ate two pieces while he sipped his tea.

They talked about walks they'd done and warned Warlow that Cadi, and Bouncer, had eaten something very dubious on that morning's ramble.

'Par for the course,' Warlow said. 'They have stomachs of iron.'

'It might have been something dead,' Maggie said.

'Or something dead that had already passed through a fellow canine,' Bruce added.

'Bruce, that's disgusting.'

'You know what they're like.' Bruce delivered this with a regretful shake of the head.

Warlow had a lot of time for the Dawes. They'd owned the cottage for almost thirty years and, though not local by origin, were now considered part of the community, with Maggie a member of the Community Hall committee and Bruce a coastal path warden. They'd retired from university jobs in Cardiff and flew the Welsh flag on St David's Day and the yellow cross on a black field of St David the rest of the time.

'Have they sorted out those damned Japanese trains, yet Evan?' Bruce asked. 'Last time we went to Bristol, we had to get off at a station to get into the carriage with a loo.'

He was about to answer in the negative when his phone rang. He looked at the caller ID. DI Jess Allanby was a colleague. He sent the Dawes an apologetic baring of the teeth. 'Sorry, I have to take this.'

He walked out into the yard.

'Jess, what's up?'

'How was your trip?'

'Good. Well, it was until I got on the train to get home. But that's another story.'

'You're on the way back then?' She was being polite. But Warlow could tell this wasn't a social call.

'Already here. Why?'

'Something's come up. Or rather washed up on a beach near Laugharne.'

Warlow paused for a beat and examined the sense of reprieve that washed through him. Work. Something he could get his teeth into. Something that might mean not having to think about Jeez Denise for a while.

'Evan?'

'Yeah. I'm listening.'

'It's not pretty. I'm already there.'

'Text me the address. I'm on my way.'

He turned back to the doorway where Bruce had come to see if all was well.

Warlow smiled at him. The dogs came back out and rinsed and repeated a more subdued version of the greeting they'd given him twenty minutes before.

'Problems?' Bruce asked.

Warlow nodded with a grimace. 'Any chance Cadi could stay a bit longer?'

CHAPTER FOUR

A MARKED BMW sat at the turnoff from the main road towards Ginst Point to divert traffic. Idiots were slowing down as they drove past to catch a glimpse of whatever was causing all the excitement.

Warlow's Jeep got flagged as soon as he indicated to turn and a Uniform sauntered over.

'No access today, sir—' he stopped in mid-explanation and grinned. 'DCI Warlow. Didn't recognise the car, sir.'

'Craig, is that you?' Warlow said. 'The hat and the Hi Vis suit you.'

Craig took it on the chin. 'Thank you, sir.' Craig Peters was one of the few traffic officers Warlow knew. Partly because the uniformed constable and Sergeant Catrin Richards from his own team were in a relationship, and partly because he'd helped Warlow out on a couple of cases and been highly effective.

'Is the better half down there?' Warlow asked.

'She is. It's easy to find. Keep going straight on a couple of miles until you get to a T junction. Turn left for half a mile and you'll see the circus.'

'What do you know?'

'Not much. It's a body, male. Not sure how long it's been in the water, but the crime scene lot has been there for a good couple of hours. They may have something useful.'

Warlow nodded. 'Witnesses?'

'Couple of lads. They're staying at Narrowmoor Farm, the caravan park across the road,' Craig pointed to his left. He stood back to let the DCI get through.

Warlow put the Jeep in gear but paused for one more question. 'Don't fancy getting closer to the action yourself? Or are you happy to let Catrin have all the fun?' The constable had been calm under pressure when they'd worked together. Warlow had been impressed.

Craig grinned. 'You never know. The feedback I get from Catrin is good so far. Good, since she's been working with you, anyway.'

Warlow nodded. One of his downturned mouth sage nods. 'Perfect answer, Craig. I see you'll go far.'

Craig laughed and waved Warlow through.

It was late afternoon now. As the road flattened, the hedgerows disappeared to reveal big fields and salt pans and a ridge of low dunes in the distance. He negotiated the open MOD gateway with no red flag flying today and took a left, passing farm buildings – some occupied, others abandoned – to the easternmost point, another gate, and a turning along a stoned lane to a parking area. He recognised Catrin Richards' grey Focus and clocked a couple of SOC vans and a signed QinetiQ vehicle.

Warlow checked his name off with the Uniform guarding the site and followed the female officer's direction to the beach. There hadn't been much breeze in Nevern, but here a south-westerly whistled in. Warlow zipped up his coat. A helicopter hovered out over the estuary, its buzzing waxing and waning in Warlow's ears as the wind wafted the sound away and back again. He headed for the blue tents on the sand, wondering how much of a performance it would have been to get them set up in this wind.

Catrin met him halfway between the car park and the tents. She was a small woman, shapeless in the bulky knee-length coat with fur-trimmed hood tied up over her face. She grimaced and turned away from the biting breeze to address Warlow.

'Lovely day for a walk, sir.'

'Where are you off to?'

'I'm liaising with the MOD lot. They're lending us one of their Land Rovers to get the body away. Tide's coming in.'

'DI Allanby?'

'She's just left, sir. The techs have cleaned up the body. They'll be glad you're here so we can get it off the beach.' Catrin shivered.

Warlow took in the enormous expanse of sand and the distant hills on the other side of the estuary. Somewhere over there, looking back at him, was St Ishmael's with its medieval church and not much else. He wondered how many bodies that Dark Age building had seen wash up.

He tried to remember the last time he'd been to a beach just for the fun of it. When the boys were younger, ten, perhaps fifteen years ago. Was it that long? They'd go further west, park up on his uncle's derelict – now reno-vated – property and head to Newport Beach. The boys loved it there. Rock pools, kayaks, a proper sandy shore. Tom and Alun would exhaust themselves and he'd play beach tennis and cricket and bloody loved it. Denise, meanwhile, would sit in the sun and set out her home-made sandwiches and crack open a bottle of wine.

Always the cooler with wine.

The beginning of the sodding end, if he'd only known it then.

'Okay, we'll catch-up later.' He waved Catrin away. She

turned and trotted off. Warlow turned the other way and ploughed on himself, filing away the bitter-sweet memory and ducking his head against the wind. The flapping of the heavy-duty, blue SOC tent set up a constant reverberation that he didn't need to see to aim for. They'd set larger windbreaks up to protect the area. Warlow followed the cordon tape and came face-to-face with Alison Povey in her away uniform of blue suit and hood. Like Catrin, she'd pulled the material tight around her red-cheeked face.

'I prefer you in white,' Warlow said, yelling above the wind.

'Weatherproof,' the crime scene manager plucked at the material. 'Sweating like a badger. Still, lovely day for a stroll on the beach, Evan.'

'You and Catrin Richards in cahoots?'

'What?'

'She asked me the same thing.'

Povey nodded. Warlow suspected she hadn't heard. He shouted back, 'Where is it?'

'Follow me.'

They'd set the tent up with the entry leeward. At the entrance, Povey offered Warlow a mask. He took it and slid it on over his ears. He'd be glad of it later. It neutered the smell and covered any faces he wanted to pull.

Inside it was calmer, though the gusting wind provided a moaning accompaniment with ropes adding a distracting tympani. Elemental was the word that sprung to mind. Highly appropriate music for viewing the remains of a human being.

Warlow shook these thoughts from his head. What did appropriate mean in these circumstances? He had no idea. All he knew was he'd rather a moaning wind than 'The Birdie Song'.

He'd seen corpses before in all kinds of circumstances. Burnt, smashed, torn to pieces from shotguns. The sights were bad, the smells worse. Sickly sweet earthy stenches that made you gag and sometimes followed you home. And here in the tent and out of the wind, something extra had joined the party. The salty ripeness of rotting fish.

'It's the seaweed,' Povey said, reading Warlow like a book.

'Can't you light a bloody match? That's what my mother taught me to do.'

Povey chuckled. 'If only.'

Warlow clenched his throat. Breathing through the mouth helped bypass the smell cells, but then when you swallowed it was somehow worse. Tom, the ENT surgeon, would no doubt have an explanation.

But no one had an explanation for what had brought the corpse here for Warlow to inspect on this bleak Sunday afternoon. That was his job.

It was a male, no doubt about that. The beard was a giveaway. Grey more than black, but darker than the blue-white skin of the face.

The face.

Catrin could have warned him. As it was, all he could do was blow out air as he took in the open mouth, the slight curl of the lip and the grey teeth…and the eyes. Or what was left of them. One lid was at half-mast but the other was open, displaying a viscid pool of dark, bloody vitreous spilling out from the ruin of one pupil.

'Gulls.' Povey said matter-of-factly.

Warlow grunted.

He turned his attention away from the face to the body. It remained clothed. A waterproofed jerkin and trousers. Both of the same make. Not expensive, but good enough for outdoors. One foot was bare, the other wore a boot. Again, a make that Warlow recognised. Mid-range but acceptable.

'Dressed for outside. Any idea of cause of death?'

'Are you asking me if this is a drowning or something else?'

'I'm asking for you to point me in the right direction.'

'Come around to the side.'

Warlow followed Povey who squatted at the head end. That bought Warlow close to the very thing he would have preferred not to be looking at. Some of the skin on the side of the face had come away to reveal grey flesh beneath, but Povey was pointing to a flap of scalp that had curled back on itself, exposing some white skull and a telltale crack on the surface.

'He may have drowned. But this could not have helped.'

'So, fell and cracked his head and then drowned?'

'That'll be for the HOP.'

Warlow wondered about that. The Home Office pathologist liked to look when there was doubt over a cause of death. 'Where is he, by the way?'

'Too far away to get here before the tide comes in. We need to get a move on.'

'So, assuming this wasn't an accident—'

'As you do,' Povey added with a grin.

'Anything else of any help?'

Povey shook her head. 'The tide brought him in and, if we don't get him away from here, it'll take him back out again.'

Warlow stood up. 'You've spoken to Jess Allanby?'

Povey nodded. 'She had the first peep. Also had the pleasure of watching us take out his wallet. The big reveal.'

'So we know who he is?'

Povey frowned. At least that was what the slight movement of the inch of forehead visible under her hood suggested to Warlow. 'You mean they haven't told you?'

'Told me what?'

'Detective Chief Inspector Warlow, meet Malcolm Boscombe.'

Warlow blinked. The name rang a big, noisy bell. 'The surgeon?'

Povey nodded.

Now Warlow understood why everyone was treating this with a hefty dose of suspicion.

His phone rang before Povey could say more.

Warlow stood, more to get away from the smell than anything, and put his finger in one ear to take the call.

'You're not going to sing a sea-shanty, are you?' Povey quipped.

Warlow sent her a scathing glance as Jess's voice came through the ear piece. 'Evan? Have you seen it?'

'Jess, where are you now?'

'About to go into Boscombe's house.'

'Where is that?'

'Near Amroth.'

'Can you wait? I can be there in twenty minutes.'

'Have you seen him?'

'I'm with Povey at the scene now.'

'What do you think?'

'Fishy,' he said, and ended the call.

From behind him, Povey said, 'Oh very good, Evan. Mind if I use that one?'

'Be my guest,' Warlow said, halfway out of the tent. He barely heard Povey shout at him before the wind took her words.

'But it's the seaweed, I'm telling you…'

CHAPTER FIVE

WARLOW PUNCHED the postcode Jess texted him into the car's satnav. He waved to Craig when he pulled back out on the B road, this time pointing the Jeep west through Pendine towards Amroth with its long stretch of groyned sandy beach parallel to the road. It even had a castle of sorts – didn't everywhere around here? The satnav sent him inland after that, along single-track roads past isolated farms and the odd bungalow until he turned back towards the coast for a quarter of a mile and found a lopsided sign on a rotten gatepost that read Moor Cottage.

He parked up next to Jess's Golf outside a stone barn that could have been spectacular but wasn't. The DI got out of her car as he pulled in. She tugged on a woolly hat and zipped up a windproof jacket.

'This his?' Warlow asked.

'Rented. Gil's trying to contact the landlord.'

Warlow nodded, and both detectives walked across a yard gone to seed. Towers of wooden pallets had been stacked in one corner next to a pile of uncollected black refuse bags. Patches of grass grew through the paving blocks that were mud stained in one corner where standing water hadn't drained away after recent rains. The small front windows needed cleaning and varnish was peeling off the front door. Warlow pressed the bell and listened.

No answering chimes.

He pulled back the rusted lion's head knocker. The hinge squeaked its resistance until he added some force. After two goes, it thudded against the backplate with a resounding crack. He knocked three times. Loudly.

Let there be no doubt that the people outside meant business.

He repeated it twice more, adding a shouted, 'Police,' after the third.

No reply. 'Do we know if he lived alone?' Warlow asked.

'We don't. In fact, we know very little other than what the press printed when his case went to court.' Jess walked to another window and peered in.

Warlow stared around at the sorry little property, recalling the case that made national news. 'What did he get, two years?'

'Twenty-three months. Served three before getting out on appeal.'

'Where was that, Cardiff?'

'Yep.'

'How long has he been down here?'

Jess shrugged that she didn't know. Behind them, a blue Mercedes SUV pulled up. The man who got out wore raspberry corduroys and a Viyella shirt under a tweed jacket. He was short and compact, with a polished face under a hairline that was rapidly retreating from his forehead.

'Detective Inspector Allanby?' he asked, fumbling with the armhole of a waxed jacket he managed, after two attempts, to slide on.

'Mr Jennings?' Jess replied.

'That's me,' Jennings said.

'This is Detective Chief Inspector Warlow.' She gestured towards the DCI. 'Mr Jennings runs the letting agency that manages this property.'

Jennings made a face. 'Not one of our most prestigious lettings, I'm afraid.'

'Who owns it?'

Jennings fiddled with the zip on his coat. 'A farm estate. The owner is quite elderly. The entire estate will be sold… eventually. For now, they're trying to maximise revenue with long-term rentals.'

'I didn't think it had much Airbnb pizazz,' Jess commented.

'No indeed. There is a great deal of competition in the holiday cottage business these days. I'm afraid the owners would need to spend a little money to get this place up to standard. Still, the current tenant does not seem to mind.' Jennings dropped his voice. 'Though, he is not the most regular of payers.'

'Oh?' Warlow prompted.

'Three months in arrears, in fact. It did not surprise me when your phone call was in relation to this property, shall we say?'

'How so?' Jess asked.

Jennings cleared his throat. 'There's been some friction between the tenant and the owner's representative. By that, I mean the owner's daughter, who has been keen to see this property show some return.'

Warlow nodded. 'We need to get in.'

'Is no one answering?' Jennings frowned.

'No,' Jess said.

'Have you tried ringing Mr Boscombe? I think I have his number.' Jennings reached inside his coat to a jacket pocket.

Warlow stepped forward and gave Jennings one of his

best stop-arsing-around glares. 'Mr Boscombe was found dead this afternoon. We have not yet told his next of kin. I'm sharing this with you on the understanding that you will not reveal this information until we release it. Can you do that, Mr Jennings?'

The letting agent's mouth dropped open and his ruddy complexion blanched. 'Oh dear…Oh, yes. Of course.'

'Good. We're hoping we can find out who to call inside. If you wouldn't mind.'

Jennings fumbled with the keys he'd held in his hands since exiting the car and stepped towards the front door. 'No, I mean…yes, certainly.'

The officers stood back and donned nitrile gloves while Jennings slid the key in, and with the front door open, Jess told Jennings to wait outside.

Things were not much better inside. A dingy living room with outdated furniture and a not very wide-screen TV gave on to a dark kitchen with a sticky floor. Unwashed dishes sat piled in a plastic bowl in the sink. If this was the place Boscombe was calling home, he needed to look up the word in the dictionary.

Warlow studied the fridge for Post-it Notes or telephone numbers but found nothing. One chair at the small table had become a repository for newspapers. He picked one up. Dated two days ago. He estimated a good month's worth lay on the seat. But he and Jess were not there to carry out an extensive search. Warlow was looking for signs of violence or a struggle.

'I'll go upstairs,' Jess said. 'Let's hope I don't catch anything.'

Warlow walked through to a mud room at the rear. Some wellies, another couple of coats, and some fishing equipment were all he could see. He opened the back door and stepped out into a small garden that needed as much, if not more, attention than the front. The grass on either side of a concrete path needed cutting a good two summers ago. But at the bottom he spotted a big shed the shape of a loaf with curved corrugated walls and a roof made of U-shaped lengths of tin.

The door, more corrugated tin screwed onto a heavy wooden frame, looked solid and padlocked shut. Warlow walked around to the side where he fended off the branches of a tree and cupped his hands around the glass to look inside. What little light there was seemed to come from this one window and a skylight towards the rear of the shed. All he could make out were vague rectangular shapes. The place wasn't empty then.

'Evan, you ought to see this.' Jess's voice drifted down from the first floor.

The stairs creaked as he took them. He noted the glossy cream spindles, and a patterned carpet with heavily varnished balustrades. A stained Turkish rug ran the length of the landing floor. Jess stood in the doorway of the last room along, looking in.

Warlow joined her and stepped through into a freshly painted room with slatted blinds over the windows and a large modern made-up bed. The plain duvet cover looked expensively ruffled.

'Linen,' Jess explained, picking up on Warlow's confusion.

To the right, an adjacent room had been set up with a desk, computer, and two certificates hanging on the wall, attesting to Boscombe's previous existence. Channelled cables ran from the computer to a router that blipped a green light at him. What struck Warlow was how clutter-free this room was compared with the rest of the house. The only other furniture comprised a wardrobe and a mirror.

'I think this is where he spent his time.' Jess picked up a list of names and glanced at it. She nudged the mouse, and the screen came to life displaying an animated logo entitled *Alternis*.

'I'd spend most of my time here too, given the chance.' Warlow walked to the side of the bed and pulled back the covers. Two memory-foam pillows side by side, but only one had a slight darkness to it in the shape of a head. 'Looks like he slept alone.'

Jess walked to the one remaining door and opened it. 'The bathroom looks tidy, too.'

'My guess is he spent a bit of his own money here. Whether or not with the landlord's permission, he made a nest for himself.' Warlow retraced his steps to the kitchen and began looking for somewhere that might hold keys. Jess joined him after poking through the other upstairs rooms.

'Anything?' Warlow asked.

'No. Nothing suggestive of an altercation.' She peered around the dingy room. 'Other than the bedroom and office, he must have missed the lecture on personal hygiene at whatever medical school he attended.'

'I'd like to think this is one man's mess. If it isn't, his housekeeper needs to retrain. Or get an eye test.'

Jess wrinkled her nose. 'I don't know how people can live like this.'

'You need to lower your expectations to my level, DI Allanby. It's never a problem then.'

Jess sent him a toothless smile.

Warlow picked up a cracked vase and peered inside. 'There's a locked shed at the back. A big one. I'm looking for a way in.'

The DI nodded and joined the hunt. Three minutes later, she called from the mudroom. 'Found them.'

She pointed to a battered-looking blue box screwed to the wall and hidden by a yellow raincoat. She pulled back the door to reveal a bank of nine hooks, two of which held bunches of keys. Jess picked one up and peeled them apart on her palm.

'Front, back, don't know, don't know, padlock.'

'Worth a try,' Warlow said. He led the way back to the corrugated shed. The key fitted and the lock opened smoothly. 'Well used and oiled,' he muttered, as he unclipped the padlock and used the hasp as a handle. The door opened outwards and late afternoon light lit up a workshop.

All three of the inner walls were lined with sturdy workbenches. A chest freezer hummed in one corner. Sacks of what looked like plant material sat under some benches. Warlow stepped in, picked up a sample, and sniffed. Not what he was expecting. Definitely not marijuana.

Under the benches to the rear, Warlow's eye caught an array of pressurised gas cylinders with tubes leading to some machinery. Next to the cylinders squatted a couple of Dewar flasks.

'Look at this,' Jess said. She'd gone right and was holding up a printed sheet picked from a pile on the floor. Warlow stepped closer. There was only one sheet, but it looked like it could be folded into a leaflet. A photo of a beach with lots of foliage and above it the words,

"ALTERNIS. The natural way to health."

Warlow looked from Jess to the workbenches and to the fridge.

'Legitimate business or something else?' Jess voiced his thoughts.

'Hardly *Breaking Bad*, but we'd better inform Povey. Get this lot looked at properly.' He picked up a packet of herbs and put it down again.

Jess nodded. 'You think this could be drugs?'

Warlow blew out his cheeks. 'Christ knows. He was doing something in here, that's for sure. Whether it's illegal, someone else needs to find out.'

'I'll give Catrin a ring. Maybe a couple of crime scene techs can come up here once they've finished on the beach.'

Warlow nodded. 'Probably better we don't tramp around here anymore or Povey'll have a fit.'

He stood outside while Jess phoned Catrin. The only thing he was certain of after having visited Moor Cottage was that Boscombe had no interest in gardening. But then neither did the owner, judging by the windblown litter and the weeds. Maggie Dawes would have a fit.

Jess joined him, pocketing her phone. 'They're driving the body up the beach now. Povey's team are packing up and coming straight here.'

'Good. That'll mean a visit to Cardiff for the post-mortem. Any idea who's doing it?'

'Sengupta,' Jess said.

Warlow brightened. 'She's good. No-nonsense. None of the posturing of the other three HOPs. Have you worked with her?'

'No,' Jess said.

'I'll go up if you like. I'll take Rhys. Best he gets one under his belt.' DC Rhys Harries was the youngest of the collection of officers who made up the Warlow/Allanby team that Superintendent Sion Buchannan had put together. Originally, so that Jess could get some big cases under her belt as part of her training to be a Senior Investigating Officer. But their recent successes had made the powers that be keep the squad together whenever Warlow caught a case.

There'd been no complaints from him.

'Yes, Rhys needs some exposure. But I'll take him,' Jess replied. 'The post-mortem is in the afternoon, and I said I'd pick Molly up from Cardiff Station around five. Saves her an extra three hours on the train.'

Warlow recalled a conversation about Molly Allanby

visiting her father. 'She's up in Manchester for a long week-end, right?'

'She is.'

'And how is that going?' Warlow also recalled that this was Molly's first visit to her father since Jess and he had broken up.

'He got tickets for a game. It was the only way she'd go. I've not asked. I've not pestered. I'm expecting a candid report tomorrow.'

Warlow raised his eyebrows. He knew Molly. Candid was an understatement when it came to the way the almost-seventeen-year-old dealt with most things. He said no more on the matter and retraced his steps, careful not to touch anything else. 'Why don't we lock the shed and leave the keys with our man in the raspberry cords? He can stay here until Catrin comes.'

It wasn't so much a request than an order Warlow gave Jennings as he handed over the keys. 'Until we know better, we assume this a crime scene. No one enters until Sergeant Richards arrives and picks these up, understand?'

Jennings nodded. 'Was Boscombe…?'

Warlow laid on the schmooze. He guessed Jennings was the type of bloke who revelled in being made to feel impor-tant. 'I can't give you any details of the investigation, Mr Jennings, as I'm sure you'll understand. But your help and cooperation would be appreciated.'

'Of course. Anything,' Jennings said, eager to please.

Jess called to Warlow. 'I'll follow you. Assuming you know the way to the campsite.'

'I do not. But I know a man who does.' Warlow slid into the Jeep's driving seat and headed back towards the turn off to Ginst Point.

CHAPTER SIX

WARLOW HAD CRAIG PETERS' number. He rang and got directions for the Narrowmoor Farm Caravan Park.

'The Maitlands are in number 107. Take the right fork as soon as you get through the entrance. They're at the end.'

'Thanks.'

'Find anything in Amroth, sir?'

'So much for confidentiality.'

'I...uh...' Craig floundered.

Warlow put him out of his misery after five excruciating seconds, through which he enjoyed a Cheshire Cat grin at the thought of the PC realising his blunder. 'Only kidding, Craig. Good to hear Catrin's keeping you abreast of the investigation. In answer to your question, nothing much. Some kind of business enterprise and a room set up for online working. We'll know more once Povey's given it the once over.'

'Right you are, sir. Oh, and the kids had a rollicking from their parents for being on the beach. They weren't supposed to be there. Thought you ought to know.'

'Their names?'

'James is the youngest. And then there's Alex.'

Warlow filed them away. 'Useful information. Thanks.'

Warlow drove into the park under a wooden archway. He recognised the Hamden Holidays logo. They were a national company, so Narrowmoor Farm was not a small concern. The place stood in stark contrast to Moor Cottage, with manicured grassy areas and topiary on every bend. The caravans were spaced well apart with trees forming screens between them. He wondered if you paid more for the secluded stands. The homes were all statics; identical green boxes in a line on one side, radiating out from a lawn area where he'd taken the fork on the other. He looked for the right number and pulled up. Jess's Golf appeared in his rear-view mirror.

'Not bad,' she said when they both stood looking south at the sea view over a bank of carefully trimmed shrubs. An upright post near a gravelled walkway had the number 107 painted on a driftwood sign.

'If you like that sort of thing,' Warlow said. 'Bit too sterile for my liking.'

The door of the caravan opened before they'd even taken a step towards it. A man and woman emerged and stood on the wooden post and rail decking outside the front door. They were dressed for the weather in fleeces and jeans, but it was their footwear that gave them away. The man in flip-flops, the woman in wooden mules. Indoor footwear which suggested they were encamped and not venturing anywhere on foot.

The woman folded her arms and said, 'If you're from the newspapers you can forget it. The boys are not talking to anyone.'

Warlow grinned. He liked the Maitlands already.

Jess stepped forward and brandished a warrant card. 'Mr and Mrs Maitland, I'm Detective Inspector Allanby and this is Detective Chief Inspector Warlow.'

A look of momentary horror gave way to hurried explanations. The press had already got wind and the site manager had been down with messages from various news sources three times already.

'Should have realised. Sergeant Richards said you'd be calling. Sorry.' Mrs Maitland's hand went to her neck where it worried at the V of her sweater.

Warlow picked up on the Bristol burr and shook his head. 'No need to apologise. And you're right, James and Alex do not need to speak to anyone except us. They here?'

They followed the Maitlands inside. The two boys were sitting on a sofa in a remarkably spacious lounge. Warlow had never been inside one of these statics before, and he took the opportunity to look around. His experience of caravans had hardly been five-star. Once, he'd taken a cramped one-room traveller with a girlfriend up to Aber-dovey. It rained the entire week, and he'd never enjoyed card games since. And he and Cadi had lived in a caravan on the building site that was now his home while he toiled at the renovations. Any romantic notion about the gypsy existence had soon buggered off never to return after a couple of months of that.

But this was a different animal. Bright and modern. It even had a bloody chandelier.

'Hello, boys.' Jess's greeting brought him back to the two interviewees waiting on the sofa.

After a brief silence, Mr Maitland stepped in. 'Well, say hello. Like I said, you brought this on yourselves. These police officers need to speak to you now.'

'Hello.' The boys spoke as one. Owl-eyed and unhappy.

Warlow was a dad. He knew the score here. The boys had transgressed. Broken a rule and gone somewhere they shouldn't. Mr and Mrs Maitland knew that his and Jess's presence in their caravan might well have had a very different connotation with two boys missing. So he could appreciate the tone. But he didn't want to be the bad man here. Things would go much smoother if the kids were on their side.

'Cup of tea?' asked Mrs Maitland.

'Milk and one,' Warlow answered without having to think.

'A dash of milk only for me, please,' Jess said, more politely.

While Mrs Maitland fussed in the well-appointed kitchen, Mr Maitland sat next to the boys. Warlow sat opposite in one armchair, Jess in the other.

'This yours?' Warlow asked with a vague hand wave.

'I wish.' Mr Maitland shrugged. 'Timeshare. We've got a week at Easter and two in August. Works out great with the school hols.' He looked at his sons and raised his eyebrows as a signal to them to speak.

The older of the two, Alex, looked at Warlow, swallowed and said, 'I'm sorry.'

Warlow frowned. 'For what, Alex?'

The boy looked on the verge of tears. 'I poked it.' He squeezed his eyes shut before correcting himself. 'I poked him. The dead man.'

'With a stick?'

Alex nodded unhappily.

'I expect I'd have done the same. You didn't know what it was, right? You thought, a dead dolphin perhaps?'

Next to Alex, James's younger eyes lit up. 'That's what we thought it was. A dolphin.'

'Natural thing to do.' Warlow nodded. 'And that's exactly the sort of information we need.'

Mr Maitland frowned at this change in the narrative, but Warlow didn't break eye contact with the boys.

'Let's get one thing straight. Neither of you are in any

trouble. And thank you for talking to us. I'm sure you must be fed up with repeating this story.'

James nodded and smiled. Alex looked a lot less miserable. It was Mr Maitland whose puzzled expression descended into disappointment. He let Warlow have his two penn'orth.

'I have warned the boys about going off alone again. It's not like them and they will be punished.' Maitland's expression stayed stern.

'Looks like having to sit here and talk to us is punishment enough,' Warlow said.

Mrs Maitland brought the tea. Warlow took a sip, nodded and said, 'So, Alex, can you remember what time you got to the beach?'

'They left here at just after one…' Mr Maitland began, but Jess put a hand up to stop him.

'It would be better if you let the boys answer, Mr Maitland.' She said it kindly, but in a way that left nothing open to discussion.

Mrs Maitland sat on the arm of the sofa and put her hand on her husband's shoulder. 'I'm sure it'll be alright, Paul.'

Her husband nodded.

Alex looked at James and said, 'About half-past one, I think.'

'And why did you go there? Just for a spin on the bikes, was it?' Warlow took another sip of tea.

Alex nodded. But James filled in the gaps. 'We were looking for treasure. Bits of shells. It's an ammunition site.'

'Munitions,' Alex corrected him.

'We were looking for somethin' we could sell on eBay,' James gushed.

Next to them, their father shook his head. Mrs Maitland rolled her eyes.

'So you went on an adventure?' Warlow probed.

James nodded. Alex kept his eyes down.

'And how soon after getting to the beach did you see what had washed up, Alex?' Warlow wanted to include the older boy who looked cowed by his dad's remonstrations.

Hearing his name did the trick.

Alex looked up. 'Almost straight away. The tide was way out. I said we should go to the water's edge—'

'And on the way we saw the seaweed we thought was the dead dolphin,' James jumped in.

'And what made you think that?' Warlow asked.

'We've seen dead dogfish on the beach before,' Alex explained. 'But this was bigger, so I thought maybe it could be a dolphin…' His words tailed off as he glanced at his father.

'That makes sense,' Warlow said. 'And then what?'

'We went to investigate,' Alex said.

'We found a driftwood stick to test it with. That's because of the loads of seaweed,' James took up the baton, living the moment. 'The seaweed was mingin', so we tried to get it off.'

'That's when I poked it with a stick and we saw it wasn't a dolphin,' Alex added.

'That's when we ran back up the beach to get help,' James said.

Warlow nodded. 'Was there anyone else on the beach when you got there?'

James and Alex looked at one another. 'There were some fishermen way off in the distance. No one on the beach near us,' Alex replied.

'What about the car park?'

'Two cars,' James said. 'No, one of them was a van. A white one and a silver car.'

Jess had her notebook out, jotting down the details as they went.

Warlow took another sip of tea. The one sugar must

have been heaped because it tasted sweeter than he usually took it. But there'd be no complaints from him. 'What about in the sea? Any boats that you saw?'

'No boats. There was a tanker but miles out,' Alex said.

'We thought we saw a whale,' James said, looking at his brother for confirmation. 'Remember?'

Alex nodded. 'James said whale. But it didn't go back under. Just a shape, like a hump in the sea, drifting. And a long way out.'

'Okay, so not a whale, but a kind of hump in the sea?' Warlow probed.

'Yeah. But then we saw the…the man, and we didn't look at the hump after that.' Alex recalled the moment unhappily. 'I'm really sorry I poked him.' A big, silent tear ran down his face.

'Well, I'm glad you did,' Warlow said.

Alex blinked at him.

'What if you hadn't?' Warlow continued. 'What if you'd walked away? We'd never have known about Mr Boscombe. That's the name of the man you found. The tide might have come back in and taken him away. Then where would we be?'

'Aren't you mad?' James asked.

'What's to be mad about? You two boys have been an enormous help to us. You should be proud of what you did. You're a credit to your parents.' Warlow looked into the adult Maitlands' faces. Mrs Maitland tried to blink away her confusion. Mr Maitland's old anger gave way to surprise.

'You have a phone, Alex?'

Alex nodded miserably. 'James dropped it.'

Warlow smiled. 'If it's on the beach, we'll find it and get it back to you. Don't you worry.' He turned back to Mr Maitland. 'I had a rule with my two. They could go off and do what they liked so long as they texted every fifteen minutes.'

'You've got boys, too?' Mrs Maitland asked.

'A lot older than these two, but yes. Two boys. So I know exactly how it is.' He turned back to the young Maitlands. Alex no longer looked miserable. He looked exactly like his dad, surprised and a little confused. He'd obviously been expecting a dressing down.

Well, let a bad day end with some element of pleasant surprise at least.

Warlow took one more gulp of tea and stood up. 'Right, that's more than enough questioning for one day.' He walked across the room and shook the boys' hands. 'Someone else will be along and write down everything that you've told us. That's only us being extra careful and so that we don't miss anything. I can't give you any treasure from the beach. I'm short on shell casings. But I can give you the Police Service's gratitude for being good citizens. Oh, and the standard reward.' He reached for his wallet and took out a couple of fivers and handed one each to the boys.

James was a grinner, anyway. The money simply made his stretch a lot wider. But Alex looked genuinely perplexed.

'Take it,' Warlow urged.

'Thank you,' whispered Alex, a shy smile banishing the tears of earlier as he took the offered money.

He thanked the Maitlands for their time and reached for his coat from the backrest of the armchair.

Outside, the wind had freshened a little more, if that was even possible. Warlow pressed his keys, and the indicators blipped on the Jeep. Jess was right behind him. He turned as she reached the cars. 'I suggest we leave it there for today. Let's get an early start. See what we've got by then.'

She didn't answer. Warlow looked up to see her staring at him with narrowed eyes.

'What?' he demanded.

'That,' she nodded back towards the caravan with a hint of admiration in her voice. 'You got the older boy to open up. I didn't think he would.'

'Years of practise,' Warlow said.

'Really? So you're not just a big softie then?'

'You believe what you want to believe. I told you, I like kids.'

Jess smiled. 'But you can never eat a whole one.'

Warlow grimaced.

'I know, old joke.' She turned away and strode off to the Golf. 'See you tomorrow, Evan.'

CHAPTER SEVEN

FOR THE SECOND time that day, Warlow pulled in to Maggie and Bruce Dawes' property, Cuddfan. There followed another five-minute, full-contact, tactile greeting from Cadi, but he turned down the offered tea and cake because he was keen to get home. He hadn't eaten properly since brunch and hunger gnawed. Not for the first time, it was as if these good people read his mind. As he walked through the door to get Cadi into the Jeep, Maggie pressed a Tupperware box into his hands.

'Sunday lunch. We had far too much left over. Five minutes in the microwave.' She beamed at him.

'Maggie, there is no n—'

'Nonsense. I don't suppose you've eaten all day, have you?'

'Brunch and now your cake.' He'd meant it to sound as if he'd had enough but his salivary glands flooded at the thought of the food in the box. He knew, in an instant, that he'd lost the battle.

'Exactly. Go on, it'll save you cooking.'

She was right. He smiled gratefully. 'Any chance I can bring her back tomorrow early?'

'I'll be up,' Bruce said. 'I'm awake with the birds. No trouble.'

Warlow thanked them again and headed home to Ffau'r Blaidd, his renovated cottage that, much to everyone's amusement, translated into Wolf's lair.

It was well after dark when he arrived and parked up under the bright security lights his arrival had triggered into action. Warlow picked up the post from the doormat as he entered and put it on the kitchen table. He gave Cadi some water, plated up Maggie's Sunday lunch and, while it heated in the microwave, had a quick shower.

Seven minutes later, he was munching through pork loin with roasties, broccoli, and carrots and skimming through his correspondence. He'd gone paperless as much as he could for utilities and banking. His post was now from people trying to sell him things or officialdom requiring physical bits of paper to give credence to a message sent. Oh, and the odd bit of fan mail. Or, to give it its proper title, despise-you-with-a-vengeance mail.

He opened the official envelope first. This was from West Midlands police force telling him they'd been tasked with investigating criminal activity in relation to Detective Sergeant Mel Lewis. Warlow stopped eating. He'd known this was coming. Even so, it made for sober reading.

Mel Lewis had taken his own life. Warlow knew this to be absolutely true because he'd been standing two yards away from the man when he'd jumped off a cliff into the sea and drowned. The criminal activity alluded to in the letter was more to do with the reasons Lewis had jumped rather than the jump itself. Warlow and he had been involved in the investigation into the deaths of two missing walkers on the coastal path. An investigation that led to the discovery of a marijuana farm hidden under an old engine house and the illegal trafficking and enslavement of immigrants and refugees.

It had been a horrible case and on the one hand Warlow wished they could let sleeping dogs lie and Mel Lewis rest in peace. But on the other, there was always the question whether or not Mel Lewis, who took money from whoever was behind the drug racket, had been working alone. This letter was giving him and anyone else involved due notice that the formal investigation by a different force was about to start.

'Bring it on,' muttered Warlow and forked another roast potato into his mouth.

The second letter was, in fact, a card. Easter was looming and early in the holiday window this year. Even though the envelope had been redirected from his old address, he knew who this card was from. He felt the contents with his fingertips before opening it. Sure enough, something sinewy and thin rolled beneath his fingers under the thick card. If that was not enough to convince him, then the handwriting did. Karen Geoghan was consistent, he had to admit. Both in the frequency of her correspondence and its contents. Cards would arrive for birthdays, Christmas, and Easter. And, since the miserable cow had discovered magical thinking, in that she thought just by saying it she was now a witch, there'd be presents in the cards. Bird's wings, a bloody feather, or, as he found out five minutes later when he'd finished eating and donned some gloves, a rat's severed hind leg.

The words she'd written were no better.

You are a bastard, Evan Warlow. I hope you and our family are sick with the plague.

Die soon for what you did to Derek.

PS. Derek has found some old friends of yours in prison. They said they'd write soon, too. Our lawyer says Derek will be out within weeks. See you then. Bastard.

As with all the other desiccated animal tokens, Warlow threw the leg in the trash, placed the card in a clear plastic bag to be added to his Geoghan collection, and filed it away.

But the remaining correspondence puzzled him. It was a card, too, but in a smaller envelope. On the off chance, he kept his gloves on while he slit it open and removed the contents.

This one was not from Karen Geoghan. He knew that right away. But that was as far as he got in determining the source. Inside, there was no signature. Just the one sentence. Capitalised.

I WILL FIND YOU

Frowning, Warlow looked at the image on the front. Four mannequins; two adults, two children, sitting around a table. Each mannequin had its eyes removed and replaced with red light bulbs. Each one, too, had one arm removed and red paint splashed on the torso near the armhole. Said arms were on a platter at the centre of the table around which the mannequins all sat.

There was no manufacturer's mark and Warlow concluded that this was no bought card. Someone had made it. He looked at the envelope. It, too, had been forwarded from his old address.

'Lovely,' he said to Cadi. 'Whoever it is, they haven't found us yet, eh girl? Long may that continue.'

He placed this, too, in a clear plastic bag for filing. One day it might be needed, you never knew.

By the time he'd unpacked, sorted himself out, and watched an hours' mind-numbing TV it was gone eleven and he crawled into bed, hoping that sleep would come. It did, but not for an hour. Not until he'd run through the day's events half a dozen times. Halfway through these ruminations, he texted Tom to tell him he'd spoken to Denise.

Tom texted back.

Have heard nothing. All good

And by good, he means not all bad. But it wasn't really good. Not when "it" refers to Jeez Denise. Not by a long chalk.

Outside, the rain had come back. It pattered against the roof slate in fits and starts as the wind blew it in. He finally fell asleep thinking of mannequins with red lights for eyes and woke up thinking about Boscombe and what the gulls had done to his.

———

HE WAS UP AT SIX, took Cadi out for a quick walk around the field that backed on to his property which the farmer had not yet filled with cows, fed her, and made coffee. While he sipped it, he fired up his laptop and punched Boscombe's name into the search engine. As soon as he pressed the spyglass icon, the page came back with twenty-one million hits. The headlines veered between the lurid to the prosaic.

Killer surgeon gets time.

Botching butcher sentenced

GMC criticised in damning report.

Warlow let out an expulsion of air and moved the arrow down over the page, finally settling on a BBC report from 2018

A SURGEON CONVICTED of killing an elderly man under his care during a botched procedure has applied for reinstatement on the General Medical Council register. Malcolm Boscombe was convicted in 2016 after admitting the manslaughter of David Spiller five years earlier. Boscombe was sentenced to two years but served only a fraction of the time after his sentence was reduced on appeal. Between the date of the manslaughter and the trial, he continued to work as a consultant surgeon at the Medfield Private Hospital in Swansea and carried out hundreds more operations. Many of those patients now claim that the surgeries he carried out were unnecessary.

Boscombe was initially struck off the medical register in 2010 after the GMC found him guilty of performing surgery 'beyond the limit' of his confidence and skill but reinstated eighteen months later on condition that he did not perform certain operations. However, Boscombe ignored these conditions and continued to operate in the private sector until the trial finally exposed his practice.

During the court case, the Old Bailey heard how an operation to remove a tumour from Mr Spiller should never have been performed by Boscombe who trained as a breast surgeon. During the surgery, the 80-year-old lost a catastrophic amount of blood from an uncontrolled haemorrhage that Boscombe did not have the skill to stem.

The GMC hearing that finally resulted in Boscombe being banned from ever practising took place in 2017. It heard how he stole the surgical register book from the operating theatre at the Medfield so that details of the events surrounding the case could not come to light. The hospital claimed the book was lost during refurbishment, but police found the register hidden among papers in Boscombe's study during their investigation into the killing of Mr Spiller. The GMC concluded Boscombe had lied about the register and acted in a way that was inappropriate, dishonest, and liable to bring the profession into disrepute.

THERE WAS MORE. But Warlow had seen enough to remind himself of the horror and, more importantly, of the kind of man they'd found washed up on the beach. He wondered, as he pulled away in the Jeep with Cadi in the back on his way in to work, who might mourn Boscombe's death and who might be silently punching the air on this cold, wet morning.

CHAPTER EIGHT

SOME PEOPLE still called Dyfed-Powys Police HQ in Llangunnor, Carmarthen Police Station. And, Warlow surmised, they'd be right, given that the town station in Friar's Park was now a shiny new Lidl. But the out-of-town HQ within sight of the dual carriageway on the A48 was where they'd set up an Incident Room for the Boscombe investigation. And it was here, in familiar surroundings, that Warlow walked through the door to find that he was not the first there.

He tried to slip in quietly and failed. As soon as he crossed the threshold, everything stopped as three familiar faces turned in his direction.

Jess glanced up and called out a 'Morning.' She had a phone to her ear, transcribing whatever the person on the other end of the phone was saying.

Opposite her and with her back to him, Catrin Richards snapped her head around and said, 'I'm just going through the preliminary crime scene report on Moor Cottage. Five minutes.' She turned back to her screen and Warlow glimpsed a set of familiar images scrolling down.

'Great,' Warlow said.

The third member of the team swivelled in his chair and grinned up at him. Rhys Harries was the youngest in the room but the biggest. You could tell that even though he was sitting down since both desk and chair seemed a little too small for his long and spare frame.

'Morning, sir.'

Warlow took in the yellow and black shiner surrounding the DC's left eye. 'Not again?'

Seeing him injured was becoming something of a habit. In his short time on Warlow's team, someone had tried to stab him, an off-road motorbike had run him over and he'd twisted an ankle in pursuit of a miscreant. 'I'm going to regret asking, but what is that?'

'You mean my eye, sir?'

'No, I mean that paper clip in the shape of *Apollo 14* on your desk.'

Rhys glanced down at his sculpted effort. 'It's not *Apollo*—'

'Of course I mean your eye.' Warlow sighed.

'Ah, right.' Rhys grinned. 'Cup match on Saturday. Semi-final against Newcastle Emlyn.'

'Did you win?'

The grin morphed into a smirk. 'Of course. Final's in two weeks' time. Narberth seconds. Local derby of sorts.'

Warlow nodded and pushed his tongue into his cheek. 'We'd better get a bed booked for you in ITU then.'

'Stupid game if you ask me,' Catrin said without turning around.

'Just because Craig is a soccer mother,' Rhys countered.

'It's soccer mom, Rhys,' Jess said.

'That's what I said...isn't it?' Rhys sent Jess a confused look.

As disparaging comments went, it left a lot to be desired, being sexist and sportiest and probably a few other

-ists that Warlow couldn't be bothered recalling. Rhys had no doubt meant to imply that soccer was a less macho sport than rugby; the game that had given him the black eye. But his understanding of American colloquialism was not his strong point. Warlow put him out of his misery. 'We get the gist, Rhys.'

A voice called out from the back room. 'Ask him about the other bloke. The one that gave him the black eye.' From around the door frame, the moon face of Detective Sergeant Gil Jones, a seasoned detective who ran the office with a steady hand, appeared, all innocence.

Warlow turned raised eyebrows back to Rhys. 'I trust there's no suggestion of assault here?'

'What? No...he broke his hand, that's all.'

'On your face?' Catrin turned her horror-filled gaze on to her junior colleague.

'Not my fault,' Rhys protested. 'It wasn't as if I threw my eye onto his fist, is it?'

'My God, what's your skull made of, concrete?' She knocked on the top of his head like a door.

Gil emerged from the SIO office with some printed images and handed them to Catrin. 'As requested, the printer cartridge is now installed and functional.'

Catrin began arranging the sheets.

Jess signalled to Warlow with a nod and pointed towards the office. Warlow, still in his coat, joined her. The DI waited until he was inside and shut the door before asking, 'Did you get a letter from West Mids over the weekend?'

'About Mel Lewis? Yes, I did.'

Jess had been on the same case. Warlow tried to read her expression but failed.

'How do you feel about it?' she asked.

'Got to be done. Someone got to Mel. I'm all for finding out who did and nailing the sods.'

Jess sighed. 'The Gowers have said nothing.'

Warlow nodded. Father and son, Rylan and Ben Gower ran the marijuana farm they'd unearthed deep under an abandoned engine house. Both were serving long sentences for their involvement. Both had decided not to cooperate with authorities. Warlow knew why. They were in prison and vulnerable. No question they'd be more worried about the criminals surrounding them than the authorities and their prison sentences.

'They won't. Not if they want to survive.'

'I bloody hate internal inquiries.' Jess's mouth was a tight line.

Warlow was about to ask if she'd been involved in one before, but then remembered that they'd reprimanded her ex-husband for unprofessional conduct. He'd been caught having a sexual liaison with a colleague while on duty in the station. Greater Manchester Police's investigation into that could not have been pleasant, even if Jess had been a completely innocent party. That infidelity and its humiliating aftermath is what led to her presence now in Warlow's office, in a different force, in a different country even.

He tried sympathy. 'I don't enjoy them much either. More than anything, it's distracting.'

Jess nodded. She was gazing out of the window, but Warlow doubted the countryside outside occupied her thoughts.

'Best we keep this lot focused,' he said after a while.

Jess pulled her shoulders back. 'You're right. It doesn't do to dwell.'

They went back into the Incident Room. Catrin stood at the front where two boards sat. One white – the Job Centre for posting actions and questions, one beige – the Gallery for images. The DS pinned up the sheets of paper Gil had given her.

Jess joined her. 'Okay, shall we start?'

Warlow threw his coat over the back of a chair and sat expectantly.

Jess indicated the Gallery, and the posted photos. Warlow had seen these images before in real life. From the beach at Ginst Point. But next to him, Rhys's face grimaced.

'Malcolm Boscombe, male aged fifty-one,' Jess began. 'Found washed up on the beach on Ginst Point, just south of Laugharne yesterday. At present, we do not know if he died from drowning or the dirty great crack on the back of his head.' She pointed at the sea-washed scalp wound. 'We've chatted to the two kids who found him. Nothing much to add from them. Pure luck that they were there.'

'Nothing at the scene?' Gil asked.

'Whatever the tide washed in might have been washed out again. He was covered in seaweed, so we think he was in the water for some time. The boys saw nothing else except for a whale in the sea.'

'A whale?' Rhys asked.

'A humped shape,' Jess explained. 'One that didn't go back under the water. Maybe nothing, or a seal, perhaps. Their imaginations must have been on fire.' She turned to Catrin. 'What do we know about the dead man?'

'What don't we?' Catrin said and ran through a more extensive version of the information Warlow had gleaned from the Internet that morning.

'So, he's a convicted killer,' Gil said when she'd finished.

Catrin nodded. 'He is. For the manslaughter of David Spiller. What's interesting is that they ordered four other manslaughter charges to lie on file.'

'What does that mean?' Rhys asked.

Jess answered. 'It means that they can be reinstated at a later date, but only with the permission of the trial judge or the Appeal Court. They're on file because no admission to the charge has been made and therefore no verdict.'

'The Swords of Damocles,' Gil muttered.

'Who?' Rhys asked.

'Played on the wing for Argentina in the World Cup.' Catrin said, feigning innocence.

This left Rhys even more baffled.

'So more than one person had reason to despise Mr Boscombe.' Warlow refocused.

'Shouldn't it be Dr Boscombe?' Rhys asked.

Warlow answered because he knew this stuff from his son, Tom, who was a surgeon. It was the sort of thing you picked up being the parent watching your kid go through medical school house jobs and exams galore. 'No, on two counts. First, the bugger was struck off and second, surgeons are misters, not doctors. Something to do with early surgeons being barbers. They were the ones asked to do the cutting up because the physicians considered themselves above getting their hands bloody. Too refined. So the bloody-minded surgeons kept the "mister" nomenclature.'

Jess pointed to another image. A cottage with a corrugated tin shed at the rear. 'DCI Warlow and I called in to Boscombe's rented cottage yesterday. The place is a sty. But there's a workshop-cum-laboratory in the garden. Suspicious looking. That's why we asked Povey to look.'

Catrin took over again. 'I think you were concerned that there might be drug-related activity, ma'am. Am I right?'

Jess nodded.

'There wasn't. Povey says that everything in the shed is harmless. They've got dried herbs and plants from the coast. The cylinders you saw contain nitrogen for packaging processes.'

'Packaging?' Warlow asked.

'Nitrogen displacement. You pump nitrogen into the

bag to displace the air. Keeps things fresh,' Catrin explained.

'What things?'

Catrin pointed to a pinned-up copy of the leaflet Jess had found in the property. '*ALTERNIS. Natural homeopathic remedies. They sell health supplements, dried herbs, and reinvigorating body butter. And, most interesting of all, the opportunity for a one-to-one discussion with their resident expert to help with natural healing.*'

'Boscombe?' Gil asked.

'That would be my guess.' Catrin shrugged.

'Looks like he was dipping his toe where it should not have been dipped,' Warlow said.

'What about the house?' Gil asked. 'Any signs of a struggle?'

Catrin shook her head.

'What about his car?' Rhys asked.

Warlow turned to Rhys and waited for the DC to lay out his thoughts.

'He must have got into the water somehow,' Rhys explained, looking suddenly nervous. 'We don't know how or where. But if he had a car, and living where he was, he must have, we'd find out where he accessed the water.'

'Makes sense.' Warlow nodded towards the Job Centre. 'Go on, run with it, Rhys.'

The DC blinked and levered himself out of the chair, glancing nervously around at his senior colleagues. Catrin stepped away as he walked to where a pasted-up map covered one-quarter of the board. 'Thinking about what you said, sir. What the boys said, too. If Boscombe was washed in on the tide, he may have been out in the estuary. I read somewhere that he fished.'

Warlow recalled the fishing equipment in the house's passage.

'And maybe it wasn't a whale that the boys saw. Maybe it was a boat.'

'Bloody hell, Rhys,' Gil said. 'What did you have for breakfast?'

'Weetabix,' Rhys said, and then added with a grin, 'well, four, actually. And a banana.'

Catrin did a half eyeroll.

'It's a thought,' Jess said.

'A good one, too,' muttered Warlow. 'Get on to the DVLA. Let's find that car.'

'Yes, sir.' Rhys scribbled something down on a pad.

Warlow turned to the Gallery again. Apart from the crime of scene photos, there were others of Boscombe alive and beneath them, set out like a family tree, were images of a woman and two younger people joined with marker pen lines in green.

'Next of kin?' Warlow asked.

Catrin flicked through her notebook. 'His wife lives in Caswell. He had a son and a daughter.'

'Anyone spoken to them yet?'

'They've been informed. South Wales Police offered a Liaison Officer, but Mrs Boscombe refused. Said she didn't need that.'

'Okay.' Warlow stood. 'Jess, how do you see this?'

'We'll know more after the post-mortem. But for now, we treat this as suspicious until we rule that out.'

Warlow nodded. 'We need to trace Boscombe's movements. Who was the last person to see him or talk to him? Phone records, obviously. Find his car if he has one. Catrin, find out if Povey has finished at Moor Cottage. I'd like to take another look. We also need to talk to his wife. So, Gil, can we leave the DVLA to you?'

Gil nodded.

'I was going to do that—'

'You won't have time because you're with me,' Jess interrupted Rhys. 'We're going up to Cardiff for the post-mortem.'

Rhys blanched. Fear or excitement, or a bit of both. 'Me, ma'am?'

'Yes, you. And because you're with me and not DCI Warlow, you won't need your stab vest.'

'Uncalled for,' said Warlow with a scowl.

Jess grinned. 'Get on to Mrs Boscombe, Rhys. See if she'll talk to us this morning. We can call on the way to Cardiff.'

Rhys nodded and swivelled the chair back to his screen and the phone.

'But before you do, there is one important thing you haven't done,' Gil said.

Rhys looked at his sergeant and frowned. The light bulb moment took ten seconds before it appeared as a widening of the eyes. Rhys got up and headed for the door.

'Same as usual for everyone?' he asked.

'A little less milk in mine, please,' Gil said, nodding his approval. Once the DC was out of earshot, he said, largely to himself, 'We'll make a copper out of him yet, mark my words. But first we'll concentrate on his tea making.'

CHAPTER NINE

THE ROOM DESCENDED into quiet industry. Tea was brought through and drunk. Phone record requests were submitted. The DVLA contacted. Warlow spent half an hour reading through Povey's preliminary report on Boscombe and Moor Cottage and ended up none the wiser. Other team members were luckier.

Gil was the first to come up with something useful. 'Boscombe's car is a blue Mazda CX-30. It's taxed for another eight months.'

'Get the registration sent out. Tell the Uniforms to keep their eyes peeled.' Warlow ordered.

'Where do you start, though?' Jess looked up from her screen.

Gil pushed back from the desk. The castors on his chair squeaked in protest. 'Let's go with Rhys's theory for a bit. I know some boys that fish out of Laugharne. It's the easiest place to moor a boat. They tie them up on the mudflats and float them out on the tide. No need for marina fees.' He laughed at his own joke and shook his head. '*Arglwydd*, imagine a marina in Laugharne. Let's tell the patrols to start there.'

Jess sent Catrin a questioning glance. She mouthed back, 'Good lord.' All a part of their usual wordless exchange whenever Gil let out an oath in Welsh. Catrin would translate for Jess who was trying to learn.

Warlow scanned the team's faces. 'Anything else?'

Jess stood up and walked to the Job Centre where she pinned up a sheet from the handful she held. 'Boscombe used to rent a house in St Clears. Fifteen months ago he reported being harassed in a Morrisons' car park by someone who claimed to be a relative of one of his patients. A very unhappy relative. There were witnesses. It was only a verbal altercation, but three days later his car and the property he was renting was spray painted with the words "Killer". Shortly after that, Boscombe moved to Moor Cottage.'

'So, his attempt at keeping a low profile failed once at least.' Gil commented.

'Spectacularly, it looks like,' Jess agreed.

'Who was interviewed?' Warlow peered at the sheet Jess had pinned up, but the print was too small to read.

'A twenty-five-year-old called Lee Pryce.'

Catrin frowned, turned back to her desktop, and the keyboard clacked once more as she typed. The team waited. When it came to DS Richards, they all knew it was usually worth the wait. Catrin's screen lit up, and she turned to Jess in triumph. 'Doreen Pryce, seventy-six. She was one of the alleged manslaughter cases left on file. She died from complications following one of Boscombe's ops.'

Warlow nodded slowly. 'Let's get him in for a chat. Where does he live?'

Jess looked at her print out. 'Last known was Station Road, Llanelli. Bit of a wild card. Arrests for drunk and disorderly and assault.'

'Ah, Tidy. A member of the aristocracy then,' Gil

muttered. 'Definitely need your stab vest there. I'll get some feelers out. '

'Any luck with Mrs Boscombe, Rhys?'

The PC sent her a nod. 'Yes, she's in all morning. I said we'd be there about eleven.'

Warlow glanced at the wall clock. It was almost ten already. Where the hell did the time go. He got up from the desk. 'Right then. Catrin, you're with me. I want to go back out to Moor Cottage and have a better look. Gil, you're here. Try not to eat too many biscuits.'

'You know that's a team pursuit. I do not fly solo when it comes to the *boîte à biscuits.*'

Warlow sent him a sceptical glance. 'You have difficulty getting up from a seated position, never mind flight. And referring to everything biscuit related in French doesn't add sophistication.'

Gil ignored the barb. '*Merde* on that. Besides, the missus baked some *bara brith* yesterday. I have a slice already slathered with a quarter inch of salted butter in a cool bag waiting for you lot to sod off.'

'That's not fair.' Rhys swivelled in his chair to glare at the sergeant. 'I love *bara brith.*'

Catrin responded again to Jess's quizzical look with a mouthed, 'Fruitcake.'

Jess replied with, 'Very apt,' causing Catrin to stifle a giggle in a cough.

Gil ignored them all. 'On the contrary, Rhys. What isn't fair is inflicting you upon DI Allanby for your first ever post-mortem. It's with that in mind we've decided that you should keep a completely empty stomach.' He reached into a drawer and threw the DC a half packet of Polo mints. 'Here. Magic pills. Take one before you enter the pathology suite, one after you've thrown up.'

'Ha, ha.' Rhys let out a half laugh, though his face

showed anything but amusement. And he pocketed the sweets.

'Let's try to make it back here this afternoon for a catch-up,' Warlow announced at the door.

Everyone nodded.

With that, Warlow stood and grabbed his coat. 'Catrin. Let's do this.'

———

THEY WENT in Warlow's Jeep. Catrin with her laptop open in the passenger seat. Diligent was one word that sprang to mind. Relentless was another. Two things that made her an excellent officer. Warlow had a lot of time for the young sergeant.

'I spoke to Craig yesterday.' Warlow flicked up the indicator to overtake a lorry. 'He looked well.'

'He is well.' Catrin kept her eyes down.

'I like Craig.'

'I'll make sure he knows.'

'I mean, still hasn't quite grown out of the fast cars thing, but that'll come with age.'

Catrin smiled. 'I'll make sure to tell him that, too.'

The radio played. A local station that Warlow had on during his drive to work that morning. He switched it off. Catrin took no notice.

'Have you had notification from West Mids about the Lewis investigation?' Warlow floated the question.

This time, Catrin side-eyed him. 'Yes. On Saturday. Craig says I should make sure my union rep knows.'

'Good idea.' Warlow nodded.

'We haven't talked about it much, sir. In fact, we haven't talked about it at all. I know he was your friend.'

'We shouldn't, strictly speaking. Talk about it, I mean. But he was a friend. Though I wouldn't say we were close.

We'd worked together on some cases. Had the occasional beer.'

Catrin nodded. 'Craig says it's important we do things outside of policing.'

Warlow thought about that but said nothing. Wise words. Though in Mel Lewis's case, it was exactly those things he did outside of policing that got him into trouble. But she was right. You needed a way to escape.

'Will they want to interview you, too, sir?' she asked.

Warlow nodded. He thought for a while and then murmured, 'Mel had us all fooled. Me anyway.'

'But you're the one who worked him out, sir. That twigged he was rigging the investigation.'

Warlow nodded again. Catrin saw it one way, he saw it another. His version was riven with guilt and regret that he hadn't seen through Mel earlier. If he had, perhaps he might have been able to do something. Stopped him from...

'We all liked him.' Catrin's mouth formed a sad smile. 'That's the trouble, isn't it? Why can't the bad ones show it on the outside? It would make life a lot simpler.'

'It would indeed.'

Warlow was saved from more maudlin thoughts by his phone ringing. Povey's name appeared on the screen.

'Alison, what can I do for you?'

'Sergeant Jones said you were on your way. I rang to tell you we're about to leave. I've got nothing to add except to say that we'll run samples from the workshop, but I don't think we'll find anything of interest. Nothing jumped out at me.'

'What about the cottage?'

'I can confirm no signs of violence. Other than against the senses of anyone with an interest in decor and hygiene.'

In the passenger seat, Catrin grimaced.

Warlow put a finger on the button that would kill the call and let it hover there. 'Okay, thanks. We'll have a quick trawl through his belongings. See if we can find someone who knew him.'

The line went silent. But then he heard some voices off through the phone's speaker. Warlow read it as unfinished business.

'Alison?' Warlow prompted.

'Did I already say it's your lucky day?' Waning and then waxing as if she'd held it away from her face before bringing it back.

'Why? Because I get to handle the belongings of a struck-off doctor with bad personal habits?' Warlow frowned.

'No, because his personal assistant has just turned up here for work. I've suggested she hang on until you arrive. I'll wait here to make sure.'

'You're a saint,' Warlow said in a voice that held not one iota of sincerity.

'Enough of the flannel. How long are you going to be?'

'Twenty minutes.' Warlow put his foot down.

'Make it fifteen. I need a shower.'

Povey didn't even wait to speak to Warlow as they pulled in. She waved to them from the front seat of a SOC van and pointed to a red Citroen parked up to the left of the cottage. Warlow pulled in next to it and got out.

A woman sat in the driver's seat, looking anxious. Warlow put her at around fifty with frizzy hair and a long, but not unattractive face. He held up his warrant card and made a winding motion with his index finger. She buzzed down her window and Warlow spoke through the gap.

'DCI Evan Warlow.'

'Fiona Needham.'

'Ms Povey, who you met earlier, tells me you're Mr Boscombe's personal assistant.'

'Yes, I am…look, can you tell me what's going on?'

'I can and I will. But can I ask what exactly is your relationship with Malcolm Boscombe?'

Fiona's hands were on the wheel. She shifted in the seat and Warlow dropped into a crouch to be at the same level as her. 'I work for Malcolm. In the workshop mainly. Packing ready for postage. I also manage the website for Alternis.'

'In there?' Warlow nodded towards the shed.

'Yes.'

Catrin joined Warlow. 'DS Richards. Ms Needham—'

'It's Mrs.'

'Mrs Needham, would it be okay if we spoke inside?' Catrin suggested.

'Where's Malcolm?' Fiona's eyes narrowed.

'It would be better inside.' Catrin stood back to make way. After another moment, an unhappy looking Fiona Needham got out of her car and followed Catrin towards the front door of the cottage, fished out a key, and let the officers in.

Warlow let her. There was bad news to be delivered here. He didn't have the heart to tell her they already had a key.

CHAPTER TEN

FIONA LED the way into the grubby kitchen. She wore jeans and a polo-neck sweater under her coat. Warlow concluded there might not be much heating in the workshop.

'It's a bit of a mess. I only come in here to fill the kettle or heat up my lunch in the microwave.'

'Could do with a bit of a tidy,' Warlow's observation earned him an incredulous glance from Catrin. She mouthed, 'bit of a tidy' with sceptical eyebrows raised. Fiona was too busy at the sink to see it.

'Malcolm is forever trying to get some help, but this place is so far away from anywhere…' She let the tap run and rinsed some mugs. At least she used hot water and a bowl full of suds.

'Why don't you leave that for a minute,' Catrin suggested.

'Almost done.' Fiona's voice sounded a little too fulsome as she scrubbed three mugs with a blue-handled brush, rinsed them under running water, filled the kettle, and thumbed the on switch. All before turning around to confront the officers. 'There,' she said. Two spots of colour flared high on her cheeks.

'You might want to sit down, Fiona,' Catrin said.

'No, I don't. I've already spoken to the scene of crime officer that was here so I know something is up. Something bad. Otherwise you wouldn't be here. So please, why don't you tell me.'

Warlow shrugged. In his experience, no matter how prepared people thought they might be, how steely their mindset, hearing it was always hard. And the distraction techniques, the mugs and the kettle, did little to make him believe that Fiona Needham was any different.

'They found Malcolm Boscombe washed up on the beach at Ginst Point yesterday. I'm sorry to have to tell you he is dead.'

There were no histrionics. No collapse. But a range of emotions flitted rapidly across Fiona's face like clouds across the moon. Shock, confusion, a shake of the head, denial. They followed one another in quick succession. 'But...I...' Words were trying to emerge from her mouth but somewhere between creation and execution the cable had snapped. What emerged instead were staccato bursts of nonsense. She swallowed loudly, looked around, and reached out.

'Perhaps I will sit down,' she said, pulling out a chair and falling into it. One hand rested on the table, the other kept moving from lap to table and lap again, like a restless child's.

'It's come as a shock, Fiona,' Catrin said.

Fiona swallowed and nodded. In the background, the kettle began its slow rumble towards a boil.

Warlow pulled out a chair and perched opposite her, leaning forward. 'When did you last see Malcolm, Fiona?'

She swallowed again, looked at him, and didn't see him. Kept looking until she blinked and focused, as if noticing him for the first time. 'Friday...I left at three. He was in the workshop.'

'You mean the shed out back? Workshop is what you call it?'

Fiona nodded.

Catrin took out her phone and showed it to Fiona. 'Mind if we record this conversation? It's a lot easier than taking notes.'

Fiona shrugged her agreement.

'What is it you do in there, Fiona?' Warlow continued.

'I help...helped Malcolm with his salt marsh products.'

'Alternis?' Catrin asked.

Fiona nodded. 'All natural. Sourced from the marshes. Samphire salt, sea fennel, oyster leaf.'

'So it's food?' Warlow asked.

Fiona looked mildly offended. 'It's all edible, but it's so much more than food. Malcolm believed that as complementary therapies, foraged products that have been fed and grown purely by nature's bounty have a role to play in the treatment of serious diseases.' She reeled off the words by rote.

There was a slight aroma of "mission statement" about it. Warlow suspected he might find it written somewhere on the Alternis leaflet. He also knew that there were bits of coast around here that got flagged occasionally by environmental health alerts. And not for being the most beautiful beach in Europe either, but because the poor bloody filter feeders in the water were too contaminated by human waste to be edible. "More moules manure than marinière," as Gil had so aptly put it.

'We've been in there, Fiona. What are all the gas cylinders for?' Warlow asked.

'You mean the nitrogen? It's used for packaging. Displacing the air when we send out freshly picked herbs. It's not cheap, but Malcolm got the machine second-hand.

Covid bankruptcy sales, you know. There's also some liquid nitrogen that we use to make the samphire salt. We flash-freeze the plants; that makes them easier to crush. We freeze-dry the powder and mix it with salt from Anglesey. It's a very popular product.'

'And how is it going? The business, I mean?'

Fiona shrugged. 'We could do with more equipment. And harvesting the herbs isn't easy. It's seasonal, as you know.'

Warlow didn't, but he said nothing.

'Is it all online?' Catrin asked.

Fiona nodded.

'It's sold as a kind of natural remedy, then?' Warlow probed.

'It's popular with people who want a holistic approach.'

'Approach to what?' Catrin asked.

'Their health concerns. Malcolm was a doctor. He knew a lot about diseases. People contact him via the website.'

He was also a struck off as a dangerous quack, thought Warlow, but he filed that away for later. Instead, he brought things back to the here and now. 'Did he tell you his plans for the weekend?'

'The weather was good, so he planned to go fishing, I think.'

'Was he a keen fisherman?'

Fiona let out a little laugh. 'He always seemed to catch things. Pollock, mackerel. Sometimes a sea bass.'

'And did he fish alone?'

Fiona nodded. 'He had a small boat he kept at Laugharne. A little thing with an engine.'

Warlow threw Catrin another glance. A signal for the sergeant to ask some questions. For him to observe the answers.

'What about your relationship with him, Fiona?' Catrin asked.

'I worked for him,' she said. 'That's all.'

'And how did that happen?'

'I was interested in the product. I researched and found that it was a local producer, so I made contact, and we met. I sort of stumbled into it, I suppose. Luckily, Malcolm was looking for an assistant.' She made to get up. 'The tea…'

'I'll make you one,' Warlow said. 'We're fine. Had one at the station before we left.' He caught the relief flashing across Catrin's face. She, like him, he suspected, would only consider drinking out of one of these cups if they'd have been soaked in bleach overnight.

'Tea bags are in the cupboard. There should be milk in the fridge.'

Warlow stood up and did the needful, all the while listening to Fiona's responses.

'And where do you live, Fiona?' Catrin continued.

'Llanmiloe.'

'Not too far, then. Do you have family there?'

'Just me and my mother. I've been looking after her for the last few years.'

Warlow sensed the change in tone at the mention of a family. He put the least cracked mug he could find from the drainer on the table with the teabag brewing inside it and the milk next to it. 'Sugar?'

'No thanks,' said Fiona. Warlow handed her a builder's brew, teabag and milk all in together. She clutched at the mug with both hands. Her knuckles were white.

Warlow sat back down. 'We know little more at this stage, Fiona. Could be that Malcolm had an accident and ended up in the water. We think he might have hit his head. But we'll know more after the post-mortem. And we'll probably need to speak to you some more. I know this is going to sound odd, but we have to know. Is there anyone you can think of who might want to do Malcolm any harm?'

'Harm? What does…do you think that someone…?'

Warlow held up a pausing hand 'We're not thinking anything yet. These are questions we ask in all cases of unusual or unexplained deaths.'

Fiona stirred her teabag. Gil Jones would have had a fit. Agitating the bag was not a part of the sergeant's tea-making technique. When Fiona next spoke, it was falteringly. 'I know that…I know Malcolm had a chequered history. I know he went to jail for what he did. But that was years ago. And even though he'd been struck off, he had all that knowledge. All that training. He was trying to put it to good use. But there were people who could no longer trust him. You know about the thing in Morrisons and the car?'

'We do,' Catrin confirmed. 'We're interested in anything you could tell us.'

Fiona extracted the teabag and Warlow reached for a plate to put it on. 'He kept himself to himself. Not that difficult out here.' She looked up and gave them a rueful smile.

'There's been no odd visitor? No strange activity?'

Fiona shook her head. 'We get deliveries. Packaging materials. Postal orders sometimes…' She hesitated before asking abruptly, 'Should I carry on here? I mean, there are orders to fill. To post out.'

Warlow sighed. 'Until we know the result of the post-mortem, I'd suggest you didn't contaminate the site. There's no evidence that anything untoward took place here. But we may need a more thorough search.'

'A more thorough search. Why?'

'That I can't answer. For now, I suggest you go home, and we'll be in touch.'

'Take the day off. Go home and surprise your mother,' Catrin said.

'She's in hospital.' Fiona looked down at her tea. A sharp, jerky movement.

'I'm sorry,' Catrin said.

Fiona waved off the apology. 'No, it's alright. She went in last week and...it's all still a little raw.'

'Sorry to hear that,' Warlow said.

'Obstructed bowel. She needed surgery.' Fiona smiled thinly. 'She's eighty-eight. Not easy at that age. But she came through okay, so I'm hoping to have her home soon. Hospitals are not the nicest of places. All those resistant bugs and terrible food.'

Warlow did his best to not let his gaze stray around the filthy kitchen. 'Forget about this place for today,' he suggested. 'As I say, we'll be in touch. I'm sure we'll have more questions.'

Fiona nodded.

'If I could take some contact details.' Catrin already had her notebook out.

Warlow left them to it and walked outside. Fiona Needham had given them more information that he could have hoped to get by a blind trawling through the house. That would still need to be done, but he'd get others to do that.

Knowing he was coming, Povey had left the workshop open and Warlow wandered into it, taking in the small, neat machines, the clear plastic wrappings, and plastic bottles ready for labelling. The definition of a cottage industry. But something didn't add up here. The cottage itself, with its grubby kitchen, looked run down and except for the bedroom, almost unoccupied.

So where, if not here, was Boscombe spending his time?

And, more importantly, with whom?

The Kinks' 'Waterloo Sunset' started up in his pocket. Tom used the iconic opening bars as a new ringtone for him and installed it over the weekend. For a second, it threw Warlow as he searched for the source. But then he reached into his pocket and took the call.

'Gil. How goes it?'

'News on Boscombe's car. It's in a car park in Laugharne. A patrol just called it in.'

'Okay. I can't remember if there were keys on the body.'

A noise like a detective sergeant clicking a keyboard followed. 'There were. Might be worth checking for spares if you're still at Boscombe's'

'Good idea.'

Warlow still had the phone to his ear when he exited the workshop and saw Fiona Needham emerge. He gave a cursory wave as she got into her car and drove away.

Catrin came out of the cottage door just as Warlow said goodbye to Gil.

'So,' Catrin said, 'do we still search?'

'No. Let's wait until the post-mortem. I think a little trip to Laugharne is called for. After we have a quick shufti for Boscombe's spare car keys.'

Catrin made a face. 'If I'd known, I'd have brought one of Povey's paper suits.'

'No need. I think I know where the keys might be.'

Warlow went back into the cottage and came back three minutes later, dangling a single key with a small torch as a fob.

'Miraculous,' Catrin said.

'Maybe Boscombe was a dirty creature. But he was a dirty creature of habit, I'll give him that.'

CHAPTER ELEVEN

Anita Boscombe lived in a house with a sea view on a hilly road in Caswell, on the south-east edge of the Gower coast, five minutes' walk from the beach and a golf course in Langland. Not the only house on the street but somehow the driveway had been constructed with high walls such that once away from the road it became secluded and quiet.

The front garden had been set up for outdoor living. Summer was a long way off, but the garden had a big patio with cushioned rattan furniture and lots of pots. Someone had also brushed away all winter's leaves. And though not to her taste, the modern building had big picture windows with, Jess suspected, gorgeous sea views.

'Pretty nice. How much, you reckon?' Rhys asked, as they drove in.

'Knocking on a million, I'd say.' Jess negotiated the bend that brought them to the front of the house and pulled up.

'I heard people have moved out of London and bought down here. I mean, it's three hours on the train.' Rhys's perplexion caused a crease in his brow. It was clear he could not understand the commuter's mentality.

'If you only have to be there a couple of days, it makes sense. Probably cheaper to stay in a hotel for two nights than live in something a quarter this size surrounded by concrete in the south-east.'

'I suppose,' Rhys said.

'But the Boscombes have lived here for years. He worked in Swansea and Llanelli hospitals, didn't he?'

'Yeah. Still, all right for some.' Rhys looked up, trying to count the bedrooms.

Jess parked next to a Range Rover and pocketed her keys. She was halfway out of the door when she said, 'Try to remember that he's dead, Rhys.'

He gave her one of his rabbit-in-the-headlights blinks. 'Yes, ma'am.'

They walked up a short incline to the front door across a bricked driveway. Jess rang the doorbell and heard a small dog bark from somewhere inside. It sounded a long way off. The door opened to reveal a woman in cropped workout pants and trainers topped off by a loose-fitting T-shirt. She carried it off well, even if the sinewy look of her arms added a hard edge not helped by deep lines between her eyebrows. Jess had once been told these were anger lines. But then, Mrs Boscombe had a lot to be angry about.

Rhys made the introductions. It had already been decided that he'd take the lead here to begin with. Mrs Boscombe's welcome stayed business-like, and she led them into a minimalist pale-grey room where they sat on high-backed chairs around an oval table. She made no attempt at offering up her first name. Jess suspected this was deliberate.

'Excuse my appearance. I was in the middle of an online class.' She blew a wisp of hair out of her face. Rhys looked baffled. Jess put him out of his misery.

'Yoga?' she asked.

'Yes. So much more convenient than a draughty hall somewhere. How can I help you, officers?'

Jess turned to Rhys. He cleared his throat and spoke. 'First of all, we're sorry for your loss.'

Mrs Boscombe nodded. 'I realise you're trained to say that, but please don't be. Malcolm's death is no loss to anyone, least of all me.'

'Had you seen or heard from Mr Boscombe at all in the last few days?'

'No. We don't communicate. My solicitor deals with his. That's as far as it goes.'

'But you were able to confirm that it was Mr Boscombe's body that was found yesterday?' Rhys asked.

'I was, and I did.' She had an aluminium bottle with her which she sipped from occasionally. Jess hoped it was water and only water the flask contained. In between sips and answering the questions, Mrs Boscombe's mouth set in a thin line. 'But if you want the truth, Malcolm has been dead to me for years. Ever since he was struck off the first time.'

'Right,' Rhys said.

Jess smiled to herself. She'd noticed that most women over forty-five wanted to mother Rhys. The younger ones saw only the physical side of him. The tall, spare rugby player. Some of them took that as permission to treat him as an easy target and tried to manipulate him. His shyness when confronted with someone his own age was almost painful to see. But with women of a certain age, he culti-vated exactly the right amount of naïve surprise. Jess felt no guilt at this Machiavellian use of the age and sex dynamics, though not in the pejorative sense. Mrs Boscombe had a boy of her own, and Jess had guessed correctly that Rhys brought out the maternal in her.

It seemed to work, judging by the way Mrs Boscombe

happily opened up to him. 'Harsh, I admit, but we have kids. A girl and a boy. When all this hit the fan, we had to move them to a private school. Somewhere they weren't known and could get the right sort of help. I can't forgive him for what they went through.'

'Is that when your relationship broke down?'

The lines in Mrs Boscombe's forehead deepened. 'No. We stayed together for three years after that. But by 2013, I'd had it up to here.' She wafted some fingers at eye level. 'Nothing was ever enough for Malcolm. That drive got him a consultancy, but it also drove a bloody big wedge between us. And before you ask, he was a philandering arse grabber, and I'd had enough of it by then.'

Rhys's head bobbed up and down like a nodding dog's. Jess decided it was time to take over. Throw her a few little verbal jabs to make sure she wasn't getting too comfortable with doe-eyed Rhys.

'So you're unable to tell us if he was suffering from any condition that might have caused him to black out or faint?' Boscombe's death remained suspicious, but the possibility that he'd fallen out of his boat for no other reason than high blood pressure needed to be factored in. Aneurisms blew at the most inconvenient of times.

'No.'

'And he'd not reported any recent threats?'

Mrs Boscombe's inscrutable expression never wavered. 'No.'

'But there had been threats in the past. Am I right?' Jess persisted.

'Many and justified. As I'm sure you know.'

'When was the last time you actually spoke to Malcolm?'

Mrs Boscombe looked away, sucking air in through her nose and squinting. 'I'd say around eighteen months ago.'

'Has there been contact with the children?'

'No. But they're not children anymore. I've left it up to them to decide how much they wanted him in their lives. They're upset, naturally. And I have the difficult job of pretending, in front of them at least, that I am as well.'

'Of course.' Jess glanced over at Rhys, who was jotting all this down in his notebook. 'We're on the way to the post-mortem. Would you like me to inform you of what we find out today?'

Anita Boscombe looked out of the window at her nice lawns and her nice car before turning back to Jess and engaging her with a cool gaze. 'I know what this looks like to you. What you must be thinking. But the house is all that's left after all those years of sacrifice. And if you marry a doctor, there is sacrifice, especially early on. You move half a dozen times, your social life is Swiss cheese and the rewards, if there are any, come late. I kept up the insurance on Malcolm. I'm putting that out there because you'll find out once you start digging. He lost us everything else. It will barely pay off the mortgage and I won't lie to you, that will be a relief. It's a home for me and the children, and the least he can give us. Malcolm was always an arrogant sod. You might think it's a trait in surgeons, but you'd be wrong. Some of them are humble. Malcolm wasn't. I won't miss him. Neither will the kids. Whatever you find at the post-mortem, it's water under the bridge for us.' She got up and reached for a sheet of paper from a bureau covered with framed photos of a girl and a boy that were a timeline of school, university degrees, and partners from what Jess could make out. The most recent, action holiday shots of a young woman and a man in their early twenties. Mrs Boscombe scribbled some names and numbers. 'And just in case, here are the phone numbers of the women and men that can vouch for my movements on Saturday and Sunday.'

Rhys took the offered sheet.

'Best to be prepared.' She smiled in response to his frown.

Back in the car and buckling up, with the front door of the Boscombe property shut, Rhys let out an exaggerated, 'Ooof.'

'Now there's a woman determined not to waste any time on grief,' Jess said.

'That was...' Rhys searched for the right word and failed to find it.

'Illuminating?' Jess offered.

'Eye-opening, definitely. She was a bit scary. I don't think she'll lose any sleep, put it that way. Funny that you could end up hating someone you married so much.'

Jess waited for him to show any sign that he'd plonked a size twelve into the conversation, but nothing happened. If he knew much about her and the ex-Mr Allanby, it was not registering in the context of the here and now. Jess had no complaints there.

'Keep that list she gave you safe. You never know.' Jess swivelled in her seat and reversed out.

Rhys tapped his jacket pocket.

Jess nodded. 'Now, I think I spotted a McDonald's on the way back to the motorway. Fancy it?'

Rhys cocked an eyebrow. 'Wouldn't have thought it was your sort of lunch stop, ma'am?'

'Oh? And why is that detective constable?'

Rhys panicked. 'It's just...you know, fries and stuff. I figured you might want something...healthier.'

Jess sent her eyebrows up but stayed silent, fighting a smile. This was too easy.

Rhys ploughed on, searching for a foothold on a very slippery slope. 'Don't get me wrong, MaccieDs or a KFC is my go-to car-journey meal venue. Happy with a sit down or takeaway, depending on how much time there is.'

Jess grinned. 'Good. So I'll have the grilled chicken

salad. Less than 150 calories.' She looked across at him. 'With a side of fries.'

Rhys's eyes lit up. 'Nice.'

But as they drove back towards the motorway, Rhys's face gradually clouded over.

'What is it?' she asked.

Rhys's swallow sounded loud in the car. 'It's just that Sergeant Jones said I ought to keep an empty stomach for the post-mortem.'

Jess dismissed that. 'You're made of sterner stuff, Rhys, believe me. Besides, best to have something to throw up than retch on empty like a braying donkey.'

The DC gave her one of his little boy stares. 'You know best, ma'am.'

'Say that to my daughter when you meet her, will you?'

CHAPTER TWELVE

WARLOW HAD BEEN to Laugharne many times. With the
boys to see the Norman castle and visit the boathouse.
With Denise to the spring literary and arts festival, which
was a kind of cut-down Edinburgh Fringe weekend.
Laugharne, the town, was never free of tourists thanks to
an alcoholic poet who called it "the strangest town in
Wales". Warlow had even been on the Dylan Thomas
birthday walk, where sections of poetry marked the route.
He'd enjoyed that, even though Denise had done it in
double time so that they could get back to Brown's pub for
a drink.

The car park stood under the castle on the waterfront
and regularly flooded at high tides. This afternoon, the tide
was out as they pulled in next to a blue and yellow Ford
Focus response vehicle. Warlow did not know the officers,
but they knew Catrin and waved a greeting as she exited
the car. A few yards away, the blue Mazda CX-30 and the
spaces on both sides had been sealed off with tape.

Warlow stepped over the cordon, slid on some gloves,
and used the key from Moor Cottage on the Mazda's door.
No alarm sounded, and it opened with a resounding click.

Catrin joined him and they carried out a quick search. Other than some plastic bags, the boot was empty. Ditto the glove box apart from a driver's manual and some fuel receipts.

Warlow stood back, took off his gloves, and walked to the foreshore. He read a sign warning against mud flats, tides, and sandbanks. Just feet away on a grassy strip was a seat where one could sit and stare out at the estuary. A boat sat low on the bottom of a dry mud channel a few yards away. It looked cartoonish, like a tiny tugboat with a wheelhouse built for a maximum of two. Elsewhere, little skiffs with oars, or neat little stick-like outboard engines folded back into the bottom, sat with ropes like umbilical cords anchoring them to buoys or stakes. There were more boats on the grassy land that would flood once the tide came in. Gil had been right. The thought of a marina here simply didn't fit.

There were regular reports of tourists being caught out by spring tides. Parking their cars in the car park and heading off for a stroll, or a quick pint, only to find three feet of water surrounding their vehicles on their return. A cause of great hilarity for the locals. But he could see how convenient this all was for a boat owner. All any sailor had to do was time his arrival, walk to his boat, and sit while the waters rose around him. There was something faintly medieval about the whole thing, especially with the castle sitting only yards away.

He turned now to look at it. Dylan Thomas called it as "brown as owls". That was all very well for poets. What he needed was a castle that was as all seeing as CCTV. He looked behind. Beyond the junction, the town stretched uphill inland. He continued pivoting, eyes roaming past the junction itself and the houses to the floodlit gardens and their wooden seats.

Floodlit.

He looked up at the lights and the pole that held them and back to search for its twin on the castle side and… there it was. Two-thirds of the way up on a discreet arm, a black dome. Supposedly vandal proof.

He called over to Catrin.

'Find anything?'

'No, sir.'

'Nor me. But there is this.' He pointed up to the camera. 'We need to find out who this belongs to and pray that it isn't broken.'

'I'll ring it in. Get Gil to check.'

'Not much point hanging about here though, is there.' He looked at his watch. The morning had disappeared. 'Ask the Uniforms to keep the car cordoned off until we hear from Jess. Too early for the post-mortem yet. Let's say we go over to the hospital in Llanelli, check out a few of Boscombe's colleagues.'

'Lunch on the way?'

'We'll grab a sandwich in Tesco's. My shout. Okay by you?'

Catrin grinned. 'Taken to lunch by the boss. What's not to like?'

Warlow bought a sandwich for himself and something with edamame beans and quinoa for Catrin. They both opted for a bottle of water to wash it down with. She insisted they sit in the car park to eat.

'It's not against the law to eat while you operate a vehicle.' Catrin opened a sachet of something spicy and squeezed it into the little bowl on her knees. 'But if you get distracted and are not in control, you can get done for dangerous driving.'

'That sounds like Craig speak.' Warlow paused between bites.

Catrin nodded.

They ate in silence for a while and Warlow let his thoughts marinate.

'Do we have any idea how successful this Alternis business was?' He took a sip from his water bottle.

'It's a swish site.' She opened her laptop, perched it on the dash and swivelled it so Warlow could see. Lots of clouds and trees appeared in tastefully muted colours, and the word ALTERNIS slowly drifted up from the bottom to shimmer right at the centre. 'It's an e-commerce site. Easy ways to pay: credit cards, PayPal, the usual. But it's Boscombe that offers a one-to-one consulting service.' She pressed a button, and a face appeared. A professional shot of the ex-doctor looking clean cut and nicely informal, smiling in an open-neck shirt.

'How much did he charge?' Warlow squinted at the screen.

'A free ten-minute chat. After that, £150 for a forty-five-minute in-depth consultation for a *"novel and fresh approach to natural health. Dr Boscombe will discuss and devise a natural, holistic plan for you to follow, harnessing your own body's natural healing. The plan will include addressing your unmet needs, including the revolutionary Alternis salt-marsh supplements foraged from the wild seashore of West Wales. Dr Boscombe trained and qualified in medicine in the United Kingdom. He has worked both privately and for the NHS for many years, but now prefers to devote his practice to a unique form of health which he defines as a state of physical, mental, and social wellbeing. An approach that requires taking the entire person into consideration"*.' She looked across at Warlow whose sandwich had paused six inches from his mouth.

'Snake oil?' Warlow took a bite.

'RM from Birmingham doesn't think so. And I quote, *"My partner refused to address his chronic bowel problems and wouldn't go anywhere near a GP or specialist"*.'

'I'd be bloody grateful if I was that GP or specialist.' Warlow grinned.

Catrin raised her eyebrows.

'Tom's a doctor, don't forget,' Warlow explained. 'I get special privileges.'

Catrin continued reading. '"*But Dr Boscombe soon put his mind at rest and prepared a selection of treatments using Alternis products that have changed his life. Thank you, thank you, Dr Boscombe. You are a saint*".'

'Jesus.'

'No, just a saint.' Catrin closed the laptop lid.

'So, he wasn't breaking any rules? Not pretending to be a surgeon.' Warlow scrunched up the sandwich's packaging and stuffed it into the plastic bag it had all come in.

Catrin shook her head. 'I haven't had time to look through all the social media sites. See if I can find real feedback on this naturopath thing.'

'You think that testimonial is fake?'

'Let's say I don't believe everything I read on the Internet.'

Warlow shoved the last mouthful of a tuna and mayonnaise on wholegrain into his mouth and chewed it thoughtfully. He took another sip of water. 'Naturopaths. What's that, bloodletting and cupping, bit of acupuncture, that sort of thing?'

'I doubt he was doing anything hands on. Too risky.'

Warlow gunned the engine. 'Can you realign someone's chakra via Skype?'

'There's probably an app for that.' Catrin scooped up the last forkful of salad and did up her seat belt.

Warlow squirted some cleansing gel onto his hands and offered Catrin a blob. She took it and gave him a smiley nod. 'Right. Prince Philip Hospital, here we come. We'll hit Costa in Cross Hands for a coffee to go.' He pulled out of the parking slot. 'Don't let it be said that I don't know how to give an officer a good time...' He winced and then braked gently to come to a stop in the middle of the lane. 'That might have come across as—'

Catrin shook her head. 'No, sir, it was all very PC. You said officer, not girl. Could just as easily have been applied to Rhys as me.'

'Point taken.' Warlow accelerated away, but the troubled expression on his face gave him away.

Catrin clocked it. 'What?'

'If I'd have stopped here with Rhys, he'd have had two lots of sandwiches, crisps, a full fat Coke, and a KitKat. Or two.'

'You're right,' Catrin said.

'So we'll have to rein that statement back in. I would not have given him a good time. I would have been a grudging, probably judgemental, enabler. But on that note, I'm sure Rhys prefers DI Allanby's idea of a good time as opposed to ours. Who wouldn't want to be ankle deep in formaldehyde and various leaked body fluids in the morgue?'

'That's cruel, sir.'

Warlow caught the smile she couldn't hold back and grinned in return. 'I know. But it's a great thought to be going on with.'

CHAPTER THIRTEEN

WARLOW FOUND SOMEWHERE to park that wasn't anywhere near the entrance. Somewhere under the overhanging branches of a tree in sight of the business end: the laundry and delivery bays. A safe bet usually. Too far for the infirm to walk and way too far for the privileged hale and hearty who, if they could not park within twenty yards of the entrance to any building, immediately went on a Twitter rant. Warlow liked to call them ranting twits.

A florid-faced man and a long-suffering woman pulled up two spaces down in a black Mercedes. They fitted the bill perfectly. Or he did, at least. As the couple walked towards the hospital, the man kept up a constant and animated stream of what Warlow assumed was invective. The fact that there was no one to hear except his po-faced companion made it, ironically, completely in-effective. But that was a minor detail.

Nowt so queer as folk, thought Warlow. But kept it to himself. You had to be careful what you said these days. What you thought, even. Still, it hadn't got to the stage where someone could read what you were thinking. Just as well, in his case. Warlow generally thought the worst of everyone, bar colleagues, the odd friend, and relatives. Years of policing had taught him that people were capable of almost anything. For example, lying through their teeth when it came to saving their own skins. It made you cynical. Of course it did. He knew he was. But insight didn't change a mindset, it only made you aware of your faults. And he had plenty of those.

The officers walked back past the lines of cars that filled every available space, and some that were not strictly spaces, on the verges.

'There's never enough room in these places.' Catrin pulled her coat around her as a stiff breeze flapped it open.

'Too many patients, not enough doctors.' Warlow quoted his son, Tom. Hardly a nuanced response, but it would do for now.

They stopped at the reception desk and Warlow asked for the surgical secretaries and was given directions for the canteen and the library upstairs by a lugubrious porter.

'They're all on that corridor, the secs.' Job done, the porter tuned to answer a question from a very pregnant mother.

'I thought we wanted to speak to his surgical colleagues?' Catrin hurried after the DCI.

'We do, but secretaries know more about their bosses than any amount of HR bods or colleagues.'

After stopping a different porter in scrubs, they found the room stuffed with four desks, three of which were occupied. Catrin made the introductions. 'We're looking for anyone who might have worked with Malcolm Boscombe.'

Two faces turned towards the back desk. A plastic nameplate read Mrs Paula Roberts. The woman behind it had abrogated responsibility for dealing with the intrusion of two strangers and, earphones in, continued typing. When she looked up and saw everyone staring at her, she took out the earphones, put them calmly down, and studied Warlow and Catrin with a slightly annoyed face.

The DS stepped forward, warrant card extended, and repeated herself. 'Mrs Roberts, we understand you worked with Malcolm Boscombe?'

Mrs Roberts drew herself up and said, 'Yes.'

Not the first time she'd been asked that, Warlow suspected. She was older than the other two secretaries by a good stretch. Older even than Warlow by a couple of years. Mature was the word that sprung to mind. But, judging by the make-up, well-cut hair, and the trim physique, someone who took pride in her appearance.

There was something severe about her, though. Something that made you think organised and capable and... judgemental. Warlow had a sudden urge to check that his shirt was tucked in at the back.

'This is DCI Evan Warlow. Is there somewhere we could have a quiet word?' Catrin switched on her *it's-not-really-an-option* smile.

The somewhere turned out to be a glorified stationery cupboard containing a photocopier and shelves laden with envelopes and paper. But it also had a desk and a phone. Somewhere for a doctor to sit and dictate unfinished notes, Warlow surmised.

He let Catrin take the lead. She took route A.

'Mrs Roberts, the reason we're here is that Dr Boscombe was found dead yesterday afternoon.'

Her face seemed to crimp in on itself before recovering. Remarkably quickly. 'I see. And it's mister, not doctor. Surgeons are mister.' Paula brushed some fluff off her trousers.

'Right. I'll make a note of that.' Catrin looked up. Warlow leant against a cupboard with arms folded.

Paula Roberts looked from one officer to the other. 'How did it happen?'

'We think he may have drowned,' Catrin explained.

The slightest wince bunched the muscles up in Paula Roberts' forehead again. 'I see.'

'How long did you work with him, Mrs Roberts?' Catrin had her notebook out, pen poised.

'Ten years. From the day he started here.'

'And have you had much contact with him?'

'None, since his second attempt at getting reinstated failed. He asked me to provide some thank-you letters from patients when he was presenting his case to the GMC.'

'And when was that?' Catrin jotted down the information.

'In 2011.' Paula was not the kind of person to forget dates.

Warlow pushed off the cupboard. 'We're trying to piece together his movements and trying to get a handle on his circumstances. You'll know there was some unpleasant-ness after he was struck off. Are you aware of anyone else in the hospital that maintained contact?'

Paula Roberts had her hands in her lap. Relaxed and in control. 'I read about the antagonism, of course. But none of the other surgeons here kept in contact. Mr Boscombe was ostracised. The whole hospital wanted to have nothing to do with him.' She remained matter of fact.

Warlow tried to recall the date, but he was no Paula Roberts. 'Didn't I read that there had been some alterca-tion in a clinic?'

Paula inhaled and exhaled slowly before answering. 'When the complaints started to emerge, there were inci-dents. One in particular where blows were exchanged in a clinic corridor.'

'Blows between…?' Warlow threw out the question.

'Mr Boscombe and the senior member of the surgical team. The clinical lead, Mr Corrigan. He felt that Mr

Boscombe had let the department down.' Paula steepled her fingers on the desk.

'Is Mr Corrigan still here?'

'About to retire, but yes, still here.'

Catrin's phone vibrated in her pocket. She checked the caller ID and mouthed an apology. Warlow heard her say 'Rhys' as she exited to the corridor.

'Do you work for Mr Corrigan?' Warlow probed.

'I do,' Paula said, her gaze even and, Warlow felt, a little challenging.

'Good. Is he here today?'

'He's in clinic, yes.'

'Any chance you might contact him and let him know we'd like to see him?'

Paula smiled pityingly. 'I can try.' She reached for the phone on the desk and punched in some numbers. The door opened six inches and Catrin beckoned for Warlow to join her in the corridor.

'That was Rhys. They've started, but Sengupta gave them an early heads-up. Alcohol and Lorazepam.'

'Is she a witch? Tox screens take—'

'Weeks, yes, sir. But she's done a rapid blood alcohol and the Lorazepam she's identified from stomach contents.'

'The actual tablets.' Warlow sounded impressed. 'I wasn't expecting that.'

'Sir, what's Lorazepam again?' Catrin grimaced to indicate her ignorance.

'It a sedative. Ativan to its official friends, the ones with genuine prescriptions. Candy or downers to the upstanding members of the public we are lucky enough to encounter on a daily basis who obtain it on the street corner.'

'Does that change things?' Catrin frowned.

'Yes, and no.' Warlow stared at the posters on the corridor wall but took in none of them.

The door to the room opened and Paula put her prim head through into the corridor. 'I'm afraid Mr Corrigan says he's hopelessly overrun, and could you make an appointment?'

Warlow waved it off with exaggerated benevolence. 'Tell him thanks very much, but we have to leave. And be sure to tell him we will want to speak to him and could he instead make an appointment with us down at the station here in Llanelli. Always prepared to meet a busy man halfway.'

'I will,' Paula said, the smile now gone.

Warlow turned and hurried along the corridor.

'Where are we going, sir?' Catrin asked.

'Back to the office. Give you a chance to get a proper look into Alternis while we wait for the post-mortem. And for me to have a little think, sergeant. IMHO, as DC Harries would say, a highly underestimated aspect of police work.'

———

FIONA NEEDHAM STOOD in the corridor leading to the outpatient department off the main reception area listening to words she only half understood. The man speaking to them held half a dozen sets of notes. A little above average height and broad chested, he wore a striped shirt, no tie, and a nice royal-blue suit.

'We're still awaiting panel confirmation of the histology, but I suspect that's academic.' He clutched a paper cup of coffee in his other hand, the notes held tight against his chest.

'Does the type of…type of cancer it is make a difference?' Fiona asked. She dropped her eyes to his name badge. Mr Alan Corrigan, Consultant GI Surgeon.

'It does.' Corrigan looked around for somewhere to put

his cup and landed on a windowsill to his left. 'But this is what we'd call late stage. The cancer has spread to distant sites. I know that one of the Juniors showed you the scans.'

'They did, but it was a lot to take in.' Fiona winced at the memory. The junior did not know how to explain things in layman's terms and she'd come away bewildered.

'There are secondaries, that means other areas of spread, in the liver, lung, and brain. They're small but extensive.' Someone raised a hand to Corrigan as they passed. He lifted his finger in acknowledgement but didn't look away from Fiona's earnest face.

'That means you can't cut them out?' she asked.

'We can't.' Corrigan shook his head. 'But there are other treatment options and we've referred Edith to the oncologists.'

Fiona dropped her gaze, too preoccupied by what was being said to see Corrigan glance surreptitiously at his watch. 'My mother doesn't like hospitals.' She looked back up. 'She wants to go home.'

Corrigan smiled. 'I've noticed.' He cocked his head back in consideration. 'She's eating and drinking well. Theoretically, there is no reason she should not go home so long as the oncologists are happy to manage her as an outpatient.'

'The bag she has—'

'The colostomy?'

'Will someone show me how to deal with it?'

'Of course. I'll speak with Sister.'

'I think that would be...' Fiona's eyes drifted across to two hurrying figures approaching along the corridor. She locked eyes with one of them and read recognition in his face.

'Fiona?' Warlow said, as he and Catrin approached.

'Mr Warlow, I...'

Warlow dropped his eyes to Corrigan's lapel and smiled. 'And you're Mr Corrigan the surgeon.'

Corrigan straightened. 'I'm Alan Corrigan, yes. And who might you be?'

'DCI Evan Warlow. We've been chatting with your secretary.' Warlow held out his hand.

Corrigan did not take it. 'Look, I'm sorry, but Mrs Needham and I were in the middle of a confidential conversation.'

Warlow dropped his hand and nodded. 'Of course. Rude of me.' He turned back to Fiona. 'How's your mother?'

'So, so. We were discussing me taking her home.' A grateful smile flickered on her lips.

'Excuse the interruption.' Warlow turned back to gaze steadily into Corrigan's face before glancing at the paper cup slowly steaming on the windowsill. 'I can see you're overrun.' He smiled and without waiting added, 'We'll be in touch for a formal chat.' With that, he pivoted and continued towards the exit.

Fiona watched him for a moment and then turned back to a distracted Corrigan. 'If my mother had come sooner. When the symptoms started, could you have…?'

Corrigan sighed. 'Edith has presented very late. Whether or not we could have done something, who knows? But these things happen.'

'Perhaps you're right,' Fiona said, and there was something in her manner that made Corrigan pause. But time was pressing.

He glanced at his watch again. Pointedly this time. 'Now, if you'll excuse me, I'm due in theatre.'

'Of course. Thank you for talking to me.' Fiona followed his departure and saw that he'd left his coffee. 'Ah well,' she muttered. 'These things happen.'

CHAPTER FOURTEEN

GIL HAD a brew on within five minutes of them getting back to the office.

Catrin immediately logged on to her computer and got to work on Alternis while Warlow shrugged off his coat and dunked a chocolate chip Hobnob – a recent addition to the Gil Jones' biscuit collection – into his mug while the detective sergeant outlined how his day had gone. Incident Room office managers oiled the wheels of an investigation and Gil was a lubricator par excellence. Warlow often wondered how many cups of tea were drunk, and biscuits consumed in the office, while he and his deputies were out there with the great unwashed.

'Had a bugger of a job tracking down the CCTV from Laugharne. You said the lights were for the car park?' Gil leant back in his chair. A carefully measured distance that allowed for straight arm dunking.

Warlow thought carefully before answering. 'There were lights, and they were next to the car park.'

'Right, but you assumed that whoever ran the car park also had responsibility for the lights and therefore the camera, am I right?' Gil's round face shone with mischief.

'I did. I will admit that.' Warlow took a slurp of tea.

'Easy mistake to make. In fact, the camera was put in place by the town council in response to complaints about stranded vehicles at high tide. But it was paid for by the Friends of the Castle. A fundraising charity. The deal, as I understand it, is that someone, I couldn't find out exactly who, had the idea of maybe having a klaxon sound when the tide came in and cars were at risk. That way visitors had a chance of recovering their cars before a dogfish drove it away.'

'High tide is hardly a tsunami. But did they?' Warlow asked. 'Put in a klaxon?'

Gil tutted. 'Did they heck, as my granddaughter likes to say. The one aspect of this well-thought-out surveillance plan they forgot to factor in was monitoring the feed. There was no one to do that. So now they're left with footage of outraged drivers splashing around their new Renault Capturs and the odd late-night reveller peeing up against the wheels of a Transit van. Nothing at all *You've Been Framed* worthy. Who would be interested in an irate underwater driver when you can YouTube a cat playing a clarinet at the click of a keyboard?'

'Did you get the footage, though?' Warlow asked.

Gil finished his biscuit and sat forward to retrieve the tea from its optimal dunking position on the table. 'Not yet. Stuff is automatically wiped after seventy-two hours, but they have a nerd – the son of a councilman who is also a Friend of the Castle – looking after that for them. He is on the satchel, as they say.'

'Satchel?' Catrin sent Gil a sideways glance.

'He means case,' Warlow explained, 'And wasn't that a Dusty Springfield song?' asked.

'Nice try, but no teddy bear.' Gil held his mug in both hands. 'You are thinking of the late sixty's classic, 'Son of a Preacher Man', as opposed to a councilman. A tune which

Mrs Jones has been known to belt out – with more enthusiasm than skill, I'd have to say – after a quart of Prosecco.'

Catrin looked up. 'Does she like Prosecco? I find it a bit sickly after a while.'

'It certainly looks sickly when it fills up the toilet bowl in the wee small hours I admit. *Ych a fi.*'

Gil snapped his head around to the office door as three people walked through it. 'Aha, the away team has beamed up.'

'Ooh, is that tea?' Jess said striding in.

'It is,' Gil said and then shouted, 'Rhys, get the kettle on.'

The DC had taken three steps into the room but pirouetted and walked back out saying, 'Anyone want a refill?'

Responses were unanimous.

A third person stepped into the Incident Room and Warlow stood up to greet her. 'Molly, how are you?'

Jess looked apologetic. 'The post-mortem finished early for once, so Molly got an earlier train and she's agreed to wait in the SIO room while we—'

'Do your voodoo.' Molly, dressed in jeans, a puffer jacket, and with a big bobble hat on her head, made jazz hands. 'That's what Rhys calls it. Though he said voodoom. I'm not sure if he was joking or not.'

'Not,' Catrin said, without looking up.

Warlow introduced Gil, who stood up and shook hands with the younger Allanby.

'How was your weekend, Molly?' Gil asked.

'Tiring. Dad's a United fan and they were playing Arsenal.' The weekend in Manchester had brought her Manc accent back with a vengeance.

'Good game.' Gil nodded. 'Saw the highlights.'

'Their centre half should have been sent off, but a 'w' is a 'w', that's what I always say.' Molly beamed. There was something slightly manic about it.

'You never say that.' Jess said.

'No, but Dad's friend does. That's exactly the sort of thing she says.'

Glances were exchanged between the team. Jess wrinkled her nose and steered her daughter towards the back of the room from behind with both hands on her shoulders. 'Rhys will bring you a cup of tea. You can sit in here and quietly steam. Half an hour, I promise.'

'Oh, and the lads gave 110 per cent. 110 per cent? That was a good one. She said it 110 times.' Molly's voice trailed off.

'The errant dad I take it?' Gil asked, as if he'd tasted something nasty.

Warlow nodded. 'First time since.'

Jess came back all smiles. 'Sorry about that.'

'Anything we can do?' Catrin asked.

'She has her phone. What else is there?' Jess took off her coat. 'I would have rung, but this is Rhys's gig and he didn't want to talk post-mortem in front of Molly.'

'How was he?' Catrin asked, a little too eagerly.

Jess was saved from answering by the man himself walking in with a tray and six mugs. Jess took one down to Molly and Gil removed the HUMAN TISSUE FOR TRANSPLANT box he used as a surreptitious biscuit tin from under his desk.

Warlow waved the offer away but said, 'I'd recommend the chocolate chip Hobnobs.'

Jess rejoined them, declined the offer of baked goods, but took her tea and walked to the Job Centre.

'First things first. We called in with Anita Boscombe on the way.'

'And?' Gil sat back down in his chair.

'Let's just say she'd win "a woman scorned prize" hands down.'

'Was she upset by Boscombe's death?' Catrin stirred a sweetener into her tea.

'No tears. No joy. Didn't bat an eyelid. The Boscombe children are post university. They do not see their father. At least not to Anita Boscombe's knowledge. I'd say no love lost for what he did to the family.' She turned to the board and wrote up Anita Boscombe's name. Still with her back to the team, she added, 'And then we went to the post-mortem.' She turned to her DC. 'All yours.'

Rhys eased his frame up from the desk he'd been perched on and took Jess's place. Despite his size and his rugby player frame, he didn't seem to know what to do with his hands until Jess stepped forward and handed him the marker.

Warlow studied him and couldn't decide if he was going to throw up or burst into song. Thankfully neither happened. But it was close.

'What an amazing experience.' Rhys's eyes glinted as he spoke.

'What?' Catrin folded her arms.

Rhys launched into an explanation. 'Dr Sengupta even showed me where the gulls had pecked at Boscombe's tongue. She said you had to be careful to differentiate between predation and self-induced trauma because the latter could imply a seizure. Sometimes involuntary clamping jaws—'

'Rhys,' Jess held up a warning finger. 'What did we talk about in the car?'

'Sorry ma'am. I know, first things first.' He turned to look at Warlow and thumbed open his notebook. 'There was water and sediment in the lungs. So cause of death was drowning. There was an un-displaced skull fracture with some bruising of the brain tissue.'

'In English?' Gil asked.

Rhys nodded. 'We know about the alcohol and the

presence of undigested Lorazepam in the stomach. Just a couple of pills in among the egg and cress sandwiches. He would have been intoxicated and so Sengupta said she first thought he'd fallen, hit his head on something hard—'

'Like the edge of the boat?' Catrin sat forward in her chair.

'Exactly.' Rhys pointed to the scene of crime photos. 'Hit his head, fallen in the water, and drowned.'

'I sense a but coming,' Gil said.

'But there was another injury to the back of the head. This one hadn't broken the skin so wasn't that easy to see under the hair. But there was obvious swelling caused by,' he consulted his book again, 'a haematoma.'

Warlow put down his tea. 'One fall is unlucky. Twice is clumsy.'

Rhys shook his head. 'But he could have been hit twice.'

'*Mynufferni*,' Gil said.

Jess sent Catrin a look. She mouthed back 'Something with hell in it' with a little rotational movement of her hand to imply an approximation.

Warlow stepped up to the board next to Rhys, to where he'd written two words under the heading "Likely cause of death." The first was: Accident? The second: Suicide? He took the pen and added: Murder?

He turned back to face his audience. 'Now we've got some work to do. Let's start by going through what we have.'

He went around the room, starting with Catrin.

'We have the victim, obviously. I'm halfway through looking at his business, Alternis. As I suspected, there are forums that are not as gushing in their praise as the testimonials on the site would have you believe.'

'Keep working on that. What else?'

Catrin glanced down at her notebook. 'Still on the

business. I'm requesting bank statements and phone records—'

'Did we find his phone?' Rhys cut across her.

Catrin shook her head. 'Not on him. Probably at the bottom of the estuary somewhere. We'll need to make do with records.'

'What about Fiona Needham?' Warlow turned and wrote her name on the board. 'Does she do any book-keeping for him?'

'No, I don't think so,' Catrin said.

'Fine. Ask if she knew if he had a laptop somewhere. Softly, softly, though, what with her mother and all.' He turned to Gil and lifted his eyebrows.

The detective sergeant sat up and arched his broad back. 'I'll get some help organised. We'll start off with half a dozen for secretarial and indexing. Oh, and I'll chase up the nerd for the CCTV.'

'Jess?' Warlow turned to the DI.

'Sengupta thinks the blow could have come from something wooden. She's getting some fragments looked at. As for Mrs Boscombe, we'll need to establish her movements. But if she was involved in this, I would have expected her to be less hostile.'

Warlow nodded. 'Rhys?'

'Do you want me to go into more detail about the post-mortem, sir? I've made notes—'

'Let's wait for the official report. But glad you enjoyed it.' Warlow cut him off.

Rhys grinned and sent Gil a thumbs up. 'The Polos were a big help, sarge.'

'Tidy,' Gil said with a nod.

'Where are we with the graffitist?' Warlow asked.

Rhys closed his book. 'I'll get on to that now, sir.'

'We should pay him a visit. Preferably unannounced. Find out known address, place of work, the usual.'

Rhys walked back to his desk and sat down but turned back to Warlow before even touching his screen. His open face registered a by-now characteristic light bulb moment 'There is one thing, sir.'

'If it's about the post-mortem…' Jess tilted her chin in warning.

'No,' Rhys waved a hand. 'The boat, sir. Where is it?'

A contemplative silence followed. It was a good point. 'Right. Speak with the coastguard or someone who knows the area. If it capsized, we ought to be able to find it. If it hasn't, it could be anywhere.' Warlow glanced at his watch. 'It's coming up to half four. Let's make a start now and then get back here early tomorrow. Boscombe might not have been anyone's flavour of the month, but someone knocked him on the head and drowned the poor sod. Our job is to find out who did that.'

CHAPTER FIFTEEN

Warlow remembered the technique had a name. Or different names. Working in bursts. Carrot and stick. Pomodoro. Whatever it was, it seemed to do the job. Everyone knew they had thirty minutes to blitz their given tasks before going home. So they got on with it. Jess, Catrin, and Rhys were staring at screens, Gil was on the phone. Warlow walked over to where the sergeant was sitting and reached under the desk for the box marked HUMAN TISSUE FOR TRANSPLANT.

Gil watched him with narrowed eyes.

Warlow took off the lid and looked into the various half-wrapped packets. And there, right at the bottom, he found the treasure he was after. He reached in and pulled out a wrapped, two-fingered Kit Kat. Gil looked suspicious, but when Warlow pointed towards the SIO office, he got a smiling thumbs up from the sergeant.

Molly sat at the desk, mobile in hand, both thumbs dancing over the screen. Her mug was empty. She looked up and offered a tired but questioning smile as Warlow entered.

'Thought you might like this.' He slid the biscuit across the desk.

'Yesss.' Jess had the wrapping off in five seconds flat. Warlow pulled up a chair. He usually sat where Molly did, but didn't make a thing of it.

Molly paused, mid-chew. 'Am I in the way?'

'No. All the troops are busy. It's cogitation time for me.'

Molly took another bite. 'Am I stopping you cogitating, then?'

'No.'

'How's Cadi?'

'She's fine. With her pal Bouncer today so no complaints from her.'

'I wish she was here, now.' Molly said, sounding a good few years younger than the almost-seventeen that she was.

'Yeah. We could all do with a Cadi wag-fest now and again.'

Molly nodded and put her phone face down. She had her mother's grey eyes and dark hair and a runner's build. She'd taken off her bobble hat and stroked her hair behind her ears. She often walked or dog-sat Cadi and Warlow liked to think they were friends. Or at least knew each other well enough for him to ask, 'So, how was it really?'

A big sigh followed. 'Dad tried too hard all weekend. The game, out for meals, shopping. The thing is those were all treats before. Most of the time with your dad doesn't have to be special, does it? It's just being normal.'

'You didn't have much chance to be normal then?'

'No. By Sunday I was glad to leave. He wants me to say that I forgive him.' Molly folded the paper Kit Kat wrapper into a long spear.

'And you're not ready to do that?'

Another sigh. 'No. Maybe I never will be. He said he wasn't trying to hurt me or Mum, but he did.'

'He's probably feeling bad about it.' Warlow watched the spear reducing in size as Molly continued her folding.

'Boo-hoo.' Molly muttered. She dropped her eyes. 'Sorry.'

'Don't be. My eldest still hasn't forgiven me for leaving his mum.'

Molly's gaze snapped up. Disappointment blazed in her eyes. 'You? You cheated on your wife, too?'

'I didn't say that.'

Molly frowned. Her mouth moved to say something, but it took a while for words to emerge. 'So if you didn't cheat, she did?'

'Yes. But not with someone else. With a bottle. Same difference in the end. Bottle, needle, person. All it means is that other thing becomes more important than you. Tough to take. But it doesn't stop you from feeling jilted.' Warlow picked up the silver Kit Kat paper Molly had rolled into a ball and tossed it into the bin.

'Good shot,' Molly said.

Warlow shook his head. 'People are complicated, Molly. That's why you and I like dogs. They aren't complicated.'

'Cadi WYSIWYG,' Molly said with a wistful smile. 'Can I take her out for a walk next weekend?'

'Deal,' Warlow offered his hand.

Molly shook it and a smile flickered at the corner of her mouth.

Someone knocked. Warlow said, 'Come in.'

Jess stood contemplating the scenario in front of her with puzzled amusement before addressing Warlow. 'I'm going to take this one home. I'm waiting on a couple of calls and I can take them in the car if they come back to me. It's after office hours so I'm doubtful they'll ring back tonight. Still, who knows?'

Molly slid out from behind the desk and followed her

mother. As she was shutting the door, she turned back and whispered, 'Have you forgiven her yet?'

Warlow considered lying. Discarded it as a bad move because Molly would sense it in a heartbeat. 'It's a work in progress.'

Molly grinned. 'Good answer, Mr Warlow.'

When the door closed, her question kept buzzing around in his head. He ought to ring Denise. Or, if not Denise, then Martin, her partner. See if they'd heard anything more about going to court.

Another knock on the door. This time Rhys's head appeared around it.

'Sengupta's sent through her report, sir. It's on the system now.'

'Thanks Rhys.' Warlow grabbed Molly's empty mug and handed it to the DC. 'So you're our go-to guy for PMs now, are you?'

'Anytime.' He grinned. 'I found it really interesting.'

'What about the smell?'

Rhys thought about it and said, 'I really enjoyed biology in school. My teacher, Mrs Ogden, offered observational dissection during lunch breaks for anyone interested. Not on the curriculum, obviously. Always roadkill. I mean, she wasn't a barbarian.'

Warlow opened his mouth but shut it again so as not to stop Rhys's enthusiastic flow from gathering speed.

'She'd scoop them up with a shovel: rabbits, the odd rat or the odd squirrel. And sometimes after being run over by a milk lorry they were very odd rabbits and squirrels. You know, bits where they had no right to be thanks to being squeezed and squashed. But never a specimen from a lab. In fact she was a member of PETA. I used to volunteer to help. The smell never bothered me. Once she brought a squished together combination of a pigeon and a cat.'

Rhys chuckled. 'That took three lunch breaks to tease apart.'

Warlow thought about saying something but fell back on his default response of speechlessness when faced with the totally guileless. Thankfully, other members of the team were less reticent. From inside the office, he heard Catrin shout. 'He's now officially the team ghoul, sir.'

Rhys turned to confront her. 'I'm interested in how the body works.'

'They say that about serial killers, don't they?' Gil's bass voice boomed out his take. 'You haven't got half a cat in your fridge at home, have you?'

'He's keeping that for the cat-sserole next week.' Catrin's pun earned her a groan from Gil.

Warlow chuckled and shook his head. Rhys was an open book. Not a comic, as some might think at first glance, but a damned good read with lots of subtext and the odd clever twist, for those who cared to delve a little deeper. The DCI said, 'Good for you, Rhys.' But when the young officer was out of earshot, he muttered, 'Takes all sorts.' Then he fired up the desktop and lost himself in Sengupta's prose.

By the time he was halfway through, he'd forgotten all about Denise's court case.

He remembered six hours later as he climbed into his bed. By then, it was too late to do anything about it.

He'd do it tomorrow. Yet he fell asleep knowing full well he was lying to himself. Tomorrow would bring its own set of priorities, as every murder investigation did.

CHAPTER SIXTEEN

WARLOW TOOK Gil's call a little after seven thirty, on his way to drop Cadi off with the Dawes.

'Lee Pryce. The graffitist from Station Road. We found out he's labouring for a carpenter on the big housing site out at Bryn. I was thinking that might be the place to have a chat with him. He'd be off his own patch.'

'Great idea. Fancy it?'

'I'll text you the directions. Meet you there?'

'Give me an hour.'

They met in the car park of a community hall where Gil had already parked up. He got out and jumped – or at least levered himself – into Warlow's Jeep. 'Starsky and bloody Hutch.' Gil said between groans of effort as he stretched the seat belt across.

'You realise that there is no one else on the team old enough to have heard of them?' Warlow backed out and eased the car into traffic.

'Not heard of the 70s iconic sleuthing duo from Bay City, Southern California?' Gil's expression bordered on the incredulous. 'We'll put that to the test with Catrin and Rhys.'

They found the site easily enough. Gil sourced a foreman and from him, the site manager in the Portakabin acting as a site HQ. Gil knocked and entered and came out five minutes later, looking triumphant.

'Pryce is hanging doors up at the furthest cul-de-sac. He's clocked in so we know he's here. Follow the road around until we can go no further.'

Warlow did as instructed and pulled up behind a light-blue Nissan Cargo with its side panel door open, showing racks of tools, extension cables, power saws, and sanders. Both officers eyeballed the path in to an opening that as yet did not have a front door. Music, or at least a series of beats accompanied by nasal auto-tuned words, blared out from the open windows.

'Shall we try here?' Gil asked.

'Why not?'

Warlow sent Gil around the back of the house and waited while the sergeant picked his way across ground that had not yet been landscaped. 'Watch you don't do yourself an injury there.' He called out, as Gil almost tripped over half a breeze block.

'Why don't these buggers clean up after themselves? Whatever happened to standards?' Gil licked a thumb and leant over to wipe a scuff mark off his shoe.

'Don't fall over now, for Christ's sake. I don't see a crane on site.' Warlow said. But, despite his size, Gil was remarkably nimble. Even in the way he showed his middle finger to Warlow before disappearing around the edge of the adjoining half of the building.

A familiar smell of brick dust and render drifted into Warlow's nostrils once he stepped across the threshold of the building. He'd spent the best part of two years reno-vating the cottage he now lived in, and the dusty bare floor and plaster-boarded walls brought back memories of the satisfying, but back-breaking work. He'd enjoyed doing it. Enjoyed it more now that it was all done.

The house stairs were already in place, the treads covered by a plastic wrapping that had already torn in several places, leaving big boot marks on the wood. It would be someone's job to clean them off before the house was signed off.

Builders, thought Warlow. It all makes work for the working man to do. That was a quote from somewhere. He twirled it around in his head for a couple of seconds, but nothing lit up. It would come back to him.

'Hello?' Warlow called up the stairs.

Nothing changed. Not the noise of hammering, nor the awful music. He took three steps up and called again, louder this time. 'Hello?'

The hammering stopped, and the music dropped a few decibels. A face appeared on what would be the landing, looking down. 'Help you?'

'Are you Lee Pryce?'

'Are you the electrician?'

Warlow hesitated. Answering a question with a different question was a skill all of its own. But in this instance, skill definitely did not apply. He thought about the electricians he knew. Most of them turned up in overalls or fleeces and work trousers with a dozen pockets. This morning Warlow was wearing a suit under a navy Crombie. Proper detective garb. On a long list of things he might look like, electrician must have been in the bottom two. Which said quite a lot about the intellect of the carpenter standing above him.

'No. I am not the electrician. Now, are you or are you not Lee Pryce?'

'Who's asking?'

Warlow flashed his warrant card.

The carpenter looked at it for longer than it was necessary before looking back into Warlow's face. 'If this is about those missing windows—'

'It's not about windows. Is Lee here?'

'He's next door.' The carpenter nodded towards the wall in front of him. 'He's in the other half, framing up. I can give him a shout.'

'No, it's ok—'

'Lee! Five O are here. They want a word.'

Warlow's mouth puckered into a shape that usually led to a terrible word emerging. Through the wall, he heard rapid footfalls. The sound of someone running down a set of stairs. He turned and ran to the door, stepped through it, and hurried along the four yards to the open doorway of the attached building next door. He reached it just as a man came barrelling towards him. On seeing Warlow, he froze.

He was young, bearded, beanie hat pulled down, a scarf over the lower half of his face. And all of that covered in a frosting of pale sawdust. In his hand was a piece of two by four, a yard long.

'Lee, I need a word. You haven't done anything—'

Warlow didn't get to finish as the two by four came sailing towards his head. He threw up an arm to bat it away, turned his head, and collided with the edge of a countertop stacked on its end ready for the kitchen installation. A sickening thud reverberated through him, rattled his fillings and brought a hissing, 'Shit,' from his lips.

He knew he was bleeding by the sharpness of the pain as he clamped a hand over his forehead. He stumbled through the house, towards the rear entrance to find Gil standing there looking very confused.

'Where is he?'

'The bloke who ran out of here like his arse was on fire, you mean?'

'That was Pryce.'

Gil nodded. '*Wedi mynd.* Gone before I'd even turned around back up the road. This joins on to the Gors Twyn estate. Bloody warren in there.'

'Looks like he's allergic to the police.' Warlow took his palm away from his head and clocked the fresh red blood that come away with it. A warm trickle began heading for his left eye.

Gil reached into his pocket for a tissue. 'You realise you're bleeding like a *mochyn.*'

'He threw a plank at me, I ducked and…'

Gil held up the tissue. Warlow flinched away. 'I was only going to wipe the blood from your eye.'

'I'll do it.'

Gil handed the tissue over. 'You're going to need more than a bloody Kleenex.'

'Okay. Take me to A&E. I'll keep the pressure on.'

'At least let me wipe your—'

'No.' Warlow said. It came out loud and petulant.

Gil stared at him.

'There are reasons,' he said. 'A&E. Leave me there with my car. Get someone to pick you up.'

Gil sighed. 'You're the boss.'

'Don't give me any of that. There's an explanation.'

'And one day you'll tell me, I'm sure. Come on, you're making a mess on this nice rubble floor.'

Twenty minutes later, and for the second time in as many days, Warlow found himself in the hospital. Gil had some words with the receptionist, and they fast-tracked the DCI through the gaping crowds in the waiting room. A bleeding man was always good box office.

'Want me to stay?' Gil stood in the space just inside the curtain that served as privacy for a corridor lined with cubicles.

'Christ, no. I want you to get Uniforms to sweep that estate and find Pryce.'

Gil handed over the car keys. 'If you're sure?'

'I am. I've nicked the skin on my forehead, that's all.'

'Is there someone you want me to call?'

'Yes. Uniforms to do a sweep of—'

Gil held up both hands. 'Okay, got the message. You're sure you didn't pass out?'

Warlow sent him a steely glare.

'What about driving afterwards? You want me to send—'

'Jesus, man. I haven't lost an eye,' Warlow barked out the protest.

'Okay, okay.'

A nurse that looked to be at least fourteen years old to Warlow appeared in the cubicle. She smiled cheerfully. 'Oh dear. What have you been up to?'

'This is DCI Evan Warlow,' Gil said. 'I found him like this. We think he might have fallen out of his pram trying to reach for one of his toys.'

Warlow shook his head. The nurse, fighting a smile and losing, began uncurling a wrapped blood pressure cuff. Gil kept standing there, watching.

'Pryce?' Warlow said, arching his eyebrows. Well, the one eyebrow that was still arch-able.

'Okay.' Gil backed out. 'I'm on it. If you need anything, give me a ring.'

When he'd gone, the nurse asked Warlow to roll up his sleeve. 'Doctor will be in to see you shortly. I'm going to get some basics done and ask you a few questions.'

Warlow glanced down at her hands. She was wearing gloves. He waited until he was sure Gil was well out of earshot and said, 'Fine. But there's something you and the doctor need to know before we go any further.'

'Oh, what's that?'

He fished his wallet out from his coat pocket and found a card. 'You need to ring Dr Emmerson in haematology.'

CHAPTER SEVENTEEN

GIL GOT to the Incident Room, an hour after leaving Warlow, to be met by a sea of concerned faces.

'Is he alright?' Jess asked.

Gil, red in the face from taking the stairs, peeled off his coat. 'The good news is we managed to get him to hospital before he bled to death. The bad news is they're not keeping him in.'

Catrin snorted.

'What happened, sarge?' Rhys's earnest expression echoed everyone's concern.

'We called to see the graffiti artist who spray painted Boscombe's car. One Lee Pryce. He ran for it and DCI Warlow managed to head-butt a worktop. You'll be glad to know the worktop is undamaged. Couple of stitches and he'll be fine. Bit precious about his injuries but insisted on driving himself.'

'No concussion then?' Catrin piped up.

Gil ran a finger around the inside of his shirt collar and huffed out air. 'No. But he'll want us to get Pryce in for questioning as soon as.'

Jess walked up to the Gallery and peered at Pryce's pinned-up photograph. 'Why did he run?'

'I'd probably run from DCI Warlow if I didn't know him.' Rhys offered up this little gem and got three sets of quizzical eyes focused on him for his trouble. 'He can look a bit intimidating, is what I mean.'

Gil pondered this. Rhys was a good four inches taller than him and six inches taller than Warlow, but the DCI had a way of putting the fear of God into people. Even the ones he liked. Never mind the buggers he didn't. 'The carpenter Pryce is supposed to be working with mentioned some missing window frames. There's been some pilfering from the site.'

Jess nodded. 'Pryce thought you were there to see him about that.'

'Either that or he killed Boscombe and panicked. Which means we let him get away.' Catrin said with exaggerated cheerfulness.

'Yes, I'd keep that one to yourself for now. Certainly until Evan's inevitable headache subsides.' Gil wiped a thin sheen of sweat from his forehead.

'Either way, he's in the wind and we need to find him.' Jess turned to Gil.

'Uniforms have been to his house, ma'am. No joy there. He has a car but shares a lift to work with a couple of others.'

'He left on foot?'

'Ran out before I could get a hand on him.'

'Must have been moving pretty fast, then.' Catrin managed to keep a straight face. Rhys failed.

'Harsh,' he said with a chortle.

'Do we know Pryce's mobile number?' Jess asked.

'We do.' Gil answered the DI, but kept his glare on Rhys and Catrin. 'And we'll get a trace on that as soon as

Rhys gets the kettle on. We'll get him. Only a matter of time.'

————

Warlow got back to HQ an hour after Gil. He'd had better mornings. The very last thing he wanted as he made his way along the corridor to the Incident Room was to be hailed by a sergeant who said that Superintendent Goodey wanted to see him. With Buchannan away, someone needed to oversee the Boscombe case and Little Miss Two-Shoes, as she was known to all and sundry in the Force, had that pleasure. The name was no reflection of her character, but with a name like Goodey, it was only to be expected. Most of the time, they dropped the 'little miss' and just used 'Two-Shoes'.

And as epithets went, it was a good one. Pamela Goodey was an advocate for women in a man's world and a tad officious. Neither of those things worried Warlow. No, it was her enthusiasm for projects that she saw as somehow enhancing the police's reputation, image, and her own chances of promotion that made him avoid her as much as he possibly could.

When he rounded the corner into another corridor that led to the superintendent's office three minutes later and saw Jess leaning against the wall, he knew something was up.

'Nice stitching.' Jess pushed off the wall and peered at Warlow's head.

'Could have been worse.' Warlow frowned. 'What's all this about?'

'No idea,' Jess said. 'I got a message to wait here for you.'

'Shall we?'

Warlow knocked and heard a muffled, 'Come in'.

Two-Shoes sat behind her desk in uniform. The place was, compared with most offices, positively spartan. Some family snaps in frames, two pot plants, a desk with a pen floating in a holder. Superintendent Goodey wore no make-up and had short black hair that clung to her skull like a cap. A career copper if ever there was one.

'Ah, Jess, Evan, take a seat.'

Warlow and Jess sat.

'So, how is it going with the Boscombe case?' Two-Shoes steepled her fingers on the desk.

Warlow took a breath. 'Early days, but it doesn't look good for an accident or suicide. Two tonks on the head rules that out for me.'

Jess nodded. 'Agreed. Somewhere, somehow Boscombe was hit on the head and ended up in the water.'

Two-Shoes zeroed in on Warlow's wound. 'Those have anything to do with the case?'

'Is there something on my face, ma'am?' Warlow feigned surprise.

'Too early for stand-up, Evan.' Two-Shoes sighed.

'DS Jones and I called in on someone known to have an issue with Boscombe in the past. He did a runner from his place of work this morning.'

'Hmm.' She smiled.

Warlow narrowed his eyes. In his experience, it was rare for a superintendent to feel anything but frustration when a case wasn't giving up many leads. He decided to say nothing. Two-Shoes shifted her gaze to Jess. 'Next steps?'

'Uh, we investigate the victim. Get a timeline established. Find our reluctant helper.' She nodded at Warlow's head. 'Full toxicology from the post-mortem is still pending.'

'Excellent.' Two-Shoes put both hands palm down on the table and kept the grin. 'Sounds like you've enough to do. I won't keep you. But I wanted to give you a heads-up. We've agreed to let a camera crew come in and film. They have permission to follow officers in the middle of a case if they deem it of interest.'

Warlow looked at Jess. This time, he did speak. 'Ma'am, this case has its own set of difficulties. Boscombe had a couple of manslaughter charges laid on file. I don't think—'

'Good. Best not to. Decision is made and came down from on high. I expect you both to cooperate fully. The crew will be small, pretend they're not there. They'll have access to everywhere, well almost everywhere. Not here, obviously.' She looked left and right and then back at the officers. 'Kelvin Caldwell has agreed to be our point of contact for them. They will be here Friday to establish a base and show themselves. Keep me posted on the Boscombe thing.' She sat back.

Neither Jess nor Warlow moved.

'Ma'am,' Jess began, but Two-Shoes stopped her with a held up hand.

'It's not open to discussion.'

Warlow sat and glared until eventually the superintendent, who had gone back to pretending to shuffle papers, looked at him.

'Something on your mind, DCI Warlow?'

He nodded, slowly. 'Lots of things, ma'am. And most of them are not broadcastable to the public.'

'They'll edit it all. You needn't worry about your clean-cut reputation.'

'They'll get in the way.' Warlow's words came out as a growl.

'We are not making exceptions. It's one for all and all

for one on this one.' She waved a hand vaguely. It could, with a big stretch of the imagination, have been taken as miming a musketeer waving a sword.

Warlow still didn't move. 'I can't say I'm happy.'

Two-Shoes rolled her eyes. 'I can't say Llanfairp-wllpimple – whatever the hell the rest of that railway station with fifty-eight letters is, but I live with it. Now, I've got work to do and I know you two have. Any more questions, talk to DI Caldwell.'

Warlow said nothing on the way back to the Incident Room. He'd decided it was better not to for fear of saying something he'd regret. Instead, he excused himself and went to the toilet, locked himself in a cubicle and quietly fumed.

There were and would always be mornings like this. Mornings when things started off badly and simply got worse. He'd worked as a sergeant with a crusty old DI who firmly believed in the rule of three. In his book, when two bad things happened, as sure as eggs, there'd be a third.

Pryce was the first. Two-Shoes the second. He could do without a third today.

He turned to the porcelain and emptied his bladder. At the sink, he washed his hands and inspected his damaged skull in the mirror. Christ, he looked a sight. His flesh bulged around the cut and looked like someone had stuffed a plum under there. He recalled Rhys's black eye. If someone saw them together, they'd wonder who'd thrown the first punch. They'd been good at the hospital and Emmerson had spoken to the A&E doctors. Warlow's stance on that had nothing to do with wanting to be treated any differently. He only wanted them to know. So that they were prepared.

They were.

Now he needed to change his bloodstained shirt and forget about this morning. He didn't mind the injury, but

A&E was such a time waster…Warlow paused and looked at his reflection afresh.

A smile broke out on his lips. He glanced around in case anyone else was there to see him. They'd have thought him mad.

Well, madder.

Time. That was the answer. There was still time.

He splashed some water on his face and dabbed away a few rivulets of bloody ooze that had snaked down from the sutures before straightening up and heading to the office.

Everyone stopped what they were doing when he walked in. Typing, natter, everything.

'What?' he said. 'None of you ever seen an episode of Game of Thrones?'

'You know nothing, DCI Warlow.' Rhys said this in a bad northern accent with an expectant grin that faded slowly as the tumbleweeds rolled.

'That looks painful.' Catrin stepped up for a closer look. 'Stitches and Steri-Strips. The belt and braces repair.'

'You and Rhys stand together for a selfie.' Gil held up his phone. 'Or sit together because of the vertical discrepancy.'

Warlow took it all with good grace. 'Alright, have your two minutes of fun. But Jess has told you about the bloody TV nonsense?'

'Will we have to wear ties, sir?' Rhys wore a pained expression.

'No. No ties. Nothing different. In fact, nothing full stop.'

Rhys's face filled with horror. 'Are we doing it naked, sir? Like in those calendars.'

Warlow sent his DC an incredulous glare. 'Now you've made me think about DS Jones in the buff so thank you very much for that, Rhys. But to answer your FSQ—'

Rhys's brows beetled.

Catrin leant in and whispered loudly in the DC's ear. 'FSQ. Effing stupid question.'

Warlow continued. 'No, we will not be paraded in front of any cameras, naked or otherwise. Not if I can help it.'

'Are we relocating then, sir?' Catrin asked.

Warlow gave her a razor-lipped smile. 'We are not. What we are going to do is get this Boscombe case sorted before this TV crew gets here.'

Gil looked at his watch. 'So by Thursday, then?'

'Exactly.'

Gil, Catrin, Rhys, and Jess exchanged glances.

Warlow stalked across to the Gallery and the Job Centre, delighted to see that there were a lot more photographs and papers stuck up than he remembered seeing the night before. 'Progress. That's what I like to see. I'm going to change my shirt, and Rhys is going to get the kettle on.' He waved a hand towards the boards. 'Then we're going to go through this thing and get it pinned down.'

He took two steps towards the back office, stopped, and turned to Rhys. 'Kettle on.'

Rhys almost jumped out of his chair.

Warlow took another step and pointed at Catrin. 'Starsky and Hutch, what do they mean to you?'

Startled, Catrin did an impression of a goldfish for a good twenty seconds. Eventually, she scrunched up her face and said, 'A very average Ben Stiller and Owen Wilson oldie film on Netflix?'

'Nothing else?'

From the doorway out of the Incident Room, Rhys stuck his head around. 'Are they a drum and bass duo?'

Warlow turned to Gil. 'I rest my case.'

Gil shook his head. 'Bloody millennials and Generation X.'

'Z, Gil. Rhys is Generation Z.'

'Them too,' Gil grumbled.

Grinning, Warlow took another four steps but then stopped a third time and pivoted back to look at Gil. 'And, by way of forfeit, we'll need the HUMAN TISSUE FOR TRANSPLANT box. This morning is shaping up to be a two-biscuit session at the very least.'

CHAPTER EIGHTEEN

ALAN CORRIGAN REVERSED his Audi into a space in the Starbucks' car park on the Tenby roundabout in St Clears. He sat there for a moment and sent off a text. An answering message came back almost immediately.

He got out and walked, head down, across the potholed car park to the entrance. The place wasn't busy. It shared a site off the roundabout with a Travelodge and a Little Chef. Not exactly isolated, but few, if any, walk-in coffee heads found their way to the place. Less chance of bumping into someone you knew. A good spot to meet someone without too many nosy buggers knowing who you were.

His assignation sat at a corner table. Corrigan waved and made a drinking movement with his hand. She pointed to the cup on the table and shook her head. Corrigan ordered an Americano and, cup in hand, joined Anita Boscombe.

He sat opposite her. She smiled. 'You certainly know how to show a girl a good time.'

Corrigan glanced around and shrugged. 'The best I could come up with. There's nowhere in town—'

She reached across the table and took his hand. 'I'm kidding, Alan. This is as good a place as any.'

They sat next to a window looking out at some shrubs and the A40 with its hissing traffic beyond. Rain drizzled against the glass. Corrigan raised the cup to his lips and sipped. 'Was it the DCI, uh Warlow, that called to see you?'

Anita shook her head. 'Mine was a woman. A detective inspector. Attractive. Looked like she should have been in the *Godfather*.'

'Warlow looks like he is the bloody *Godfather*.' Corrigan tutted. 'He worries me.'

Anita picked up a spoon and stirred her coffee. 'Malcolm was an evil bastard, Alan. I'm not shedding any tears over him. You did what you had to do. We both know that.'

He massaged his forehead with a thumb and forefinger. 'What if they find something?'

'Like?'

'I don't know. Something about us?'

Anita pulled her hand back. 'Does that worry you?'

'Yes. Warlow is a suspicious bastard. Every sodding policeman I've ever known is. I wouldn't put it past him to try to—'

'What? Malcolm drowned. They found him washed up on a beach wrapped in seaweed. I had to identify his body, remember?'

Corrigan sighed and offered his hand again. 'I'm sorry.'

But Anita didn't give him hers back. 'We stick to the plan. There is no need to panic.'

He gazed back at her.

Anita shook her head. 'What have we got to hide?'

'Nothing, I suppose.'

'Then why are you worried?'

'The police make me nervous. You know what work is

like. I remember the last time, what the department went through when Malcolm was suspended. They turned the unit upside down. And the press...the press tarred everyone with the same brush. It took months for us to recover. Some patients stayed away. Some patients probably died because they were frightened off by what Malcolm did.' He paused, breathing heavily in and out through his nose. 'I've got another five months. After that, we'll be away from here and they can run as many inquiries as they want. Write about what they like. I just wish this had happened nearer to me finishing.'

'Malcolm made his bed. Now he's lying in it.' Anita's face was as hard as her words. 'Are we still on for Saturday?'

Corrigan relaxed. 'We'll have all day.'

'I'm looking forward to it. Just you and me. Now drink your coffee before it gets cold.'

'Yes, miss.' Corrigan smiled.

And, for the first time since arriving at the coffee shop, so did Anita.

CHAPTER NINETEEN

'OKAY.' Warlow sat in a chair facing the Gallery and the Job Centre with a cup of tea and an array of biscuits tastefully arranged on a plastic plate within grasping distance. He'd taken a couple of paracetamol, and the throbbing over his eye was subsiding. 'Ready when you are, Catrin.'

The others had arranged their chairs to face front, and Gil had one eye on Rhys, whose long arm had already filched a couple of custard creams. He'd received a slapped wrist on the third sortie.

'Everyone's read the summary of the Path report?' Catrin arched her eyebrows.

Nods all around.

'Any thoughts?' Warlow half turned in his seat. 'Anyone come up with a scenario where he falls and hits his head twice?'

'What if he fell backwards, hit his head, got up a bit stunned and then fell again?' Rhys asked.

'*Arglwydd*, he wasn't made of rubber,' Gil muttered.

Jess had a more considered response to Rhys's suggestion. 'There is that possibility. But the wounds were the same angle and shape. Caused by the same blunt object. If

he'd have fallen twice, wouldn't he have hit his head somewhere else?'

Rhys nodded, lips pursed.

'So,' Catrin continued. 'We have phone records. And
these show a loss of signal at 10.17 am. four days ago.'

'On the Saturday morning?'

Catrin nodded. 'The assumption is that's when he fell
into the water.'

'But we haven't found his phone?' Gil reached over for
a biscuit. Rhys followed his every movement with accusing
eyes.

'No. He wasn't wearing a coat, if you remember. The
assumption is that the phone is in the coat. Or fell out of
the coat. Either way, there is no signal. But it gives us more
information on a timeline.' Catrin turned to the map and a
line of red string. 'The phone pings towers that morning as
soon as it's switched on. We have it here, which is Moor
Cottage on Saturday morning. Then it's tracked to Laugharne at 5.30 am. and then we can see it going out to sea
until the signal is lost at 10.17 am.'

'Looks like he definitely went fishing.' Rhys muttered.

'And something happened at 10.17 am.'

'No sign of the boat?' Warlow dunked a biscuit in
his tea.

'Not yet,' Gil answered, dunking his.

Warlow chewed thoughtfully and then stood up,
staring at the map. 'So, we know he was in Laugharne at
about the time the tide came in and phone tracking
confirms he went out to sea. The question is, did he go
alone?'

'CCTV might help there,' Gil suggested. It earned him
a questioning glance from the DCI. Gil held up both hands
in surrender. 'He's promised he'll get it to me today. If not,
I'll arrest the bugger myself.'

'Who are we talking about?' Rhys asked.

'The nerd in charge of the Friends of the Castle's surveillance camera,' Gil explained.

'There are other questions that need answers.' Jess sat forward. 'Why would he have Ativan in his system if he was going fishing? Surely he'd want to be awake and alert. And not only Ativan, there was alcohol, too.'

Catrin shuffled some papers in her hand. 'I've got some bank statements for Alternis. I'm going through them, and it was doing surprisingly well. There are lots of BACS payments in.'

'From whom?' Gil asked.

'Different individuals. I'm concentrating on finding regular payees for the same amount. Lots for £150. A few for a lot more.'

'Would it be worth having a chat with Fiona Needham again? She'd know all about the business side of things.' Jess narrowed her eyes. 'She might give up a bit more information about Boscombe, too, if she knows this is a suspicious death.'

'Good idea.'

Jess nodded. 'I'll keep it light. Visit her at home. Easier that way with her mother in hospital.'

Warlow reached for a marker pen and wrote on the board, speaking the words out loud as he wrote.

'Number one, fishing. Was he alone or did someone go with him? If he was alone, did he meet someone out at sea.' He turned to the team. 'That means we need to check who else might have been out late morning catching the tide. Number two, Lee Pryce. I presume we've got someone watching the house. In the meantime, let's get a background check. See if he has access to a boat.'

'I've got a number three for you, Evan.' Gil spoke up. 'Povey rang. They've taken Boscombe's car to the lab. There was treasure under the passenger seat. A laptop.'

'His?'

'We think so. It's with the technicians. They've accessed it and are cloning the hard drive. Should be with us today or tomorrow.'

Warlow turned to Rhys. 'Can you chase that up?'

The DC nodded.

Warlow turned back to the board again. 'Number four. Mr Alan Corrigan. The colleague who seems very keen not to talk to us.'

Catrin spoke up. 'I've rung his secretary again. She's said he's busy all day and that she'll get back to me.'

Warlow looked at her. 'Did she say where he is this morning?'

'In clinic at PPH.'

Warlow glanced at his watch. Almost midday. 'Right. Chop Chop. Jess, you take Catrin and visit Needham. Rhys, Laptop. Gil, CCT bloody V.'

'What about you, sir?' Rhys asked. 'Do you want me to get some ice and a tea towel for your head?'

Warlow's eyes narrowed as he searched the DC's expression for signs of a snigger. He found one on Gil and Catrin's faces, but the young DC looked completely genuine.

'Thanks, Rhys, but no. Good to see you actually care about your senior officers.'

'My mother made me put a bag of frozen peas on my eye last night. It helped.'

'And a carrot up your nose?' Catrin asked.

Warlow silenced her with a glare. 'As I say, thanks for your concern, Rhys, but I'm fine. All I need is another biscuit and for some Uniforms to do me a little favour.'

————

HALF AN HOUR later in the SIO's room, Warlow gingerly palpated his forehead. The swelling wasn't any less. Under his fingers it felt like a grapefruit. Perhaps he should have taken Rhys up on his offer. He'd spent a little time checking the tide times for last Saturday. He'd done it despite knowing full well it was unnecessary, as Catrin had already written it up on the board. It was simply a way of avoiding the call he needed to make.

But there was no avoiding it in the end. He picked up his mobile and scrolled to his contacts, chose the one he wanted, and called it.

'Martin,' Warlow said when it was answered, 'It's Evan.'

Martin Foyles met Denise on a cruise. The cruise she'd taken four months after Warlow had announced that he was leaving. He felt no rancour or ill feeling towards Martin, wishing only he'd known the guy before the poor bugger had met Denise on a dance floor in the middle of the Aegean. He might have given him a briefing. Too late now.

'Evan, how are you?'

'Funny you should ask. Nursing a sore head thanks to a minor accident, but otherwise good. You?'

'Not bad.' Martin was outdoors. Warlow could tell from his breathing and the crunch of footsteps.

'How's Denise?'

'Worried. About the court thing.'

'Does she have a solicitor yet?'

'This is the second one. The first one she didn't like. Told her to plead guilty.'

Warlow could just imagine how that had gone down. 'What does this one say?'

'He thinks there may be grounds for mitigation.'

Great, thought Warlow. He'd been in a hundred courts where the defence lawyer pleaded mitigation. A blameless record, a momentary lapse, a good life. He'd also seen judge and jury glaze over because all they had to do was look to where the victim's relatives sat, grieving, or angry, or hungry for justice. Mitigation my arse. And though there were no victims in a case of refusing to supply a sample, her lawyer would no doubt try to paint Denise as one par excellence.

Good luck with that.

'Is he being honest with her, with you both, about what the consequences of a conviction would be?' Warlow demanded.

'Yes. He thinks she might go to prison.'

'What does Denise say to that?'

'She doesn't say anything. She's a river in Egypt. You know, in Denial.'

Denial. Big joke. But he didn't hear anyone laughing, though Martin snorted, enjoying his own lame humour. The bloke was a hopeless optimist.

Warlow tried again. 'Did the lawyer tell you that if she pleads guilty, she'll get a reduced sentence?'

Martin stopped walking. 'He did. But Denise is like a dog with a bone.'

Indeed. 'Is there a date?'

'End of next month.'

'Tell her she can ring me any time if she wants advice. You too.'

'Appreciate it, Evan, but don't stay by the phone. You know what Denise is like.'

He did. Stubborn. Manipulative. A warm, exuberant, life-lover when sober. A bitch when she was on the sauce. He hung up and was still wondering what sort of lawyer would advise a client to plead not guilty in situations like this when Gil stuck his head around the door.

'Call for you.' He handed over a handset and did it with a smile bordering on a smirk.

Warily, Warlow put the phone to his ear. 'Yes.'

'Is this your idea of a joke?' There was no disguising

the anger or the authority in the voice. This was someone used to giving orders. Then Warlow placed it and smiled.

'Mr Corrigan, what can I do for you?'

'You can get these bloody shock troops out of my clinic for a start.'

'Shock troops? Do you, by any chance, mean uniformed police officers?'

'Christ, what are people going to think? They've been loitering outside my door for half an hour.'

'They were in the vicinity. I asked them to call in to find out when you might see your way to popping into the station to answer a few questions.'

'What questions?'

'I have a boil on my neck that's irritating me. I thought you might give me your opinion.'

'Are you mad?' Corrigan's voice went up two notches.

'No, but I'm getting there with every wriggling moment of you avoiding us.'

'So you don't have a boil on your neck?'

'I do not. That was my attempt at cutting sarcasm. But I'll give you three guesses who we might want to question you about.'

'I don't know.'

Warlow sighed. This was proving to be a tough morning indeed. 'How about Malcolm Boscombe?'

After a three-second beat, Corrigan spoke. His words thick and low. 'Look, I'm sorry to hear about Malcolm. It's tragic. But it has nothing to do with me. A boating accident I heard—'

'You heard wrong, Mr Corrigan. We're treating Malcolm Boscombe's death as suspicious.'

All the bluster, spit, and vinegar ceased like someone had thrown a switch. 'Suspicious?' The word croaked out as a hoarse whisper.

'We'd like to get some background, talk to his

colleagues, see if we can establish a timeline and perhaps an insight into Mr Boscombe's state of mind. So, when can you come in?'

'I…uh…'

'I can arrange for the officers to call in everyday on the off chance you might be free if you like? They'd be happy to bring you across in the response vehicle.'

'That won't be necessary.' Corrigan's answer was swift. 'Where would you like me to come?'

'We could have done it closer to you, but we're not in Llanelli anymore. I'm in Carmarthen today. You know the headquarters in Llangunnor?'

Corrigan swallowed. It sounded loud in Warlow's ear. 'I've driven past it. I can be there in an hour.'

'We're five minutes off the A40. Look forward to seeing you.'

CHAPTER TWENTY

FIONA NEEDHAM LIVED in a tiny bungalow in a 'little boxes' development of similar properties on Woodside Close, Llanmiloe, near the resort of Pendine. The property was modern, painted white with a red-tile roof. Inlaid bricks provided hardstanding for the red Citroen parked next to a collection of paint-flecked garden gnomes. The area got its name from the woodland atop the hill behind the house. Elsewhere, the flat land marched off towards the sea, fields eventually giving way to woods and then marsh.

'Nice spot,' Catrin said when Jess parked up.

'I don't know this bit of the coast well. Is it a destination resort?' Jess had commented on the caravan townships on both sides of the main road as they'd driven in.

'Cheaper than trendy Tenby. You've got Pendine and then Saundersfoot. Lovely in the sun. Not much to do when it rains. And it does that here, ma'am. You'll have noticed, I'm sure.'

'Even more than Manchester, and that's saying something.' Jess had made the move to the Dyfed-Powys area from the northern city a couple of years before. So far, apart from the weather, she'd had no regrets.

Jess knocked and Catrin introduced her when Fiona Needham opened the door.

Judging from the scruffiness of her clothes, they'd interrupted her in the middle of some messy work.

'You'll have to excuse the garb. Thought I'd give Mum's bedroom a lick of paint before she got back from the hospital.' She was make-up free and the dark smudges under her eyes told of sleepless nights. She led the way into a small but spotless kitchen. Within minutes, they were seated with the kettle on and coffee offered.

'How is your mum?' Jess asked.

Fiona offered a tight smile. 'So, so. She survived the surgery but it's been a rocky recovery. I put that down to her age.'

Jess had filled Catrin in on the way and got her up to speed with the situation so there was no need for her to ask for elaboration. Instead, she looked around at the neat kitchen. 'This is a nice little place you have.'

'Thanks. I try to keep it tidy. I'm grateful for it. Don't know what I would have done with Mum otherwise.'

'You're her carer, I take it?' Jess declined the offer of a biscuit. Rich tea. Old school, as Gil would have said.

'I am. She's been with me five years. This was our place, my husband Mike and me. After he passed, I lived here alone for a couple of years until Mum couldn't cope on her own. Made sense to bring her back here.' Even though she'd measured the time in years, a fresh pang of grief flashed over her face when she mentioned her husband's name.

Jess took in the sparkling worktops. Such a contrast to the mess in Moor Cottage. 'It looks very comfortable.'

Polite niceties over, Fiona drew her chair up to the table opposite the two officers. 'You said you had some questions about the business?'

Catrin nodded. 'I'm trying to get a handle on Alternis.

Am I right to assume it was split into two main divisions? The online sales of herbs and salt that you handled and one-to-one health advice offered by Mr Boscombe?'

'Yes. I handle the sales. I couldn't help with the advice side of things. That was all Malcolm. But we ran the herb business together. Picked them, checked the samphire beds—'

'Checked them?'

'Yes. We don't…didn't farm them. Samphire grows on the salt marsh. Usually in awkward places. It can be dangerous. You need to know how to walk between the channels where the sea runs in. People can get caught out by the tide. Or step in a channel and not get out again. The mud could swallow you whole. Spring is when samphire appears. Sometimes, after big storms, the land-scape can change so it's always necessary to mark out where we'd pick…' Her words ran out of steam.

Catrin filled the gap. She fished out the bank state-ments. 'Most everything was done online though, is that right?'

Fiona nodded, 'Purchases by credit card or PayPal. Sometimes BACS if people are more comfortable with that. More often than not, people paid that way when Malcolm held one-to-one sessions.'

'Turnover of almost forty thousand last year, is that about right?'

'Yes.'

'And these payments of £950 per month to FN, that's you?'

'A pittance, I know. But I enjoy it…' She paused for a correction. 'Enjoyed it. I liked making the product.' Her mouth turned down. 'I don't suppose I'll be doing it anymore.'

'What about the equipment?' Jess asked. 'Did you have a stake in that?'

'No. It's all Malcolm's.'

Catrin spread some sheets out on the table. 'I noticed regular payments of £150 from an Edith Morton. Isn't that your mother's name?'

Fiona grinned. 'It is. That's pretty good detective work, sergeant.'

Catrin sent her a wry smile. 'Why we get paid the silly money, Fiona.'

'It was Mum who contacted Malcolm first. It's through her I ended up working with him in Alternis. Mum was a sceptic when it came to conventional medicine. She's scared stiff of hospitals and doctors. That's why I want her home as soon as possible.' Fiona paused for a sip of coffee. 'But she's always looked for a different way to treat her ailments. Malcolm used to give her therapy sessions. Psychological mainly. Advice on supplements, too. She used to love her little chats with him. That's how we met. He realised we were local, and he was looking for some help. I brought some marketing skills from my old job.'

'Your mother paid £150 a month for two years?'

Fiona shrugged. 'It was her money. Some people spoke to him every week.'

Jess took a sip of coffee. Freeze-dried stuff. Too bitter by half, but she didn't let it show. 'We found evidence of alcohol and prescription drugs in Malcolm's blood. Did you know he was on medication?'

'I did. He had trouble sleeping. Drank too much, too.' Fiona saw Jess's eyes widen and was quick to qualify her statement. 'By his own admission.'

'Would you say he was depressed?' Catrin probed.

'A little. But I'd say moody more than depressed. Losing his licence to practise annoyed him. He was trying to save enough to see if he could set up abroad.

'I thought he'd been struck off?' Jess glanced at Catrin for confirmation.

'In the UK, yes.' Fiona popped a sweetener into her coffee. 'But he still had all his qualifications. The Middle East remained an option. And some parts of South America were a possibility.'

'So, was that the dream?'

'It was.'

'And how was that going?'

Fiona stirred her coffee and tapped the spoon on the rim of the cup to dispel drops. 'I wouldn't know. He didn't talk about that side of things much. Ours was a working relationship. Alternis kept me busy. Busier than I thought it would. Three days a week usually ended up being more.'

Catrin smiled. 'I've seen the website. The testimonials. But I've also seen the forums. The complaints.'

Fiona nodded. 'I know. No pleasing everyone, that's for sure.'

'A lot of his advice – from what I've read – had to do with bowel problems. IBS, chronic constipation, that sort of thing.' Catrin scanned the sheets.

'I'd say that if my mother is anything to go by, bowel problems are a national pastime. It's a major issue for a lot of people. More than that, it's an industry worth millions if not billions. Malcolm knew that. And patients get fed up of prescription medications when they don't work.'

Catrin looked up. 'Peppermint oil? Sea fennel infusions? Homemade enema kits?'

Fiona smiled. 'One of our best sellers. Along with the Samphire salt.'

'Do you use the salt in the enema kit?' Jess asked.

Fiona put on a horrified face. 'No, we do not.'

Catrin took out her notebook and riffled pages until she found an entry and read out, "Don't let this smooth talker fool you. I spent £300 for two consultations and bought the irrigation kit. I could have got the whole thing for £40 in Wilkes. Rip Off."

Fiona shrugged. 'As I say, you can't please everyone. Look I'm sad and upset over what happened to Malcolm. He wasn't an easy man to work for, but drowning...it's such a horrible way to die.'

Jess sipped her coffee. 'And apart from the online complaints, there were no physical threats? No one turned up at Moor Cottage?'

'Not that I saw.' Fiona narrowed her eyes. 'Why would you ask that?'

Jess kept her gaze steady. 'We can't rule out the possibility that Malcolm Boscombe's death was not an accident or suicide.'

Fiona blanched and kept blinking. 'What are you saying? You think someone killed him?'

'As I say,' reiterated Jess, 'We're considering all possibilities for the moment. So, did any disgruntled customers ever turn up at the cottage?'

Fiona's breathing had become shallow and rapid. 'No, I...we made sure of including a disclaimer in everything we sold or that Malcolm did. He always pointed out that no one should misconceive Alternis as medical advice.'

'But I bet people did. I mean, the guy was a surgeon,' Catrin said.

Fiona sent her a horrified glance before nodding. 'It didn't do any harm when it came to getting people to sign up, admittedly.'

'Did it bother him? The complaints of charlatanism?'

Fiona looked rattled. 'It didn't seem to. He was pretty thick-skinned. As a surgeon, he had to be, I suppose.'

Jess tilted her head and picked up on the comment. 'Did it bother you, though?'

Fiona let her eyes drop and brushed a few sugar granules off the table before returning Jess's gaze. 'I tried not to think too much about it. He wasn't forcing anyone to contact him. It was a business.'

'And that's all it was? Between you and him, I mean. A business?'

For the first time, Fiona's controlled expression gave way to a flash of something else. Was it annoyance or regret? 'He tried. More than once. But I wasn't interested. I haven't been since Mike...' Her lips zipped shut.

'Did he ever talk to you about being struck off?' Catrin asked.

'No. I was an employee, not his confidante. I just got on with it.' Her reply came out sharp and brittle and to the point.

'What about his wife? Did you ever see her at Moor Cottage?'

'No, I...oh, perhaps once. A long while ago. I heard shouting, and they were having a go at one another outside.'

'Did he ever talk about her?'

'No. I honestly can't remember ever hearing him mention her.' She let out a little exhalation of frustration. 'When I was there I'd be busy in the workshop. Malcolm had calls in the room we'd set up for online comms. He'd come over to the workshop to help when he wasn't busy. As I say, I was an employee.'

Jess took one more polite sip of her coffee and put her cup down. 'Is there anything else you can think of? Anything that might help?'

Fiona shook her head and came back with a question. 'Who could have done this?'

'That's what we intend to find out.' Catrin stood up. 'Would it be okay to use the loo?'

Fiona nodded and pointed towards a door. 'It's at the end of the corridor. Excuse the mess.'

Jess got up, emptied her coffee into the sink with her back to Fiona, and put hers and Catrin's cups on the drainer. 'Thanks for the coffee.'

Fiona nodded half-heartedly. The revelations about Boscombe's potential murder had affected her badly. That was clear to see.

'Here's my number if you can think of anything.' Jess turned back and handed over a business card.

'But murder? Are you sure? Who would want to do that?'

'You'd be surprised,' Jess said. 'You must be aware of Boscombe's past. He had enemies, that's for sure.'

'I can't believe it. No one gets murdered down here.'

Common misconception, thought Jess. Fancy a walk in my shoes for a couple of months? But she said nothing of the kind. Instead, she offered her hand and said her goodbyes and went out to the car. Catrin arrived two minutes later.

'She looked pretty upset,' Catrin said, pulling on her seat belt.

'She did. Probably the last thing she wanted to hear.' Jess gunned the engine. 'Last thing anyone wants to hear, in my experience.'

Catrin reached for her laptop to begin typing up the interview. 'I had a peep into the bedroom she's decorating. She had plastic sheets on the floor and that funny tape over the windows and skirting boards. It looks frighteningly efficient.'

'Preparation. It's more than half the battle.' Jess turned out of the street to join traffic on the Carmarthen road.

'That's the bit I hate.' Catrin's laptop chimed as it booted up. 'All that sealing up and protecting. Such a faff. I'd rather pay someone to do it.'

'Not if you're an unemployed Fiona Needham you don't.' With one glance in the rear-view mirror, Jess accelerated smoothly away.

CHAPTER TWENTY-ONE

'THANKS FOR COMING IN,' Warlow said, offering the ghost of a smile to Corrigan, who sat opposite him with a rigid expression.

'Can we get you something?' Rhys, sitting next to Warlow, asked. 'Tea, coffee, some water?'

'I'm fine.' Alan Corrigan didn't bother with a thank you.

Warlow noted it and chalked it up.

He studied the surgeon. They were almost the same age, Corrigan perhaps a couple of years older. He'd checked with Tom. The earliest you could retire from the NHS and commute your pension was fifty-five. Corrigan's secretary had mentioned that impending likelihood. The suit he wore looked five times more expensive than the one that Warlow dusted off each morning. He was clean shaven, with short dark curly hair greying at the temples. He wore black-rimmed glasses that Warlow suspected were designer. They made him look neat and competent, but his body language betrayed an annoyance at being summoned.

'I have two questions. How long is this going to take, and should I have a solicitor?'

Warlow put his elbows on the table. 'It shouldn't take long. As for a solicitor, you're not under arrest, Mr Corrigan. You're here because we're investigating Malcolm Boscombe's death, and you were a colleague of his. We're trying to get a picture of the man. That's where you come in.'

Corrigan shook his head. 'What exactly happened?'

Warlow sat back. 'I'm not at liberty to divulge the details of the case.'

'I thought he'd drowned,' Corrigan insisted.

Neither officer answered. Warlow looked across at Rhys who had a list of prepared questions in front of him. The DC took his cue and cleared his throat. 'When was the last time you spoke to Mr Boscombe?'

Corrigan huffed out air and shook his head. 'A couple of years ago.'

Rhys nodded. 'Under what circumstances?'

The undercurrent of annoyance that oozed out of Corrigan's cross-legged, arms-folded body language flashed over his face. 'You want the details?'

'If you wouldn't mind, sir.' Rhys unclipped a ballpoint pen and leant his big frame forward, ready to write.

Corrigan gave a half-shrug. 'Malcolm got it into his head that he could apply for reinstatement on the medical register. He came to the hospital to get some paperwork. Turned up out of the blue. The secretaries were surprised, to say the least. He wanted copies of letters of support that some of his patients had written.'

'What did the secretaries do?' Warlow asked.

'What they always do whenever there's a problem. They ring the team leader. Me.' Corrigan emphasised the 'me'. He wanted it to sound like a burden, Warlow guessed, but hinted at how important it was in the same breath. 'I got some security, and they escorted Malcolm off the hospital premises. He had no right to be there.'

Rhys started jotting down notes.

'How did he react?' Warlow asked.

'The way he reacted to anyone that challenged him. With bluster and threats.' Colour rose in Corrigan's cheeks. He looked directly at Warlow when he spoke. 'You'll have done the background on him. You'll know about his conviction and prison term. But even that's only half the story.'

'What's the other half?' Warlow asked.

Corrigan dropped his chin, and a fixed smile spread over his lips. 'He left a stain that no amount of scrubbing can erase. On the department, the hospital, the profession. He's a sociopath. To begin with, the administrators thought he was the answer to all their prayers. He operated quickly, had a glowing CV, charmed the birds from the trees. But for quick, read slapdash. He bragged about the number of cases he could do on a list. And as for charm…' Corrigan let the implication simmer. 'The old heads, the theatre sisters, they saw right through him. Malcolm was careless. He gave the difficult cases to his underlings so that poor results did not reflect on him. He bullied them. Belittled them. Terrified the nurses and the junior staff. Worst of all, he pressurised patients into having private surgery.'

For a moment, the noise of Rhys quickly turning pages as he recorded what Corrigan said filled the room.

'Is that what caused the fight?' Warlow leant in.

'The fight? Ah, yes, the fight. That's all anyone remembers, isn't it?' Corrigan's lips quivered around his mirthless smile. 'Let me tell you about the fight. I was in theatre, finishing up a hernia op. One of the Juniors wanted to see me, and I found her outside my operating theatre doors in tears because one of Mr Boscombe's patients had collapsed on the ward. She'd tried to get hold of him, but he was in his private rooms and he told her to put up a drip and deal with it. A drip. A trainee four months out of medical school, terrified with nowhere to turn to. I don't think she ever recovered from that.'

Rhys had stopped writing. 'What happened?'

'I checked the patient personally. Massive internal bleeding. She bled out in fact. On a ward, in an NHS hospital two hours after Malcolm Boscombe nicked her liver in one of his super-fast cockups. I didn't even change. I got in my car in the scrubs I was wearing and drove to the private hospital, confronted him in the clinic in front of his patients. And yes, we came to blows. Do I regret it? Not for one solitary minute.'

Warlow had read the report. Neither man had been seriously injured. Neither had needed hospital treatment. They'd ended up on the floor in a scuffle, trading insults and blows. Highly embarrassing for the hospital, and for the 'senior consultants' as they were lovingly labelled in the press.

'And when did that happen?'

Corrigan didn't have to think. 'Ten years ago. He was struck off for that, but some lawyer got him reinstated until he was finally convicted in 2017 for an even worse balls up. Not at our hospital, thank God.'

Warlow slid over a letter they'd found in Boscombe's study. Corrigan read it. His only reaction was a tiny snort of derision.

Warlow waited until everything was read. 'Did you know he was trying to get a job abroad?'

'No. And if I had, I'd have done everything I possibly could to stop it happening.'

'Legally, you mean?' Warlow pressed the point home.

'How the hell else?' Corrigan shot him a look brimming with challenge.

Warlow said nothing.

Corrigan sat back, frowning. 'I am not going to answer that.'

Warlow picked up a pencil and inspected it. 'Dare I ask where you were last Friday night and Saturday morning, Mr Corrigan?'

'At home. Asleep.'

Rhys looked up again. 'And there is someone who can confirm that, is there?'

'No.'

Warlow frowned. 'You're married, Mr Corrigan?'

'I am. My wife is away with her family in Ireland. Has been for the last month.'

'I see. So you were at home alone?'

'Yes.'

'Do you sail, Mr Corrigan?' Warlow pulled back the letter and slid it into a file.

Corrigan's chin went up. 'I have a small dinghy.'

'And where is that kept?'

'Llansteffan. The boat club.'

'That's the same estuary that feeds into Laugharne, is that correct?' Warlow asked.

'You know it is.' Corrigan re-folded his arms.

Warlow put the pencil down. 'Did you take the boat out on Saturday?'

A simple question, but it threw the surgeon. 'Did I... no, no I did not.' He sat up. 'Why do I get the impression this is more than just a chat?'

Warlow shrugged. 'You tell me.'

'No. No more. I'm not saying anymore without a solicitor.'

'Good, because we have no more questions for you.' Warlow pushed back from the desk. 'As I say, thanks for coming in. Rhys, can you show Mr Corrigan out?'

Rhys stood up.

Corrigan stayed seated, clearly confused by this sudden change. 'We're done?'

'All we need are the details of your dinghy? Make, model, where exactly it's berthed.' Just in case we need to dot a few i's.'

Corrigan glared back at the DCI, still annoyed.

'And you're sure there's nothing else you'd like to tell us?' Rhys asked evenly.

'Nothing.'

Warlow nodded to his DC, who knocked on the interview room door. It was opened from the outside by a uniformed sergeant. Corrigan stood and hurried out without a backward glance.

Rhys followed but then stopped and turned back to the DCI, half closed the door and whispered, 'What's your take, sir?'

'That Mr Corrigan was not a Malcolm Boscombe fan.'

'The dinghy? Should we go out and look at it, sir?'

Warlow shook his head. 'Contact the boat club. Confirm the details. It's busy there. Someone would have seen something if Corrigan had sailed on Saturday. Let me know.'

Rhys nodded and ducked out, leaving the DCI alone at the table with his thoughts. He was still sitting there ten minutes later when Gil stuck his head around the door.

'The nerd has come good. We have the CCTV footage from the car park.'

'About bloody time,' Warlow said and jumped to his feet. 'Will there be popcorn?'

'No, but I could arrange an ice cream in the intermission.'

'Really?'

'Not a snowball's. But I could stretch to tea and biscuits.'

CHAPTER TWENTY-TWO

IN THE INCIDENT ROOM, Catrin and Jess were back and already adding information to the Job Centre.

'How did it go?' Warlow asked.

'Useful, but nothing earth shattering.' Jess filled the team in on the meeting with Fiona Needham.

Gil zoned in on the fact that her mother paid the dead man £150 a month for his expert opinion.

'*Iesu*, what was it he was telling her?'

'How to overcome chronic constipation. The crock of gold.' Catrin chimed up from where she was writing on the board.

'More like a crock of S, H to the one, T, as my nephew would say.' Gil grinned. It earned him a pained look from Warlow.

'We did learn that Boscombe's wife visited once, and they had a barney. Catrin's already typed up the interview. It's on HOLMES, but knowing how much you hate to read screens, she's printed off a version for you.' Jess handed Warlow a couple of sheets.

'What did you make of Fiona Needham?' Warlow pulled out a chair and sat.

Jess shrugged. 'If there was anything between her and Boscombe, she's hiding it pretty well.'

'Hmm,' Warlow muttered.

'She's more concerned over losing her job and her mother.' Catrin slid the chair from under her desk, sat, and opened her laptop. 'She's also a doer. She's redecorating her mother's bedroom and I bet she'll do the whole house. Her way of coping.'

'I hate redecorating.' Gil said.

'Next time call Fiona Needham. She does it the proper way. Sheets on the floor, masking tape everywhere. It's…' Catrin turned from the board and watched Gil tutting and fussing with his screen. 'Anything I can do, Gil?' she asked.

'The nerd from Laugharne sent me a link to the uploaded CCTV files. But it's proving elusive.'

'Want me to try?'

'Why?' Gil kept his eyes on the screen. 'Because you're younger than me and think you're more tech savvy.'

'Mainly, yes.'

Gil turned and grinned. 'Thought you'd never ask.' He got out of the chair and Catrin took his place. While they played in the cloud, Rhys returned.

'Well?' Warlow threw out the question before the DC had taken half a dozen steps into the room.

Rhys blinked. He'd worked with Warlow long enough now to be prepared for an ambush. 'I spoke to someone called a moorings officer, and he said there were a handful of people around at high tide last Saturday morning at the club where Corrigan keeps his boat. He made some calls. No one remembers seeing him.'

'Damn. Get the numbers and double check.' Warlow tried and failed to hide his disappointment. It would have been very convenient to have Corrigan out on the same stretch of water as Boscombe. Good to have been able to have the supercilious sod in their sights. But murder inquiries were seldom convenient in their course.

'Got it, sir.' Catrin called out from the workstation. They crowded around the screen, staring at a grainy black-and-white image of the Laugharne car park in daylight with cars and people moving at breakneck speed as Catrin scrolled through the hours to get to the time period they were interested in. The quality was not good. It didn't look like they'd cleaned the camera lens recently. Rhys kept pointing things out and laughing. Warlow wondered if he'd ever seen a silent film.

'This could take a while, sir.' Catrin leant forward, concentrating hard.

Warlow sat back and turned to Jess in a low whisper out of earshot of the others. 'How's Molly today?'

'Bear, sore head, you know the phrase.' Jess gave him one of her trademark overbright smiles with eyebrows raised. 'She says she's never going again. I'm saying she shouldn't be too hasty, but all the while there's a tiny gleeful and vengeful part of me that's making a triumphant fist and thinking tough shit matey. You pay your money, and you take your choice.'

'That's understandable,' Warlow said. Molly's father had paid a price for his indiscretion. Rick had become dirty Rick overnight. He could only imagine what Jess had to put up with at work after something like that.

Jess wrinkled her nose. 'Understandable, yes. But also mean and petty.'

Warlow nodded. 'Does that mean you've forgiven Richard?'

'It's Rick. Was Rick.' Jess shook her head. 'I haven't forgiven him, and I won't. But I don't want Molly to be the stick I beat him with. That's too easy and not fair on her.'

'No. That won't work,' Warlow agreed.

Jess kept her eyes on the fold in her trousers, running

her thumb and forefinger along it as she spoke. 'At first, I wanted nothing but for him to wake up in her bed and realise what a calamitous mistake he'd made. But that passed. Because the fact that he wanted not to be in our bed broke what we had and there's no glue in the world that can fix that. I've come to terms with it. But Molly can't. Perhaps she never will.'

Warlow watched the car park CCTV images rushing by a few feet away. It was like being in a time machine. 'Does she need a Cadi fix?'

'Ooh,' Jess cooed. 'Does she ever. We both do.'

'That can be arranged.'

Catrin called over her shoulder. 'Five-thirty Saturday morning as a start time, sir?'

'Why not?' Warlow wheeled his chair closer to the desk the team was working at. The CCTV images showed a dark car park, the estuary completely black beyond the pool of light above the camera, illuminating two-thirds of the space. At 5.32 am., a car pulled in and parked in a space close to the water's edge.

'That's a Mazda CX-30,' Gil said.

Warlow sat forward. A thin drizzle swept across the scene. They all watched as the car's parking lights flared in the smeary image. The driver-side door opened, and someone emerged, back to the camera, hood up against the rain, swathed in a baggy coat and shapeless, water-proof trousers. Boscombe paused for a moment, facing the sea, while he zipped up his coat. He walked around to the back of the car and opened the boot. Light flared again. He took out what looked like a rod and some bait boxes. Another light, from a flashlight in Boscombe's hand, danced over the car park. He slammed the boot shut and turned away from the car. A flash of distant blurry white showed a face half covered by some kind of wrap against the cold.

The car's lights blinked twice before Boscombe walked away to the right side of the car park, following the circle of light from the torch.

'Can we zoom in?' Warlow asked.

Catrin did something with the keyboard, and the grainy image got bigger and grainier. But not any clearer.

Warlow glanced at the time on the screen: 5.38 am. Catrin was already marking it down. They all watched for another five minutes before Catrin fast-forwarded the tape. No one else arrived until 6.15am. Time enough for Boscombe to be well away. It wasn't until 6.30am that natural light began to seep slowly into the image.

'Not much doubt about that,' Gil said. 'He arrives alone. Leaves for the boat. There is no one else around to witness it.'

'So we have a confirmed timeline,' Catrin said. 'This is the last time Boscombe was seen alive.'

Warlow ran it back a couple of times, but there was nothing else to see that would help. Zooming the image did bugger all. 'Get some uniforms out there for the next couple of mornings. Check if there are regular fishermen.'

'Won't it depend on the tides, sir?' Rhys asked.

'It would. So that's your job. Check times, liaise with uniforms.'

Gil sat back and arched his back. 'So, we know he went out first thing, but didn't come back.'

'Catrin, we'd better run through the rest of this footage to make sure he didn't return to the car.' Jess got up and walked to the Job Centre and wrote the action.

'Rhys and I can share that, ma'am.' Catrin sent Rhys a false smile.

The DC didn't object. Warlow knew he enjoyed the technology side of the work. Plus, seeing people dash about at silly speeds tickled his funny bone.

Warlow got up and joined Jess at the Job Centre,

massaging his lower lip as he thought. 'That leaves us with two big unanswered questions.' He pointed to an image that Catrin had found and pasted up. Something one of the Laugharne regulars had provided, showing an array of boats at low tide. Boscombe's boat had been circled in red.

Warlow jabbed a finger at the red circle. 'Where the hell is Boscombe's boat?'

'And where the hell is Lee Pryce?' Jess added.

Gil's phone rang. Everyone knew it was the DS's phone as he'd chosen the 'William Tell Overture' as his ringtone. Often, he'd let it ring much longer than was necessary simply for the hell of it. Or 'for the William Tell of it', as he quite liked to say. Mainly because, like the tune itself, saying it annoyed everyone in the vicinity who'd heard both the tune and the saying at least a dozen times. But he did not let it ring today. Gil accepted the call, stood, and walked to the far corner of the room to take it.

'We've got the coastguard and local sailing clubs on the lookout for the skiff.' Catrin confirmed.

'Is there a chance it's gone out to sea?' Jess asked.

'Or sunk,' Rhys offered.

Warlow nodded. 'Both are possibles. But we'll give it the rest of today before we call for help from the frogmen.'

Gil's voice reached them from the other side of the room. He was grinning. 'Right, we have an answer to one of your big questions.'

'The boat?' Jess took a stab.

'No. Lee Pryce. Would you believe he's just walked in to Llanelli nick and given himself up?'

Three pairs of astonished eyes turned in his direction.

Warlow's hand went involuntarily to the lump on his head. Everyone saw it. No one commented.

'I suspect that you'll want to interview him yourself, Mr Warlow?' Gil asked.

'Jess and I will go,' Warlow said. 'I want him to look me straight in the stitches when he confesses.'

CHAPTER TWENTY-THREE

JESS PHONED THROUGH TO LLANELLI, spoke to the desk sergeant and asked him to give Pryce a cup of tea and pop him into an interview room. He hadn't asked for a solicitor and she made sure the sergeant emphasised he wasn't under arrest. They'd be over as soon as they could.

Catrin handed Warlow a file as he put his coat on.

'I've printed off some threads from the forums I found. There's an action group with a thousand signatures trying to get recompense for the other cases involving Boscombe. Part of what they do is out him. That's what happened when Pryce confronted Boscombe in the supermarket car park. He calls himself the Butcher's Bane online.'

Warlow growled out a 'Hmmm.'

'What are they after on these forums?' Jess asked.

Catrin shrugged. 'They're angry. There's a bit of vigilantism. A bit of revenge. Worry that he might be allowed to practice again. Anger that he hasn't had a stiffer sentence. They think it's wrong that other charges have not been brought.'

'Like what?' Rhys asked.

Catrin answered. 'Assault. GBH, that sort of thing. There are lots of pissed off patients on there.'

Warlow made a mental note. With serial offenders, people were always confused as to why a hundred charges weren't brought. The fact was that less serious charges could often lie dormant where more serious charges were used to prosecute because they elicited the bigger sentence. It worked better for the courts, but perhaps not so well for the individual left feeling betrayed by the system.

As Warlow turned to leave, someone walked through the Incident Room door. The third bad thing in today's shitty triptych. DI (no longer acting DCI) Kelvin Caldwell. Known as Kev to his friends. Known as KFC – Kelvin Fucking Caldwell – to 99.999 per cent of the remaining Dyfed-Powys Police Service population, Warlow included.

He walked in, gazing around, short-sleeved with his tie done up. His poppy eyes looked small through his wire-rimmed glasses and made him appear more like an accountant that had taken a wrong turn out of the lift than a senior officer.

His gaze finally found its target and zeroed in on Warlow. 'Ah, Evan. Glad I caught you.'

Warlow continued sliding on his coat. 'Well, you'll have to catch me another time. We're off to Llanelli.'

'The Boscombe case?'

Warlow wanted to lean in and say, *None of your business*. But that would have been rude. Instead, he said, 'Which bit of we're leaving did you not understand?'

Gil frowned. Catrin turned away. The sort of thing you did when you saw senior colleagues jousting. And not amiably.

Rhys, being Rhys, looked on unperturbed.

'I'm only here to introduce myself to the team ahead of the TV crew appearing on Friday.' Caldwell continued. 'Superintendent Goodey feels it would be an excellent example of coordinated police work. I understand you've involved the coastguard?' Caldwell grinned. Or at least some muscles either side of his mouth make the skin indent a little.

Warlow fought down the urge to retch. 'I doubt we'll be able to help. The case is quickly coming to a conclusion. I suspect we'll be done by Friday.'

Caldwell frowned. 'I understood this was a complex investigation?'

'It is. But we believe in keeping it simple.' Warlow walked towards the door and right past Caldwell. 'Gil has the details. He'll fill you in on as much as you need to know.'

Warlow took the stairs. Mainly because it was quicker. But also because if they took the lift Caldwell might want to share it and he didn't want that. You didn't stay in the same room as a rattlesnake if you could help it.

They took the Jeep. Half an hour up the A48 and then the M4. As they approached the Cross Hands roundabout, Jess broke the silence. Or rather, cut it with a hypothetical knife. 'Is there any point me asking?'

'What?' Warlow shot her a glance.

'Why you almost bit Caldwell's head off? Why the mention of him makes your nose quiver like someone's just taken a dump on the tea trolley?'

'As bad as that?'

Jess waited.

'Tea trolley? Really?'

Still, Jess did not respond.

Warlow sighed. 'Okay. He's a lazy, out-of-his-depth prat.'

'And?'

'And one day he's going to cock up and someone innocent will pay for it.'

Jess frowned. 'Is this still about him not trying hard

enough to identify that refugee they found floating in the water?'

'That's one of a string of things.' Warlow kept his eyes on the road. Jess and he had once broken a drugs ring. The same case that had involved the death of DS Mel Lewis that West Mids was about to investigate. But the unidentified body Caldwell had not bothered to dig too hard into had turned out to be a refugee from the illegal marijuana farm he and Jess had stumbled upon. That refugee's wife and son had been trafficked and perhaps, just perhaps, if Caldwell had done his job then one thing might have led to another and who knows. A stretch, Warlow knew it was, but it still rankled. As did the other things that Caldwell had done, or not done, over the years.

'But you're not going to tell me, are you?' Jess asked.

Warlow shook his head. 'All I'm going to say is that if you ever work with him, trust him about as far as you can spit.'

'I can't spit for toffee,' Jess said.

'I rest my case.'

───────

'SORRY ABOUT THIS MORNING.' Lee Pryce's eyes flitted from Warlow's cut head and back to the DCI's eyes like a metronome on speed. Good, thought Warlow. Let the bastard sweat.

They sat in an interview room in Llanelli police station. Not that different to any other that Warlow had sat in except that it was older and a little smellier, despite the air freshener in the corner.

'No need to apologise, Lee.' Warlow kept it light. 'I could have been anybody. Your mate thought I was an electrician. What about you? The cartel, possibly? Me and my henchman DS Jones?'

'Now you'd be forgiven there,' Jess added. 'I mean DS Jones looks like something out of Narcos.'

'Or nachos.' Warlow smiled at his own joke.

'I'm going to write that down.' Jess repeated 'nachos' and scribbled something in her notebook.

Pryce watched this exchange with varying degrees of bemusement. When a silence opened up, he launched into it. 'I thought you might be one of that lot.'

'The cartel?' Warlow asked.

Pryce wore a rugby shirt with a hole in the sleeve. The red and green stripes were still dusty from his morning's work at the construction site. A dragon tattoo on his neck was only half visible thanks to the sawdust. He sat with his big scarred hands clasped around a coffee mug.

We have that in common at least, Warlow surmised. Builders — and he lumped carpenters in with the whole — were like coppers. Never turn down the offer of refreshment.

'No,' Pryce said. 'I have a couple of payday loans owing. I thought maybe…you know. Sometimes these sharks can get antsy, like.'

'How much do you owe?' Jess asked.

'Five hundred. Not that much, but it's a few weeks overdue, like.' Pryce pursed his lips, barely visible in the middle of his beard. He had ruddy cheeks and freckles. Warlow decided he looked more like a farmer than a carpenter's mate.

'What made you change your mind, Lee?' Jess had her phone on the table recording the chat. She'd asked, and he'd agreed. Though he'd volunteered to be interviewed, he was still under caution. Pryce glanced at the phone intermittently while he answered.

'I read about Boscombe. I reckoned that's why you wanted to see me.'

Warlow and Jess looked at each other and nodded. Jess

spoke next. 'Smart move. Saves us hunting you down, right?'

The word hunting did it. Pryce let go of the mug and brought both hands up, palms forward. 'Whoa. Hunting? Come on.'

Jess smiled. 'Just an expression, Lee. To go with the Narcos thing.'

Warlow said. 'I mean, there's no need for us to hunt you, is there?'

Pryce bristled. 'No, definitely not. I haven't done anything.'

Warlow's lower jaw jutted forward. 'Not strictly true that though, is it? There was the Morrisons' car park thing.'

Pryce exhaled. 'That was stupid. I lost my head. I saw him there and I lost it.'

Jess opened the file on her desk. She'd bulked it out with a couple of magazines, but only one sheet held any relevance. One sheet was all she needed. 'It was your nan, wasn't it? The one that suffered?'

At the mention of his grandmother, Pryce stiffened. 'Yeah. My nan. She looked after me when I was a kid. After my mother got ill.'

Warlow knew the story, as did Jess. But they wanted Pryce to open up, so they sat back and listened while the man opposite did the talking.

CHAPTER TWENTY-FOUR

PRYCE STARED down at his empty coffee mug as he spoke. 'My nan…she was lovely. Her and my grandad were good people. He started in the steelworks as a boy, like, and worked there until he was made redundant in the eighties. Then he worked in a radiator factory – you know, car parts – until he retired. He did okay, worked every day of his life. They were worried when my nan got a pain in her side, like. They went to see…' Pryce stopped. He looked up. 'I can't say his name, I can't. He'll always be the Butcher to me. It was my nan's bad luck to end up under his care. In the NHS. They did tests and he told her it was her gall-bladder, and she needed an op. And then he told her it would be months, but if she went private and paid cash, like, he could do it in a week.'

Warlow glanced at Jess. She'd folded her arms against what she was hearing, her expression rigid.

'Two grand he wanted. A lot of money then for anyone, never mind pensioners.'

'And this took place at a private hospital?' Jess asked.

'In Swansea, yeah. The Butcher worked there. She was in and out in two days, like. Didn't bother her at all. But then six months later she got the pain again. Worse this time. Of course, she waited. It couldn't be her gallbladder because that had been removed. Bad indigestion, she thought. But it weren't. It was a cholecystitis.' Pryce said the word carefully. Like he'd practised it a hundred, if not a thousand times. Woken up in the small hours of the night with it on his lips. 'An infection of the gallbladder the Butcher was supposed to have taken out.'

Pryce's lips quivered. 'She collapsed. By the time they got her in the infection had spread, like. An abscess and then peritonitis. They tried but it took over. She died in hospital because that bastard Butcher lied to us.'

'That must have been tough for you and your grandad.' Warlow said.

'It broke him. He had a stroke. He's still in a nursing home. Can't talk or walk, like.' Pryce shook his head as if he still couldn't quite believe it. He looked up then, forcing them to listen. 'And the worst thing of all was that he wouldn't even admit he'd done anything wrong. For weeks he wouldn't even talk to us, but we forced the hospital to meet us face to face. He said he'd opened my nan up and not done anything because he'd found nothing wrong. Even though he told us he'd taken it away. He lied as quick as you and me breathe, like. He lied so that he didn't have to say sorry. I don't think he's ever said that. To anyone.'

Warlow recalled the transcript of the trial and of the GMC hearing that led to Boscombe being struck off. The words arrogant and lack of remorse had stood out then. They clanged around inside his skull now like the clapper of a bell. 'But Boscombe went to jail. Not for what he did to your grandmother. But he went to jail.'

'He did. And I'm grateful to you lot for that.' Pryce gave an emphatic nod.

That was Jess's signal to slide over a sheet of paper for

Pryce to read. 'And when he came out, you and others set up a group to monitor him, yes?'

Pryce glanced at the paper. A blown-up screenshot of a Twitter feed. A message under the handle 'Butcher's Bane' had been highlighted.

@BUTCHERSBANE

I'll throw him in the river if anyone sees him at the station again. Txt me. #banthebutcher

We got an address. DM me. Fun tonight with a spray can #banthebutcher

JESS leant forward and pointed to the handle. 'That's you. Butcher's Bane? Isn't it?'

Pryce sent her a calculating look. 'You know it is. This stuff was all shown in court.'

Warlow pushed back and arched his neck. 'And you got a suspended sentence for threatening behaviour.'

Jess pulled out another sheet. 'You cornered him in a car park. You said you were going to pour petrol over his car and set fire to it. Burn the Butcher. Is that right?'

Pryce dropped his hands to between his legs with a resigned, unhappy expression. 'It was the first time I'd laid eyes on him since my nan…' He stopped, his mouth tightening. 'You know all this.'

'And you were warned to stay well away, yes?' Jess pulled the sheet back across.

Rapid nodding from Pryce. 'I have. I've stayed away from the bastard. I haven't seen him since the supermarket.'

'But it hasn't stopped you from being active online, has it, Lee?'

Pryce glowered.

Jess slid another sheet of paper across. More blown-up texts from a Facebook page. 'These are from a group calling itself Killswitch.'

Pryce frowned and looked down. 'How did you get this? It's a private group.'

Warlow tutted. 'We have a whole army of nerds, Lee. They're very good at this stuff.'

Jess leant forward and stabbed her finger at the sheet again. 'This is from last month. From a post entitled *Hacking Alternis*. You knew he was online, didn't you?'

'Everyone did.'

'But not everyone threatened to burn down the Butcher's shop once they found it. You did.' She moved her finger down and rested it on the highlighted text. 'Here.'

Pryce was defiant and kept his eyes up. 'Yeah, I said we should torch the place, like. But I didn't do it. All kinds of people say all kinds of stuff here. It's somewhere to let off steam.'

They sat in silence for a while; a good half minute until Warlow said, 'You a sailor, Lee?'

Pryce stared back at the DCI for a moment and then started nodding. 'Yeah. I'm out all weathers, me. Got a spot in the America's Cup Crew next year, plus my thirty-metre cruiser in Monte Carlo.'

Warlow suppressed a smile. Despite everything, he was beginning to warm to Pryce. 'I'll take that as a no then.'

'What do you think?'

'How about fishing?' Jess took up the baton.

'I do a bit of carp fishing up at the reservoir, like. Can't be arsed with fly. The licence is a pain, and the kit is too expensive, though my grandad used to…' Pryce's words tailed off at the mention of his grandfather. It remained a raw wound.

'What about sea angling?' Jess continued. 'Ever been out on a boat?'

'Couple of times. Mackerel and that. One of the boys I go and watch the Scarlets with goes out around the Mumbles. I've been with him a couple of times. A gang of three or four of us and a few beers, like. It's a good laugh as long as the weather isn't too tasty.'

'What about the Towy estuary? Around Laugharne?'

Pryce shook his head. 'No, I…' He stopped, suspicion clouding his eyes. 'That's where you found him, isn't it? Somewhere around there?'

'It is.'

Pryce nodded. 'So was he shot, stabbed, strangled, what?'

'You tell us, Lee.' Jess held his defiant gaze.

Pryce dropped his voice. 'If I'd have been there, it would have been all fucking three. To make sure, like.'

'You forgot setting fire to the boat. Arson seems to be your thing.' Warlow said.

'Good idea. I'll remember that the next time.' Pryce pretended to recall something and held a finger up. 'Oh, hang on, there won't be a next time because the bastard is dead.'

'Where were you on Friday night, Lee?' Jess asked.

'I was with my partner. We went out for a curry and watched a film.'

'What film?'

'*Three Billboards*. One of our favourites.'

Jess pushed a pen across. 'Write down your partner's contact details.'

'And while you're at it, that mate of yours with a boat. We'd like to have a chat with him as well,' Warlow added.

'This is bullshit,' Pryce said, as he took out his phone and wrote numbers and names from his contacts.

'Bullshit it may be. But it's bullshit we'll be checking,' Warlow said.

Pryce looked up from where he was leaning close to the

paper. 'I didn't kill him. But I'm not sorry he's dead. He killed my nan, almost killed my grandad, and fucked up my life for a while. First thing I did when I heard was jump up and punch the air. I'm not going to apologise for that. The world is a better place without him. End of. Oh, and the next time we have a little chat, I'll want a solicitor.'

CHAPTER TWENTY-FIVE

It started to rain on the way back in the car from Llanelli nick. The Jeep's wipers struggled to keep up with the deluge and the spray from passing traffic. Warlow noticed a persistent smear on the windscreen on the passenger side. That wiper would need changing. He stayed in the slow lane. He'd seen too many accidents from drivers not adapting to the conditions to play silly buggers with the big lorries in front.

'The more I hear about Boscombe, the more I don't like him. I know we shouldn't pass judgement, but this time, I can't help it.' Jess had been texting on her phone, but put it down now to express an opinion.

'Tom, my youngest, sometimes tells me stories. The odd near miss he's seen. The medics have words for the cockups – "Never events". Mistakes that should never happen, like leaving bits of kit inside, or operating on the wrong side. Difficult to believe they could, but it's a stressful job.'

'Are you making excuses for Boscombe?' Jess sounded surprised.

'No. The opposite. Cockups are one thing. Incompetence and hiding behind the big, "I'm the expert" disguise is something else.'

Jess sighed. 'Being wrong in that job is no joke. But not admitting to it is worse.'

'Criminal even.'

'Pryce is still very pissed off.'

Warlow nodded. 'But pissed off enough to follow Boscombe out to sea and clobber him? I don't see it.'

'Neither do I.' Jess agreed.

Warlow's phone rang through the car's speaker system. He glanced at the caller ID as a name popped up on the Jeep's dashboard display.

He let out a yelp of surprise. 'Hah. Owen Cargil. A blast from the past if ever there was one.' He turned to Jess. 'Mind if I take this? Owen's an old DCI I worked with in South Wales Police.'

'Carry on. As long as you don't mind me hearing it?'

'I'll tell him you're in the car. So he won't discuss the drugs or the sex tape.'

Jess narrowed her eyes.

Warlow reached forward to the dash and accepted the call. 'Owen. What can I do for you?'

'On the way back from the golf course, are we? That's what retired buggers do, isn't it?'

Warlow grinned. 'I'm in the car with a colleague after nine holes at Llanelli. Or as we like to call it in police parlance, interviewing a suspect.' He waited a beat before adding. 'I'll have you know.'

'What? So rumours of your retirement are greatly exaggerated then.'

'I went and came back.'

'Wasn't it Lazarus that said that?'

'I have been called that. Though I was away for more than four days.'

'Who's the colleague?'

'Jess Allanby. DI.'

'Hi, Jess.'

'Hi, Owen.' Jess answered.

'Sorry to hear you're shackled with the Wolf. Just stay away when there's a full moon.'

Warlow shook his head. 'The old jokes are the best ones, eh, Owen?'

'Talking of old jokes, there's a reason for the call. Remember Derek Geoghan?'

'How could I forget since I get cards from his missus at least four times a year. Got one last week in fact. One without dried shit in it this time, just a rat's desiccated leg. So an improvement on the couple before.'

Jess stared at Warlow, her nose wrinkled in distaste.

'Ah, so you know then.' Owen Cargil said.

Warlow frowned. 'Know what?'

'He's out. Applied for an early parole and has been let out on medical grounds. Some kind of leukaemia they say.'

Warlow pondered this. Karen Geoghan's cards had mentioned no illness. He understood that she'd kept up the attack as a means of psychological warfare. But threats were threats. 'I better lock the front gate then.'

'I wouldn't rush. I don't think he's much of a threat from what I've seen.'

Warlow let out a hollow laugh. 'How do you know? Have you been to visit?'

'I asked the prison service to send me a snap. He's coming back to my patch. I want to be able to recognise the git. I will now, but you wouldn't. He's lost three stone and walks with a stick.'

Warlow pondered this information and tried to apply it to the big, bruiser of a man that they'd sent down all those years ago and who appeared in his memory banks whenever he thought of Derek Geoghan. Cargil's information wouldn't compute. In

Warlow's head, Geoghan would always be a slobby, overweight monster who it took three burly officers to subdue.

Owen paused to allow Warlow time to assimilate all this before asking, 'Alun still in Australia, is he?'

'He is.'

'My niece is, too. Sydney, though, not Perth. Her partner has a term for the moribund. Anything on its last legs is "cactus". Derek Geoghan looked pretty bloody cactus as he came out of prison two days ago, if you ask me.'

'What about the lovely Karen?'

'I doubt you'd recognise her, either. Well, apart from the voice of hers. Pure nails on a blackboard, that woman. She's gone the other way and put on five stones at least. It's like a bloody Stephen King novel. Plus, she needs one of those things on wheels to get about. What do they call them, wheeled walkers, is it?'

'It is,' Jess said.

'Thank Christ you're there, Jess. Evan doesn't do small talk, as you will have noticed.'

Feigning betrayal, Warlow glanced at Jess. She kept her eyes on the traffic.

'I never had to with you there.' Warlow growled and made a moving mouth shape with his hand, flapping it open and shut a few times.

Jess's eyes never wavered, but a smile cracked over her lips.

'That's gratitude for you,' Owen continued. 'We both know Geoghan threatened to come for us once he got out. So, I'm doing my duty, Evan, like a good colleague should. Letting you know the tiger is out of its cage. Or from what I could see, the sloth is off its branch.'

The conversation drifted away towards family, other colleagues, many of whom had actually retired, and sport.

When Owen finally rang off, Jess turned to Warlow. 'Who is Derek Geoghan?'

'The term lowlife doesn't do him or his wife justice. Parasites. Worms. Bottom feeders. Take your pick.' Warlow explained about how he and Owen had investigated the case and uncovered a cesspit of fraud, manipulation, and abuse with the Geoghans the chief architects targeting the vulnerable and elderly.

Jess listened, shaking her head with each new revelation. 'How long has he done?'

'Nearly thirteen years.'

'Were there any children? I've seen cases where the kids can be worse than their parents when revenge comes into it.'

'No kids.' Warlow slowed as they reached the Point Abram roundabout. 'If ever there was justification for mandatory sterilisation, the Geoghans were it. Thankfully, nature, for once, saw sense.'

'What about friends?'

'Not the friendly type, the Geoghans. Karen recently won some money on the lottery. She may have used that to help get Derek out.'

'Enough left over to put a contract out on you?'

Warlow's side-eye glance across at his colleague dripped derision. 'That's the sort of question Rhys would ask.'

Jess grinned. 'Still, it's nice of Owen to let you know.'

'He's one of the good ones.'

They lapsed into silence as Warlow let Owen's intel marinate. It sounded as if Derek Geoghan was one less thing to worry about on balance. But even as the thought fired, another one pushed it out of the way. A jarring one that he couldn't quite hold on to. Something he'd read or seen recently that plucked at his subconscious.

Jess's phone rang and the moment passed. Warlow

couldn't name her ringtone, but it was something by Adele, he knew that much. He wasn't a complete philistine.

'It's Gil.' Jess put the phone to her ear. 'Hello?' She listened for fifteen seconds before turning a wide-eyed expression towards Warlow. 'Gil, I'm in the car with him. Let me put you on speaker.'

The DS's voice broke in at full throttle halfway through a sentence. '...for the last ten minutes. Who's he been talking to, the Pope?'

'He wasn't in,' Warlow said in his best talking-to-some-one-on-speaker voice. 'I had to speak to Owen Cargil instead.'

'Cargil. Is he still around?'

'Alive and well. Sends his regards.'

'Never mind that. I've had Povey on the phone. They think they've found Boscombe's skiff.'

The car lurched forward as Warlow's foot jerked the accelerator. 'Sorry,' he muttered as he regained control.

'Where?' Jess asked.

'On a sand bank on the other side of the estuary. Near Tywyn Point where the River Gwendraeth opens into the Tywi.'

Jess looked bewildered. Warlow tried to picture it in his head. 'Is this anywhere near Cefn Sidan?'

'Not far. You're in the right neck of the woods.' Gil answered.

It wasn't really an answer because Cefn Sidan was immense. The literal translation was silky ridge. Eight miles of sandy beach fronting the Pembrey Forest.

'But come back around the corner towards Kidwelly and on the other side of the estuary, or the middle of it, if you want to be really accurate. There are big sandbanks there opposite that gigantic holiday park. Picture that and you'd be thereabouts,' Gil added.

'How the hell did it get there?'

'You'll have to ask Povey. She's in touch with the coast-guard. Someone spotted it and rang it in. Rhys and Catrin are on their way. The boat's completely inaccessible so the coastguard is waiting for the tide to come far enough in so that they can tow it in to the quay at Kidwelly.'

Warlow weighed up his options. There'd be little point in the four of them waiting on the tide for a boat to come in. 'Okay. We're on the way back. We'll see what Povey thinks once she's had a look.'

'Any joy with Pryce?' Gil asked.

'Joy isn't exactly the word I'd use.' Jess held the phone in front of her at arm's length to allow Warlow to hear Gil better.

'We've got a couple of things to follow up on, but Pryce doesn't do it for me.' Warlow flicked the wipers up to max as the spray from a big car transporter flooded them. He eased out to overtake.

'We'll be back in twenty minutes,' Jess said.

'Tidy. I'll get the kettle on. Gil out.'

Jess ended the call with a patient smile. 'Tell me where you found him, again?'

'DS Jones? I didn't. He found us, remember? Superintendent Buchannan told me he was a keeper. A bit like a stray dog that wanders on to your porch for a drink of water and before you know it he's sleeping at the bottom of your bed.'

'Now that's an image I prefer you not to have shared.'

Warlow grinned. 'Any time.'

CHAPTER TWENTY-SIX

'I SUPPOSE it's luck the boat ended up on the sandbar.' Rhys stood at the very edge of the walled area at Kidwelly quay, next to the concrete ramp leading into the water, looking left towards the open sea.

They'd cordoned off the quay car park and parked next to Povey's Scene of Crime van. A big Land Rover stood on the ramp, its trailer in the water awaiting its prize.

'Why luck?' Catrin looked across the river to the brown mudflats and the farmland above them. Neat and tidy little green patches divided up by hedgerows.

Rhys didn't shift his gaze. 'I mean, if it was drifting, isn't there a chance it might have gone right out. To sea, I mean. A few miles and you're in the Bristol Channel and then it's the open Atlantic and next stop Newfoundland.'

Catrin turned to glance up at the DC. 'How do you know this stuff?'

'I like geography. I like to work out where I am. The current would have to take you south of Ireland, mind.'

'Have you put all that in your Tinder profile? Six two and a bit, plays rugby, likes geography and post-mortems.'

'Don't do Tinder.'

'No, of course you don't.'

The rain had stopped, but out on the horizon a grey sheet was moving left to right, blurring the definition between sky and sea.

'I think it's going to miss us. That squall.' He nodded towards the sheet.

'How do you know that?' Catrin thrust her hands in her pockets against the chilly wind.

Rhys nodded towards the west. 'It's the clouds. They're moving in that direction.'

'Oh, and a weatherman too? Why does that not surprise me?'

Rhys turned, his genial expression unperturbed by his sergeant's prickliness. 'Go back to the car, sarge. It's cold out here.'

'No, I want to be here when the boat comes in.'

There wasn't long to wait. An orange inflatable RNLI Inshore lifeboat came bouncing up over the waves, pulling a small skiff. Rhys pointed a finger. 'There's something draped over the front of the skiff. Maybe that's the hump the kids saw.'

Once the vessels were near the ramp, ropes were transferred, and the skiff attached to a launching trolley. The Land Rover pulled the lot out of the water and set it on dry flat standing. Povey appeared from out of her van with another two techs in blue suits, all gloved up.

Rhys and Catrin stood looking down as the crime tech did a quick examination. Catrin had her notebook out ready.

'Right. First things first. The name on the boat is "Miranda".' She looked up. 'Does that help?'

'It's the right one,' Rhys confirmed.

'Okay. That's a good start.' Povey walked around

examining the boat's exterior. She spent a lot of time on the top edge. 'Gunnel caps look clear. No sign of blood or tissue. We'll have a better look when we get it inside, obviously.'

Catrin shot Rhys a questioning glare and whispered, 'Gunnel?'

'The top edge of the circumference. The bit you step over to get in.'

Catrin couldn't help being annoyed, more so for not knowing quite why.

Rhys picked up on it. 'I like history. All types. Naval included. A gunnel, or gunwale, is the part of a boat that supported the guns.'

'Of course. Silly me.' Catrin batted her eyelids.

Rhys shrugged. 'I watch National Geographic. I read stuff. All sorts. Patrick O'Brien is great if you want to know about boats.'

The afternoon light was beginning to fade. Povey flicked up a headband light while one of the other techs held up a big flashlight and followed her around.

'I see an electric outboard. A small one. Still attached. The bottom of the boat contains a little water. Possible rain from the last couple of days. I see no obvious bloodstaining. That's a rib cover over the prow to keep the weather off.' She reached across and lifted the flap of tarpaulin, leant over and peered in. 'Some water bottles and a box. Probably a tackle box.' She groaned with the effort of not trying to touch anything and maintaining an awkward position. 'Nothing else I can see.'

'No weapon then?' Catrin asked.

'Nothing obvious.' Povey glanced over her shoulder. 'I don't like the look of this weather. She's been out for days as it is. Better we get her to the lab I think.'

'Should we come with you?' Catrin asked.

'No. No point. We won't be rushed. Warlow will have to make do with this as a prelim for now.' She grinned up. 'I'm sure you'll be able to keep him sweet between you.'

The two officers exchanged knowing looks and said nothing.

Rhys drove on the way back to Carmarthen while Catrin wrote up some notes. 'Why did you join the police, Rhys?'

'It's a good job. I enjoy helping people. And now that I'm working with DCI Warlow, it's…' He frowned, as if surprised by his own words.

Catrin paused and looked up, waiting for him to finish. When he didn't, she prompted him. 'Crap, mad, long hours. What?'

Rhys's brow cleared. 'Before it was a bit boring. I'd worked with DI Caldwell and Llewellyn and some others, but with DCI Warlow it's non-stop. You feel like you're about to find out something new any second.'

Catrin nodded. 'He's different, I'll give you that.'

'I asked him once why they call him the Wolf?'

A peel of laughter burst out from Catrin's lips. 'What?' she screeched.

'He didn't mind. He said it's because his house is called Ffau'r Blaidd. Some old name for an old property. I said I'd heard he got the name because once he's got the scent, he never gives up.'

'I think you're watching too many films, Rhys.'

The DC thought for a moment. 'Possibly. I look after my cousin a lot. He likes films.'

'Hmm. How old is he then?'

'Thirty-one.'

Catrin replayed the last two sentences and fought through being flummoxed to ask, 'Did you say thirty-one?'

'Yeah. Cai's a Down's. He's brilliant. His favourite film

is *Wreck-it Ralph*. I can quote probably two-thirds of the dialogue on that one.'

Catrin turned back to her notes but didn't write anything down. Rhys had a knack of repelling all boarders when it came to taking the Micky. Even Gil sometimes struggled. No one had the right to be so straightforward and genuine. It wasn't normal. She'd seen it when he interviewed people. Victims especially. He made them think they were being listened to. Genuinely and wholeheartedly, without artifice. That was him. From top to toe; the genuine article. But she worried about that in a job that took sarcasm to another level whenever the opportunity arose. Ah well, Rhys was her junior. She'd have to put in a bit of extra training to make sure he got up to speed on that one.

'How about you, sarge?' Rhys asked. 'What do you read?'

'Do magazines count?' Catrin didn't lift her eyes.

'Yep. National Geographic is a magazine.'

'I'm more of an audiobook person if I am honest.'

'Ah, like Gina.'

For the second time in almost as many minutes, DS Richards paused in her composition to stare in open surprise at her colleague. 'Gina as in Officer Gina Mellings of the blonde hair?'

'Yeah. You know Gina?'

'Yes, I do. But I didn't know you and she were—'

'It's only been a few weeks, but it's going great. She's a big Blue Planet fan. Loves JK Rowling. We have lots in common.'

Catrin once again turned back to her laptop. Mainly to hide her smile. A mischievous part of her wanted to ask if they'd played hide-the-wand-in-the-chamber-of-secrets to the accompaniment of David Attenborough saying "I wish it was twice as big and half of it was still unexplored." She smiled, and without looking up simply said, 'Know what a "not entirely light equine" is Rhys?'

His eyes lit up. 'A crossword clue? I like crossword clues.'

'Almost. A puzzle, anyway. Let's leave it at that.'

CHAPTER TWENTY-SEVEN

WARLOW WALKED through the door to the Incident Room to find it eerily quiet. Yes, there was the clicking and clacking of keyboards, but no buzz of noise, no one on the phones. No one actually saying anything. The word that sprang to mind was ominous.

'Christ, Gil. Who died?' Warlow asked only to find the DS coughing in response. Warlow had never seen him cough. And it was a good one. A wheezer of the first water. Gil's fist came up to cover his face, while his eyes became large warning orbs and his other hand extending an index finger pointing to the desk opposite. One that wasn't visible to Warlow until he pivoted and saw that it was occupied by a uniformed Two-Shoes, with her eyes firmly on the screen in front of her. A woman, Warlow decided, who did not like wasting time.

'Ah, Evan. You're back.' She didn't look at him while she spoke, but continued typing for a good half a minute while everyone stood silently waiting. Jess and Warlow exchanged one puzzled look before Two-Shoes sat back finally and turned towards them.

'Been busy I see?' Her lips parted to show a lot of unusually white teeth. It was a stretch to call it a smile.

'Always, ma'am,' Warlow replied.

'A word in your office, Evan?' She stood up. Warlow and Jess followed. But Two-Shoes stopped and wrinkled her nose. 'No need for DI Allanby. Just the two of us.'

'Cup of tea, ma'am?' Gil called from the front.

'No. Never touch the stuff.' She turned and marched towards the SIO room. Warlow lingered for a moment, taking in the expression on Gil's face. Horror didn't even come near. Lucky there was no cream nearby or it surely would have curdled.

Two-Shoes waited for Warlow to enter and then shut the door.

'Have a seat,' she said and stood, arms folded with her back to the door. 'How's it going?'

Warlow sat. 'Lots of threads, ma'am. Most are breaking off when we pull them. But we've found the boat. That's something.'

'Good, good,' Two-Shoes nodded in a way Warlow suspected she thought of as sagely. 'Lots of interest in this case of yours, Evan. The surgeon fallen from grace. An avenging angel.'

'I wouldn't go so far as calling a murderer an angel, ma'am.'

Two-Shoes backtracked. 'No, of course not. Not my words, but the sort of words they use on TV, correct?'

Warlow's nostrils flared as if he'd smelt something bad. 'One reason I don't watch it much. It's always lurid and overblown. As far as I can see, on TV so long as someone cries, everyone's happy.'

Two-Shoes blinked but didn't move. She cleared her throat. 'And that's precisely why I'd like a chance to portray the truth. Let them see the nitty gritty of an investigation.

Fly on the wall, warts and all. From what I'm hearing, yours would be ideal.'

'What is it you're hearing, ma'am?' Warlow didn't have to try too hard to sound frosty.

'You know, a mystery that needs unravelling. Not much forensics to go on. The detective running with his instincts. They'll lap it up.'

Jesus Christ on a bike, thought Warlow. She thinks it's an episode of bloody Poirot. 'I'm not sure I'm the right person to be in front of a camera, ma'am.' He could have added, *because I'm likely to shove the bloody thing where they'd need powerful lighting and a little camera on the end of a bendy scope to remove it, given the slightest opportunity,* but sensibly didn't.

'It would only mean one or two one-on-one pieces,' Two-Shoes insisted, excitement flickering behind her eyes. 'We'd both need to do that. But after the event. Showing your thought process, and mine of course, once the case is put to bed. You could do that, Evan.'

'I know Jess could. She'd be ideal.'

Two-Shoes sucked air in through her teeth. 'Not sure she's quite ready.'

'She is.'

'No, not quite.'

'Ma'am, Jess is one of the most—'

'As I said, not quite ready yet.' The smile that wasn't a smile came back with a vengeance and carried a, that's-the-end-of-that warning with it. 'So, I'll tell Kelvin Caldwell that we've had this little chat and that you're still on for Friday. Looks like progress is going to be slow on this one. What I'm trying to say is, don't rush it. Take your time.'

Despite knowing he shouldn't, Warlow responded. The words he spoke next came out stiff and low. 'Are you asking me to slow down the investigation, ma'am?'

Two-Shoes' eyes widened. 'No, of course not. Press on.

But as you say, lots of threads to pull. Let's do all that in front of camera, eh?'

'I—'

'Good, good. Glad we've had this little chat. My door is always open, if you ever want a chat, Evan. And I appreciate your cooperation in this project. We all do.'

Warlow didn't answer. He had no idea who "we all" were. There was no one else in this room but the two of them. He sat, analysing this little bollocking masquerading as a pep-talk and not liking it one bit. Caldwell had carried tales. No surprises there. But what did surprise him was Two-Shoes' reluctance to make Jess the focus. You'd have thought, given her agenda, that she'd have jumped at the chance of using a face and personality like Jess's to portray the modern side of policing in Dyfed-Powys. And it would do Jess's career prospects no harm... he clamped down his jaw and felt the muscles tighten as his thoughts froze just like someone had pressed the pause button.

That was it. Two-Shoes, for all her talk, was using this as a vehicle for self-promotion. Literally. Why have the limelight stolen by an up-and-coming star with a face that could stop traffic like Jess's, when what you really wanted was to make it your own little carefully chiselled next step up the ladder?

He sat, letting all this whirl around in the spin dryer of his head, keeping eye contact with Two-Shoes until the superintendent's comfort threshold was well and truly exceeded.

She dropped her folded arms. 'Right, I'll be going. Keep up the good work. Let me know how it goes with the TV crew.'

'I will, ma'am,' he said with the same degree of sincerity that oozed out of one of Two-Shoes' smiles. He could play at that game as well.

—————

WARLOW WORKED in the office answering emails and other necessary evils until Catrin and Rhys got back. Catrin was posting stuff up on the Job Centre when he emerged.

Everyone looked up when he entered, and the normally animated team fell silent.

'What?' Warlow said. 'Is there something on my face?'

'Apart from the dirty great lump with stitches in it, you mean?' Gil handed him a cup of tea.

'So why are you all staring?'

'You've been in there half an hour,' Jess said. 'We wondered if Two-Shoes had turned you into a frog.'

'Luckily, I had a clove of garlic in my top drawer.'

Gil chortled. Catrin and Jess smiled. Rhys, however, only frowned. 'Strictly speaking, sir, garlic is useful against vampires. For witches, you need to put something metallic under their chair. Something iron is best. Though I've read that a pair of scissors would do.'

A different quiet descended. One full of astonishment at Rhys's fount of useless facts. 'Thank you, Professor Dumbledore,' Catrin said.

'Only saying, I…' Rhys's face tightened with panic.

Gil shook his head. 'Don't apologise, Rhys. We like having a pedantic mythology nerd on the team.'

'Yeah, right,' Catrin muttered.

Warlow sipped his tea. 'Okay, the boat.'

Rhys, glad of the distraction, went over what Povey had told them. Which wasn't a great deal.

'So no evidence of injury, no traces of blood?' Jess asked.

Rhys shook his head. 'We'll have to wait and see if they find anything else.'

'If there is anything to find, she's the one to do it.' Warlow agreed.

'What about Pryce, sir?' Rhys asked.

This time it was Jess's turn to fill them in on what had taken place in the interview room at Llanelli. She pointed to the board. 'We need to chase up Pryce's boating contacts. Wait for Uniforms to come back with regular users of the car park in Laugharne, too.'

'I'm still wading through bank statements, sir.' Catrin told the team. 'A couple of things stand out. The first is that I've picked up several £450 payments in. Almost a dozen in all over a period of eighteen months.'

'Multiples of the £150 he charged for an hour's online consult?' Jess suggested.

'That's what I thought, too. ma'am. Plus, he sometimes stayed in the Easystay at Llandarcy.'

'Is that the big hotel you can see from the M4?' Gil asked.

Catrin nodded. 'It's just after the Briton Ferry bridge.'

Warlow mused over this new information. Somehow, he felt it was important. 'Was there a pattern?'

'No. It looks pretty random.' Catrin scanned the sheet. 'Always just the one night, too. I've put it all up on the case records.'

It was well after five. What Warlow wanted to do was to say to the team that it was a Tuesday evening and they had forty-eight hours in which to sort this case out before Big Brother descended. But instead, he took a breath and gritted his teeth. 'Superintendent Goodey is keen for us to cooperate with the TV crew when they arrive on Friday. That was what she wanted to discuss with me.'

Rhys piped up. 'How do you feel about that, sir?'

Warlow's lids stood at half-mast. 'I'd rather pull my own teeth out with some rusty pliers.'

Rhys opened his mouth to reply, but brought the shutters down on that smartly.

Gil shrugged. 'Okay, so we get down to it. The glamorous stuff. Man the phones. Chase the paper. Everyone alright until six?'

They all nodded and drifted off to their desks.

Warlow turned to Jess. 'How's Molly?'

A mini eyeroll followed. 'Threatening to cook supper. I'm staying here as long as possible.'

Warlow snorted and shook his head. 'No. We work until six and then I'm calling it a day.'

'You should get some rest.' Jess sent a pointed look towards Warlow's forehead. 'Don't tell me that doesn't hurt.'

Warlow's fingers strayed to the injury. It did feel tender. 'I'm fine.'

'You don't look fine.' Jess focused in on the bump and wrinkled her nose.

'I've just turned back into a human from being a frog, remember? What the hell do you expect?'

At six fifteen, Warlow called a halt and sent everyone home. They needed a break in the case, but it wasn't going to come with everyone knackered.

He called to Jess as they were leaving.

'What's Molly cooking?'

'Something on toast, I expect.'

He nodded, mind made up. 'Right. I'll pick Cadi up and call in to Narberth for a fish supper. I promised Molly she'd see the dog, so I'm inviting myself over. How about it?'

Jess grinned. 'She'll be thrilled.'

'Does she like mushy peas?'

Jess's eyebrows went skywards. 'She's from Manchester. What do you think?'

CHAPTER TWENTY-EIGHT

An hour and a bit later, Warlow was as good as his word.

He parked in front of the Allanby's rented property in the aptly named hamlet of Cold Blow. The car smelt of vinegar and oil, and Warlow's mouth had watered all the way from the fish shop. He'd barely turned the engine off when the front door opened and Molly walked out to the rear of the Jeep and popped the boot door.

It was difficult to tell whether Molly or Cadi was the most excited, vociferous, and physical as girl and dog reunited in the confines of the boot.

'Hi Evan,' Molly cried between licks and whines. 'Thanks for bringing her over.'

'Looked like you needed it. I didn't think you'd last until the weekend.'

'Good detective work there, chief inspector. Come on, Cadi.'

Dog followed girl into the house and Warlow retrieved the cardboard box with the food and followed. The kitchen table was already laid, and Jess was just putting salt and vinegar out.

Warlow paused on the threshold and made a face. 'I didn't bring any wine.'

'With fish and chips?' Jess shook her head. 'I've got some Moretti, or would you prefer a Corona with lime?'

'The Moretti please.'

Molly passed him the beer, peered at his head, and frowned. 'Does that hurt?'

'It did. Not anymore.'

Molly grimaced. 'Looks ready for an alien to burst out of it at any moment.'

'I'll let you know if I feel any rumbles.'

They sat down and ate. Cadi like a salivating sentinel at Molly's side, patiently waiting for the odd scrap she knew, despite Warlow's disapproving looks, would come. They were all hungry and conversation took a back seat while fish and fried potatoes were consumed with relish. The beer was cold and refreshing. Fish and chips and beer. What a guilty pleasure was all about.

Later, while Jess whipped up a fresh fruit salad for dessert, Molly fondled the dog's ears.

'If anything happened to you, will you leave Cadi to me in your will?'

Warlow shook his head. 'I'm wise to your tricks. I say yes and find arsenic in my tea. Forget it.'

Molly turned a pair of pleading grey eyes in Warlow's direction. 'Please?'

'You better talk to your mo—'

'Already has,' Jess said without looking up.

'I'll think about it,' Warlow sat back. 'That way, I'm safe from assassination attempts.'

Molly looked peeved. 'We would not assassinate you.'

'You say that, but you've cooked for me once, remember?'

She shook her head. 'That's so unfair. I told you the oven was playing up.'

'That chicken almost walked off my plate.'

'Mum, tell him.'

Jess's shoulders were moving up and down with silent laughter. She did not respond.

Molly persisted. 'Mum's made a will. I get everything.'

'Is that why she's stopped you cooking?' Warlow kept his face as straight as he could.

Molly pretended to be offended. 'Mum, this man is being mean to me.'

'No, he's being pretty smart.'

Jess dished up the salad.

'School okay, Molly?' Warlow asked. 'Are you considering uni?'

She nodded and spooned a chunk of kiwi fruit into her mouth. For someone so thin, her appetite was amazing. 'Criminology, maybe,' she eventually said.

'Wow.' Warlow was impressed.

'I've seen how Mum works, so I thought I'd learn how to do it properly.'

Jess could only shake her head.

'What does your dad say?' Warlow knew this was thin ice but saw no reason not to test it.

Molly looked momentarily taken aback, but then said, 'He doesn't know yet. He has asked, but I told him I might take a year off and walk the length of North Korea.'

'Molly.' Jess gave her daughter an admonishing look.

Warlow reached for a spoon. 'You ought to tell him. After all, he'll be paying some of your fees.'

Again, Molly looked momentarily annoyed, but then shrugged. 'Suppose.'

Later, with the plates cleared and the chip wrappers in the bin – bagged up in their own bag and put outside so as not to torture Cadi – Molly took the dog upstairs for what had become a traditional game of hide the stuffed rabbit.

Jess and Warlow sat down to finish the beers. He had a quarter left. Jess was on her second.

'Cadi never gets tired of that game. She's good at it. Molly could hide that thing on the moon and that dog would find it.' Jess heard squeals of laughter from a bedroom.

'The giveaway's in the name. Retriever. It's in the genes.'

Jess nodded and sipped her beer. Warlow noted the change of gear in the way her face became serious. 'What do you make of the boat, Evan?'

'The Marie bloody Celeste of Carmarthen Bay.' Warlow muttered.

'It's driving me mad, too. Boscombe set out from the car park in his boat in the dark. Is it possible he collided with something? I don't know – a bigger boat?'

'Now you're sounding like Chief of Police Martin Brody in *Jaws*. You're not suggesting a Great White got Boscombe, are you?'

Jess had her bottle to her lips and almost choked on her beer. She grabbed a tea towel and wiped up the spill from around her mouth. 'I love that film. Mol says the CGI is pants, but it still scared me silly.'

'I did wonder if Boscombe hit something. Not a shark, but there are no big ships in that estuary either. Far too shallow.' Warlow dabbed away the remnants of grease from the corner of his mouth with a paper napkin.

'I can just imagine what a TV crew will make of that,' Jess puffed out air. 'All the crank theories. For God's sake, don't mention the Marie Celeste to them.'

Warlow played a drumbeat on the table with his fingers. 'There's an answer to this. I know there is.'

'I'm glad you're so confident.' She glanced at his beer. 'Another?'

Warlow smiled. 'No thanks. I'm going to hit the road. If I can get my dog back.'

Jess went to the stairs and yelled up. 'Molly, Evan's leaving.'

'Five minutes.' Molly's voice came back down the stairs.

Warlow laughed softly. 'She seems fine.'

Jess sent him a wistful smile. 'She's tough. She'll survive.'

'Anything I can do to help, just say the word.'

'You're helping already. I've been scared to mention her dad since she's come back. You managed it in twenty minutes.'

'That's because I'm Cadi's daddy. I'm untouchable.'

Jess smiled warmly. 'Thanks for bringing her over. Mol's perked up no end.'

'Cadi therapy. Works wonders.'

LATER, in his own bed, Warlow couldn't sleep, his mind churning with the day's events. The empty boat, Pryce's sorry history, Corrigan. They all lined up for inspection. Trouble was, as soon as he'd considered one and processed it, another stood up in its place, elbowing its way to the front for inspection and consideration.

And each time, hovering in that state between wakefulness and sleep, he thought he had an answer to the Boscombe mystery. He knew something loitered in the shadows, but for now it stayed hidden, like a single cut stalk in a field full of corn ready to be plucked. The difficulty was finding the little bastard among all the identical uncut acres.

He turned over in the bed and his bruised forehead met with the pillow.

Wincing, he turned back and closed his eyes.

Behind his lids all he could see was an imagined sea scape with an empty boat floating gently upon it.

What happened out there, Mr Boscombe? What is it you're not telling me?

He dreamt of a shark circling his bed, the rug rippling where it swam beneath, a big fin surfacing now and again. But when he and Povey – he'd never tell her she made his dreams – used a gaff to pull the thing in, it was only a mock rubber triangle strapped to a dead body covered in brown seaweed.

When he turned the fronded mess over, a pair of sightless eyes stared back at him.

But the mouth was open, lips pulled back in a rictus smile, the teeth grey and stained from debris. That image of Boscombe's mocking face stayed with him while he showered himself fully awake and kept returning as he drove to the Dawes.

It took a dose of America's *Ventura Highway*, on extra loud, to finally get rid of it.

Much underrated, music therapy. Perhaps it couldn't cure the common cold but it did wonders for the mood.

CHAPTER TWENTY-NINE

HALF AN HOUR LATER, Warlow pulled in to a lay-by just outside Whitland and fired off a text to Gil to tell him he'd be in a bit later. Not much later because it was still early. A glance at the dashboard clock showed 7.43am. But a thought had struck him as he'd set out after dropping Cadi off. The Marie Celeste theme had been with him as he'd drifted off to sleep the night before and there again as soon as he'd opened his eyes that morning – albeit usurped by Jess's we're gonna need a bigger boat theme.

He needed to see for himself.

And so, twenty minutes later, instead of turning off the A48 towards HQ, he continued on towards Kidwelly; a castle town like many along this south-west coast. Another Norman fortification against the native Welsh princes' futile attempts at ousting the invaders.

But Warlow wasn't interested in the castle. He got there just as the town was coming to life, took a left along Station Road and kept going across the railway line. Five minutes later he stood on the elevated rampart of what once must have been the foundations of a building, staring out at the same view Rhys had contemplated the day before.

A green public footpath sign pointed along the southern shore. Warlow followed it into the park, keeping as close to the water as possible. Was this shoreline or river bank? Difficult to say where river became estuary. He had a photograph of where the boat had been found on his phone and opened it now, orientating himself. He walked around to the nearest point on the path and looked out. The tide was in. Water lapped at the edge of a fractured border of marsh grass and mud channels. With the tide out, beyond that low-lying edge would be mud and the sandbank where the boat had finally beached.

A desolate spot. Nothing but fields and the odd sheep for a good mile behind him.

He'd wanted to see if it was possible for someone to have been in that boat. To have beached it and walked off. It might have been possible if the tide was out, but then the sand and the mud were an unknown. An invitation to disaster. And who would there be to hear your cries for help if you got into trouble?

Was that what happened to Boscombe?

Had he hit his head, become disorientated, beached the boat, and tried to walk out only to get stuck, floundering in the sucking mud until the water came in and drowned him? Washed him of all his sins and delivered him up to be found by two kids who thought he was a dead dolphin?

It didn't seem likely, but then this case was proving to be anything but straightforward. He turned and was retracing his steps when the phone rang. Povey.

'Alison.' Warlow said. 'You're an early bird, too.'

'Thought I'd catch you before your day began.'

'I'm at Kidwelly quay checking out where they found Boscombe's boat. Tell me you've got something useful?'

Povey sighed. 'I wish I did, Evan. There are bloodstains

and we thought we'd get something from the bottom of the boat, but I'm sorry to say it isn't human.'

'None of it?'

'No. I've been caught out before waiting for DNA analysis in situations like this. Identifying a stain as presumptive blood is all well and good. But then sending it for analysis only to find it's a squirrel's gets my bosses hot under the collar. So now we run our own Raman spectroscopy on samples like this. The stuff at the bottom of Boscombe's boat is all fish blood I'm afraid.'

Warlow stood with the phone to his ear, looking out to sea. His continued silence triggered a response from Povey.

'Evan? You still there?'

'I am. Trying to swallow my bitter disappointment. Doesn't look like forensics are going to help us much on this one, then?'

'Sorry. There is one negative that might help. The gunnels on this skiff are made of oak. The wood taken from the wounds on Boscombe's skull were elm. He didn't hit his head in the boat, Evan.'

'Okay. That settles that, then.'

'I'll get this emailed over by mid-morning.'

Warlow thanked her again and rang off. Another box ticked. But even more questions unanswered. He was pondering those on the way back to the car when the phone chimed a second time. A text from Gil this time.

Boscombe's Laptop cloned and back from the techs. Ring me!

A Gil exclamation mark was always worthy of a response.

Warlow rang back immediately.

'What have you got, Gil?'

'Pandora's bloody box it looks like.'

And there, looking out to the low sun glistening on the

surface of the incessant grey sea, Warlow listened as Gil's words turned the case on its head.

———

FIONA NEEDHAM LISTENED TOO as the ward Sister talked.

'I know Mr Corrigan has spoken to you about your mum.'

Fiona remembered the quick five minutes in the corridor. Better than nothing, she supposed.

'But that discussion often leaves people with more questions than answers, I've found.' A big woman, Sister Mared Williams looked capable but tired as she gazed earnestly at Fiona. 'That's why I thought we'd have this little chat.'

They sat in the sister's tiny 'office'. One chair, one desk, one computer workstation, a printer, and a filing cabinet. Hardly the royal suite. Thank you cards and two big calendar planners dominated the wall behind. Both plastered with coloured stickers, one labelled 'Holidays', the other, 'Off Duty'

Sister Williams had shut the door, but it had opened three times already. Twice the sister's withering look had magically caused it to shut again. But the third time it had stayed open for a minute while whoever was there sent the sister a silent message to which she'd replied, 'Best ring the mortuary, then.'

Fiona didn't want to be there. Who in their right mind would, unless they were being paid to do so? Mared Williams had arranged the meeting for 10am. 'To chat about your mum.' Not the most relaxed or conducive surroundings, but Fiona was grateful, nevertheless. It didn't stop her feeling like an interloper, though.

'What's the plan for Mum now?'

'She's doing fine post-op. Oncology came last night

and they'll want to speak to you about treatment. It's Stage 4C so there'll be chemo and radiotherapy.'

Fiona winced. 'Mum's not that keen. Her sister went through this fifteen years ago. She's been terrified ever since.'

'I know, love, I know. But it's her best chance.'

'Is it?'

Sister Williams put her hand on Fiona's. 'This is hard. For the both of you. But what choice do you have, really?'

'There may be alternatives.' Fiona pulled her hand back.

Sister Williams smiled sadly. 'Read all the magazines you want, love, but there aren't any. Not really. Not when it comes down to it.'

Fiona dropped her gaze. The Sister was right. 'Will you talk to Mum?'

'We have spoken.'

'What did she say?'

'She said she didn't want to be poisoned.'

Fiona snorted gently and looked away.

'We have good drugs these days.' Sister Williams persisted. 'Things to make it tolerable.'

Fiona nodded.

Sister Williams stood. 'Will you talk to her? She needs to understand.'

Fiona said nothing. She'd make no promises. 'Is it okay to call in now?'

Mared Williams replied with a relieved smile. 'Yes, of course. There's a ward round due, but who knows when that'll start. I'll shoo you out if you get in the way.'

Edith was in the bed nearest the door of a four-bedded unit with three other women. When the patient in the far corner noticed Fiona approach, she said, 'Nurse, I need the toilet.'

She'd said that every time Fiona had visited her mum.

One reason she wanted them both out of there as soon as possible.

Edith Morton looked tiny in the bed. As if it was swallowing her.

'Hi, Mum. I brought you some Lucozade and some of those tarts you like from the bakery in St Clears.' Fiona put the food on the locker. 'I've been chatting with Sister Williams. She says there'll be more treatment.'

Edith started to cry. She looked so frail, like a broken bird. Not that she'd ever been strong. Not for as long as Fiona could remember. Polio had seen to that in the 1950s. It was a miracle that anyone had wanted to marry her with her clackety callipers, she said. But somehow she'd found George Morton, and they'd produced Fiona, who'd loved them both.

And now Edith was dying and she was scared. When she stopped quietly sobbing, she reached for Fiona's hand. The same one that Sister Williams had grabbed a few minutes before.

Her voice was thin and cracked. 'I don't want to be in pain, Fee. I don't want to feel sick for weeks on end like June was. I've been wondering, do you think Malcolm would come and see me? He's been so good to us, hasn't he?'

Fiona had known this moment would come and had decided not to stress her mother further with the news of Malcolm Boscombe's death. There was no TV in the four-bedder, and her mother had been too ill to take much notice of newspapers. Like so many others, she'd believed in him. Spent money on his rejuvenating supplements that had done her no good in the end.

Edith had listened avidly to his authoritative voice talking about gastro-intestinal health and the benefits of oceanic plant supplements. Fiona had heard him do it to dozens of subscribers. And of course Fiona had gone along with it. She was complicit because they needed the money and, if people wanted to buy samphire salt, why not? After all, it was she who carefully folded and placed the disclaimers in the boxed-up packages that went out from Alternis. The salt and the plants they sold did not profess to be a magical cure for anything.

And if Malcolm Boscombe wanted to charge £150 to talk to someone about their irregular bowel habits, why not that, too? He knew what he was talking about, after all. What harm could it do? None, so long as he was honest and knew his limits.

But Malcolm didn't hold much store in limits. His ego knew no bounds. He'd seen himself as a surgeon without a scalpel. But the same slapdash, money-grabbing attitude he'd shown when he was practising medicine was still there. Still sacrificing clients on the altar of greed. Deep down she'd realised it was only a matter of time until someone woke up to the fact that he cared little for the people who believed in him.

Fiona smiled down at her mother. The lie came easily. For the greater good. 'We'll see, Mum. The important thing now is to get you home. We can talk about all this when you're in your own bed.'

Edith squeezed her daughter's hand and nodded with a brave smile.

A group of people appeared in the corridor outside the door. A retinue of white coats, nurses and, leading the charge in a smart suit, Alan Corrigan.

Fiona glanced around. There were no other visitors on the ward. Perhaps she'd get a chance to chat with him again. One of the white-coated doctors was reading from some notes while Corrigan listened. The consultant nodded and looked up, caught Fiona's eye, and frowned as he tried to place her.

But the moment shattered when he looked down at the

phone in his hand. He turned away from his little group and walked up the corridor to take a call. Fiona watched the expressions on his face change by the second. Surprise became concern and then out-and-out panic.

He ended the call, strode back to the group of medics and nurses, muttered a hurried explanation that Fiona couldn't hear, and half ran out of the ward.

'Is that Mr Corrigan?' Edith asked.

'It was him, for a moment at least,' Fiona followed his hurried progress.

'I like him, but he's not a patch on Malcolm. Doesn't have the bedside manner.'

Fiona wanted to correct her then. Explain as she had done in the past that Malcolm was not a doctor. But she was spared when Sister Williams appeared in the doorway. 'I'm going to have to ask you to leave now while the ward round takes place.'

Fiona stood. 'I'll be back later, Mum. Once I've done a few chores.' She leant in and gave her mother a kiss on the cheek.

'Don't forget what I said,' Edith whispered.

'I won't. I promise.'

As she exited the main entrance and made her way to the car park, a red Mercedes drove past in an obvious hurry. She saw the driver, but the driver didn't see her. Alan Corrigan was too busy going to where he needed to be.

CHAPTER THIRTY

ANITA BOSCOMBE OPENED the door of her sea-view house with her mobile in her hand.

Warlow looked at it and then at her. He did so pointedly. Perhaps their arrival had interrupted a call. Or perhaps seeing them pull up had precipitated a call. He'd no doubt find out in due course.

Next to him, Jess spoke. 'Mrs Boscombe. Thanks for seeing us.'

'Us?' Anita Boscombe gave Warlow the old once over. Slowly, as if he was a wet dog.

'This is Detective Chief Inspector Warlow. He's leading the investigation into your ex-husband's death.'

'Suspicious death,' Warlow said.

This drew a sharp look from Mrs Boscombe. She recovered quickly, though. 'Haven't we already talked about this?'

'We haven't talked,' Warlow said, emphasising the *we*.

'Even so—'

'Some new information has come to light,' Jess explained. 'Can we come in?'

Warlow had his "unless you'd like to come down to the

station" spiel already prepared. But in the end, it wasn't necessary. Mrs Boscombe sighed but stood aside to let them in. 'You were lucky to catch me in.' She spoke, glancing over her shoulder, emphasising how inconvenient this was.

A small dog barked to make sure they knew it was here, and they were encroaching on its territory.

'Sounds like a Westie,' Warlow said.

'It is.' Anita Boscombe didn't elaborate.

Warlow gave Jess an eyebrows-raised look. She shrugged in response. She'd warned him that conversations with the police didn't rank highly on Mrs Boscombe's list of attributes.

Warlow knew Boscombe's age, but his wife, probably through rigorous gym work, an expensive haircut, and no doubt a syringe or two of Botox, looked younger.

To be fair, she did appear to be dressed for imminent departure. The heady aroma of an expensive perfume followed in her wake. Her trousers were tight-fitting, the knitted cashmere top she wore less so. Her hair looked washed and styled as she led them to the same tasteful grey room and sat them in the same chairs around the oval table while she sat opposite and regarded the officers.

'How can I help?'

Jess reached into her satchel. 'We found your husband's laptop. We wanted to ask you about some photographs.'

Mrs Boscombe pursed her lips. 'If it's his porn collection, I do not want to know.'

'It's not porn. It's these.' Jess clicked some buttons on her own laptop, inserted a thumb drive containing the copied material from Boscombe's laptop, and an image formed on the screen. They'd found a great deal of information on his machine, but of particular interest were his photos app and the albums he'd curated. Jess clicked one open now to reveal thirty images that were easy to scroll through like a carousel. The first one showed two people sitting at a window seat in 'Y Cwpan'; an artisan coffee shop in Swansea's SA1 Dockland Brownfield Development site.

It had been a bright day when the photo was taken. Sun lit up the two people in the window. They were smiling, leaning in over their cups, the fingers of one hand intertwined with elbows on the table. Both people – a man and a woman – were smiling.

Jess swivelled the device around so that it faced Mrs Boscombe. She stared at the photograph without expression before looking up into the faces of the officers in turn.

'That is you, am I right?' Warlow asked.

'Yes.'

'And the man with you is Alan Corrigan, correct?'

'Yes.'

Jess nodded. 'There are more images, if you'd like to scroll through.'

Anita Boscombe stabbed at the directional buttons on the laptop's keyboard. Warlow watched her eyes follow the series. She gave nothing away except for the odd nod, and once a shake of the head. He'd already seen the images in the car with Jess when they'd met in a Costa at Junction 47 Services. He'd left the Jeep and travelled on to Caswell with Jess in her Golf.

Mrs Boscombe went through the whole album without speaking. When she'd finished, she swivelled the laptop back around and sat perfectly composed. 'All those images are of me and Alan Corrigan. Walking on the beach, in a coffee shop, once or twice simply meeting in a car park.'

'You are having an affair.'

Her chin came up. Defiant. At least that was the impression she was trying desperately to give. But her breathing was a little too rapid to pull the whole thing off. 'Yes.' A one-word answer clipped and to the point. Once again, she looked from one officer to the other, finally settling on Jess. 'When we spoke on Monday, you said Malcolm had drowned.'

'He did.'

'Then why this?' A manicured finger pointed at the laptop.

Warlow answered. 'Because your ex-husband did drown. But only after being hit on the head. Twice.'

Anita Boscombe dropped her head and took in a deep and ragged breath. When she looked back up, something had changed. Her features had somehow softened. Her guard less rigid. 'Would you like a cup of tea?'

Jess looked taken aback. Warlow simply smiled. 'Is he on his way?' the DCI asked.

Anita Boscombe's eyes narrowed, but then she nodded. 'Five minutes.'

'Then yes, I'll have a cup of tea. Jess?'

'Why not.' The DI nodded.

Mrs Boscombe stood and walked out of the room. Jess stood to follow, but Warlow put his hand up. 'Leave her be. We've scratched her nice paintwork. She needs time to touch it up.'

They heard the chink of cups, the kettle rumbling to a boil and half a second of whistle before it shut off.

'Nice place.' Warlow observed.

'If you like that kind of thing,' Jess nodded. Her phone chirped and she read a message before looking up. 'The full toxicology report on Boscombe showed nothing else in his system. Only the Benzos and alcohol. But enough Lorazepam to knock him out.'

'The sort of thing you might find in someone wanting to drift off into never land and never come back. But we've found no note of any kind?'

Jess shook her head.

'And it's a bloody clever suicide who manages to hit his head twice.'

This time Jess's response was a snort and tiny nod.

Mrs Boscombe was carrying in a tray when the doorbell rang. She put the tray on the table and answered the door. Thirty seconds later, Alan Corrigan joined them in the grey room. The surgeon nodded a greeting. Warlow didn't get up. He waited while Corrigan looked around, the man's face showing much more concern and worry that having two senior police officers in your home had given to Anita Boscombe.

He sat on the same side of the table as she did, silent while the tea was poured. Warlow sipped his while Jess showed Corrigan the carousel of photos Anita Boscombe had scrolled through. All the while explaining again how they were now treating Malcolm Boscombe's death as foul play.

Powerful words, foul play. Corrigan flinched when he heard them before sitting back, shocked. Although Warlow had hinted at their last meeting that they'd wanted to know where he was the day Boscombe went missing, the impact of knowing they were investigating a murder hit home only now.

Foul Play.

Warlow leant forward. 'Right, now that we're all acquainted with the situation, why don't you tell us all about why Malcolm Boscombe had photos of you two cosying up on his laptop? In your own time. But now would be good because we're busy people. And much as I like a cup of tea, I need to get on. So, my question is this. For how long had he been blackmailing you?'

CHAPTER THIRTY-ONE

CORRIGAN PALED. 'NOW, WAIT A MINUTE—'

Anita Boscombe put her hand up to cut him off. 'No, Alan. There's no point us denying it.'

'It's not what you think, though.' Corrigan protested.

Warlow took out his phone and found a recording app. Showed it to both Corrigan and Mrs Boscombe, pressed the record button and placed it on the table. 'We're listening.'

Corrigan dropped his eyes to the phone. Mrs Boscombe remained the composed one. And it was she who decided to answer Warlow's questions.

'I suppose it started when Malcolm was suspended by the GMC in 2010. That first time was hard. Difficult to believe it's over ten years ago. He played the aggrieved innocent really well. I stood by him at the start. But things had not been good between us for a while, and we'd already separated. But he convinced me that what everyone said, his colleagues especially, was all down to jealousy. He believed he was the best and talked the talk. And I was his wife. But then the police were investigating the manslaughter case, and I began to have my doubts.'

She turned to Corrigan. 'It was me who approached Alan when the police started asking questions. I needed a fresh perspective. I suppose I was fed up with being lied to. Alan told me the truth and was a great support to me.'

'We never planned for this to happen.' Corrigan sighed.

'By this, you mean the affair?' Jess asked.

'Yes. And it's only been these last eighteen months that we've become serious.' Corrigan worried at his thumbnail.

'When did you know he'd been watching you?' Warlow kept his attention on the woman.

Mrs Boscombe frowned at the recollection. 'Ten months.'

'How did you find out?' Warlow pressed.

'A text. There was no demand for money. No warning to stop. The words he used were, "Look what I took a photo of". Something like that. It's a power thing. He wanted me to be aware that he still existed and could still exert some kind of hold over me.' She sat up. 'That's the sort of man we're talking about here.'

'He never asked you for money?' Jess asked.

Mrs Boscombe smiled. 'No. If he did, he'd be doing something I'd use to get back at him. Blackmail in the truest sense of the word. But this was something else. Manipulation. Bullying. Psychological warfare. The next text he sent asked, "I wonder what Oscar would say?"'

'Oscar?' Jess asked.

'My…our eldest,' Anita Boscombe replied.

'What about you?' Warlow turned his gaze on Corrigan. 'Were you aware this was happening?'

Corrigan nodded. 'Anita showed me. But I didn't have to wait long for him to target me, too. I'm chief architect of his downfall, don't forget.'

'So, he contacted you, too?'

'Of course, he did.' Corrigan's reply emerged tight

lipped. 'Same sort of thing. Texts that wondered if Bernice – that's my wife – knew what I was up to in my spare time. Wondering if I had been contacted yet from the recruitment company trying to get him work abroad. Never direct threats. Only questions.'

'So what did you do?' Warlow asked.

Anita Boscombe answered first. 'What do you think I did? I could either let him dictate to me like he always had done, or I could hit back. So that's what I did. I told the kids. They said I should do what I wanted to do. That I had a life to live.' Tears flooded her eyes in a rare show of emotion. She blinked them away, wiped the corners with a knuckle. 'Easy for me. Not so easy for Alan.'

Corrigan smiled at the woman next to him. 'I didn't know this was going to happen to me. Meeting Anita, I mean. I wasn't looking for it. Bernice and I, we were happy. At least I thought I was. But something was missing. I found it in Anita. What a bloody cliche, right?' Corrigan forced out a laugh. 'And Malcolm knew what that meant. He knew what it would do. Where I work is a small community. Infidelity is hardly a crime, but it affects how people look at you, think about you. That may be old-fashioned but some of my work, the private stuff, is all word of mouth. Malcolm calculated that. Used it as his leverage.'

'He wanted you to help him get a job overseas?'

'He did.'

'And did you?' Jess asked.

Corrigan hissed out a derision-filled expulsion of air. 'I did not. He's a liability. I could not, in all conscience, inflict him on anyone else.' He inhaled deeply and let it out slowly. 'Six months ago, I told Bernice that I was seeing Anita. I handed in my notice. I'm taking early retirement. There's a new clinic opening in Cardiff, and I've bought a flat up there. Anita will keep this place for her kids, but we'll be together, and I'll do the odd locum, do some private work. A new chapter.' He sent Warlow a defiant glance. 'I'm not sad that Malcolm's gone. But he changed my life. I wouldn't say I was grateful, but we weren't prepared to let him walk all over us. Getting rid of him now, after all the trouble he's caused, would serve no purpose for us. He was poison, but we found the antidote.'

Anita reached over and gave Corrigan's hand a squeeze.

Warlow gave an understanding nod but didn't ease up. 'It would have been a lot better if you'd have told us this right from the start.'

Corrigan nodded. 'I suppose we were hoping it would all go away. Like the man. We should have known better.'

'Someone like Malcolm leaves a big stain when he goes,' Warlow said. 'It's surprising what you find when you rub off a bit of the dirt and see what's underneath.'

'I can assure you neither of us were anywhere near Laugharne last weekend.' Corrigan held the DCI's gaze.

'No, we know. We've checked.' Jess's no-nonsense statement drew strained looks from the two on the opposite side of the table.

'But that doesn't mean you weren't involved. If he was blackmailing you, it's still possible that you paid someone else to get rid of him.' Warlow threw it out casually, wanting to see how much of a splash it made.

'Would you like to see our bank accounts?' Anita asked.

'It might come to that,' Warlow answered. 'Then again, it might not.'

'Surely, that's over the top.' Corrigan tried a dismissive laugh.

Warlow didn't reciprocate. 'We'll need you both to come in and give a statement.'

'We've told you everything there is to tell.' Mrs Boscombe objected.

'That's what Mr Corrigan said last time.' Warlow slowly opened his hands. 'And yet here we all are.'

Neither of them responded to that.

Warlow picked up his phone and stopped the recording. 'Thanks for the tea. We'll see ourselves out.' He followed Jess to the front door, hesitated and turned back, 'Oh, and if either of you think of anything else that might be helpful, you have DI Allanby's number. Don't let me have to come looking for you again. Next time there'll be a charge of obstructing the police.'

CHAPTER THIRTY-TWO

JESS WAS ALREADY BELTED up behind the wheel of the Golf when Warlow climbed in. She slid the key into the ignition and fired up the car.

'What do you think?'

'Of Romeo and Juliet?' Warlow sighed. 'Neither of them are Malcolm Boscombe fans. But neither of them are idiots. They knew we'd find this out eventually. Too risky to get rid of him. Besides, they have alibis.'

'What about your paid assassin theory?' Jess had a half smile on her face.

'Hey, I watch the TV too, you know.' He clicked in his seat belt. 'They didn't blink an eye, did they?'

'No.' Jess pulled out and pointed the car north towards Swansea. 'There are a lot of images on the laptop. It'll take an age to track them all.'

'Agreed.' Warlow knew Jess was fishing. 'What do you have in mind, DI Allanby?'

'Well, since we're over halfway there, I thought we might extend our road trip.'

'It's still early, why not?'

Jess explained as she drove. They stayed south of the

city, the sea on their right, Singleton hospital and the university on their left, and drove on past the gigantic Amazon warehouse up through Jersey Marine to Llandarcy. The Easystay Hotel sat off junction 43 of the M4. Easy access to the motorway. A nondescript, cheap hotel favoured by business executives and travellers on their way to and from the Irish ferries much further west. A place to break the journey.

Jess and Warlow walked up to reception and introduced themselves to an angular receptionist called Jakov, with a clean sharp chin and jet-black hair. Five minutes later they were sitting in an office behind reception talking to Leanne Parks, the duty manager.

Jess did the explaining. She was brief and to the point. Leanne was keen to help. She sat behind a desk, pale from night-shifts, the cheap corporate uniform looking dated, but clean. She had her head half turned away from the officers, staring at the monitor on her workstation as she spoke.

'What date was that again?'

Jess had Catrin's printout of when Boscombe's account had been debited by the hotel and read out the information. Leanne clicked a couple more buttons and looked back at them, beaming.

'You're in luck. Jakov was on that day.'

'The man on reception today?' Jess asked.

'Exactly. I'll relieve him. You can have a chat.' Leanne stood. She was a pretty girl with a bit too much make-up. The kind that stopped somewhere underneath her chin so that her neck was three shades lighter than the rest of her face. But she had a killer smile. She left and, less than a minute later, Jakov came in and sat in Leanne's vacated seat.

Jess didn't waste any time. She had Boscombe's face up on the laptop screen already and once again pivoted the device so that Jakov could see. 'It's a long shot, I know, but do you remember seeing this man six weeks ago?'

Jakov looked at the image, and then up at Jess with a quizzical expression. His accent matched his appearance. From somewhere in Eastern Europe, Warlow assumed. Maybe Croatia. His English, as with so many continental workers, was very good.

'But of course. This is Doctor Beamish, no?'

Jess and Warlow exchanged glances. 'Beamish?' Warlow asked.

'Yes. Doctor Beamish. I've met him several times. Very pleasant man. He explained to me how he arranges to see some of his patients at the hotel because it was convenient for them. Some have travelled far, and so he would book a room and see a patient. Sometimes two.'

'He paid by card.'

'Always. Never a problem.'

Jess ran a finger down the bank statement. 'The last time he was here was six weeks ago. Do you remember that?'

Jakov held his hands open. 'I have excellent memory, but I would lie to you if I said I remember that day precisely.'

'Understood,' Warlow said. 'What we're really interested in is who his visitor might have been.'

'All I remember is that he would arrive perhaps half an hour before his patient.' Jakov explained. 'I would ring him in his room and he would come and meet her.'

'Her?'

'Yes. Always her. A gynaecologist does not have many men patients.' Jakov grinned at his own joke.

Jess sent Warlow a side-eyed glance.

'But can we find out what time he checked in?' Jess wondered.

'Of course.' Genial Jakov nodded. 'It will all be on record.'

Jess's shoulders slumped. 'But his guest wouldn't have signed in, would she?'

'No.' Jakov nodded. 'But there is someone who could tell you.'

'Oh?' Warlow sat forward.

Jakov pointed to a camera in the corner.

Warlow's brows knotted. 'Hotels usually keep CCTV for only one month.'

'True. But we have problems with many cars being broken into last year. We now keep for two months.'

Warlow grunted, turned to Jess, and smiled.

Jakov was good at his job. Unlike the car park in Laugharne, the Easystay had a professional security set-up. Everything was up on cloud servers and all Jakov had to do was log in and punch in the date. Jess and Warlow had moved their chairs so they could all see the screen as the images appeared.

'Earliest check-in time is 1 pm. We start there, yes?'

'Good idea.' Warlow agreed.

Jakov pressed the fast-forward button and a stream of check-out guests arrived at the desk, handed in keys, and left as the time in the top left-hand corner of the screen sped by. As the clock approached 13.27 pm., Jess pointed to the screen. 'There.'

Malcolm Boscombe had dressed for the part. As Dr Beamish, he wore a suit and tie and carried a small leather case. The tape had no sound, but the exchange between Boscombe and Jakov, or at least the back of his head, which was all that could be seen on tape, seemed good natured and pleasant, punctuated by smiles from Boscombe. With the registration done, he moved away towards the lifts.

Warlow leant forward a further inch. Jakov sped the

tape on. At 13.43 pm., a woman – early forties and pulling an overnight case on wheels – came through the door and stood at reception. Jakov froze the image. Jess took her phone out and took a photo.

'Recognise her?' Warlow asked.

Jess did not.

'She is also registering,' Jakov pointed out. 'She would not be one of Doctor Beamish's patients.' He sped the tape on again until the timer showed 13.54 pm. and another woman appeared. Smartly dressed, sunglasses on, a little older but equally well groomed. She had no luggage, just a large handbag slung over her shoulder. She stood at the reception desk, smiled and spoke silent words.

Warlow leant in. There was something about her. The way she held herself. The way her mouth, after smiling, became set.

And then she took off her sunglasses, reached down into her bag and exchanged them for an un-tinted pair before looking up.

'What?'

Jess turned to look at him. 'You know her?'

'I do. I mean, I do not know what all of this means, but I know who this woman is.'

Jess took another photograph of the screen. They thanked Jakov again and Jess checked Boscombe's bank statement to make sure no more dates were covered by the two months of tape and asked that a copy of said tape be sent to Warlow's email address.

'Someone from the technical department will be in touch about access. We appreciate your cooperation.'

Warlow thanked Leanne on the way out of the reception and started punching numbers into his phone before he'd even got outside.

Gil answered after three rings. Jess stood, desperate to

ask the question that she'd dared not while they were in the presence of the hotel staff.

But Warlow held up a finger.

'Gil? It's Evan. We're at the Easystay Hotel. We found Boscombe on their security tape. He told the staff here he was using the room he booked to see patients.'

'Believe it?'

'I don't know what to believe yet. Especially after seeing who it was that met him there.'

Warlow told him. Next to him, Jess frowned.

'Huh. Another dark horse, or should I say filly?' Gil said. 'Want me to ask Llanelli nick to open up their best interview room again?'

Warlow recalled the scruffy room. 'I think that would be just the job,' he told the sergeant.

And got a trademark, 'Tidy,' by reply.

CHAPTER THIRTY-THREE

DS GIL JONES came out of the SIO office shortly after having spoken to Warlow and got some Uniforms in gear for the task at hand. He found Catrin and Rhys busy at their desks working on Boscombe's laptop, as they had been non-stop since coming in that morning.

'How are we doing?' Gil asked.

Rhys looked up. 'Still trawling through stuff. I found some images that Boscombe has classified. He's put them in albums. For instance, this one is named "Golden Eggs". And at least half a dozen of the names here tally with payees into Boscombe's account.'

'How many photos in that file?'

Rhys did a quick count. 'Twenty-one.'

'Do they have anything in common?' Gil asked. He'd been at this point in cases many times before. Floundering around in a vast snowscape of information where nothing had any shape until someone picked out a juicy handful of something and threw it at you. Before you knew it, things began to roll, and you ended up with a great big snowball trundling downhill.

Catrin answered from her desk. 'Apart from paying Boscombe a lot of money, no. None that I can see.'

'Hmm.' Gil walked to the Job Centre and stared up at the lists. 'DCI Warlow found out that Boscombe used the Easystay Hotel as a venue to meet with clients, patients, victims. Whatever you choose to call them.'

'For what?' Rhys piped up.

'One to one…something.' Gil turned around; eyebrows raised.

'All sounds a bit sleazy.' Catrin shook her head.

'Sleazy at the Easy…stay.' Rhys quipped.

Catrin rolled her eyes.

'Keep at it,' Gil urged. 'Not the rubbish puns, the proper digging. You never know.'

'I'm working through the names and…' Her words petered out. 'Wait. There's one here I recognise.' She called up the associated image and sat back, staring.

Gil joined her.

'I know who this is,' Catrin said. 'Her name is up there on the boards linked to Boscombe's.' She got up, walked across, and pointed to a stuck on Post-it Note that had already been actioned.

Gil followed her progress and then dropped his gaze to the photograph on her screen, a slow grin spreading over his face. 'Send this over to DI Allanby. It looks like we may finally have caught a break.'

———

Paula Roberts was not happy to be at the police station.

Warlow wasn't exactly enamoured, either. But needs must. He'd taken pity on her and not used the interview room where they'd interviewed Pryce. This one still had a table, but the chairs were more comfortable. The smell less pungent. But he wanted her to know that it was still under caution.

They'd swapped roles from when they'd talked to Pryce. This time, Warlow sat back, like in a doubles tennis match: observing from the backcourt, waiting for the lob, while Jess went for it at the net.

'Thanks for coming in, Mrs Roberts.' Jess was niceness personified.

'Did I have any choice?' Paula shifted in her seat.

'Always,' Jess said.

'What, with two big policemen in uniform standing in the office, asking me to come with them?' Paula's eyes blazed.

'Did they not explain?'

'They said there'd been a development in Malcolm Boscombe's case and could I spare an hour to confirm some information.'

Jess smiled. An icy one, Warlow noticed. She did great icy. 'And here we are doing exactly that.'

Paula sat, waiting.

Jess had the laptop open. She'd recorded the appropriate section of CCTV on her phone. It came out remarkably well. Still smiling, she swivelled the laptop around so that Paula could see, leant over and pressed play.

The officers observed as Paula watched herself arrive at the reception desk at the Easystay, her lips getting thinner by the minute, her eyes closing in an elongated blink when it had all finished.

'This is the bit we wanted confirmed.' Jess manoeuvred the laptop back around. 'This is you at the Easystay Hotel and the date stamp is correct, yes?'

'Yes. Do I need a solicitor?'

'Do you want one? If you've done anything wrong, it would be a good idea.'

'I've done nothing wrong.'

'You're not under arrest. Simply answering questions.' Jess opened her notebook. 'When you spoke to DCI Warlow, you said that you hadn't seen Mr Boscombe since 2011. That's clearly not true.'

'I was referring to in a professional capacity.'

Warlow spoke. 'So this meeting in the Easystay wasn't professional?'

'No. It was…personal.' She regarded Warlow with her chin up.

She was a cool one alright.

'So you were sleeping with him.' Warlow said.

'I wouldn't exactly…' Paula paused, reconsidered and said, 'Sometimes.'

'Were you aware that Boscombe used the hotel to meet with other women?'

'No.' Paula blinked a couple of times. More a flutter that kept her lids shut.

Warlow quickly realised that this was a tell. A little tic that told him when she was caught off guard.

Jess moved the pointer to the Golden Eggs album Rhys had sent her. The one containing an image of the woman that sat opposite them now whom Catrin had recognised, too. A new set of photographs appeared on the screen. Each with a name beneath it. All women. By and large older than Paula Roberts, but all with the same well-groomed look. Once again, she swivelled the laptop around for Paula to see.

'Do you recognise any of these women?'

Paula studied the photos and shook her head. 'Should I?'

'Is that a no?'

'It's a no.'

'And yet, Malcolm Boscombe had you filed away with all these women in an album he's labelled, "Golden

Eggs". Mean anything to you?' Jess pressed Paula for an answer.

Paula winced. 'I met him half a dozen times. I told my husband I was doing some work for him. I'd prefer it if he didn't find out.'

'What's there to find out?' Warlow sat forward.

'When we met, it was always to discuss old times. Work. It's what we had in common. He wanted to know about his colleagues. How they were getting on.'

'Alan Corrigan?'

'Amongst others, yes.'

'Did he ever try to blackmail you?' Warlow fired off the question.

The flutter came back. 'That's a nasty word.'

'With good reason. It's a nasty thing to do. So did he?' Warlow persisted.

Paula swallowed. It looked, from the way her Adam's apple bobbed, to be a difficult manoeuvre. Like she was attempting it on empty with a dry mouth. 'He sent me a video. Just a few seconds long, of him and me in the hotel room engaged in something that I'd prefer he had not taped.'

'Did he ask you for money?' Jess asked.

'No. But when he asked me to meet him again, I felt obliged. I wanted to see him and make him promise he wouldn't show anyone else that snippet. Promise me he wouldn't tape anything else.'

'And you believed him?' Jess couldn't help but sound sceptical.

'What choice did I have?'

'Half a dozen, from the sound of it.'

Paula ignored the jibe and looked at Warlow. 'Is it really necessary for that video to come out? Is it evidence?'

'I suppose you've got rid of the clip he sent you?'

She nodded.

'Good,' Warlow said.

Paula closed her eyes and then opened them slowly. 'My husband, he isn't well. Hasn't been for years. It's a kind of muscular dystrophy. I'd prefer to spare him the extra pain of knowing that I'd…'

Warlow nodded. 'We'll do what we can.'

There were more questions. The number of times they met. How long she stayed. Where she'd been on Saturday – childcare with her granddaughter. Easy to check and said with no eyelid flutter. But Jess was thorough.

When Paula finally left, Warlow and Jess sat pondering their morning. At every turn, with every layer they peeled away, Boscombe was being revealed as a despicable shit.

'I'm beginning to feel that if I'd ever met this bastard, I'd have hit him on the head myself.' Warlow said in a low growl.

Jess was scrolling through the "Golden Eggs" album again. 'These poor women.'

'We don't know that they were being blackmailed for certain.'

Jess sent him a sceptical look. 'You're right, we don't. That's why we need to see one of them. Here, Katherine Young.'

A face appeared on the screen. Mid-fifties. Smiling. Sharp-featured but with large expressive eyes.

'Why her?' Warlow asked.

'Because she lives about four miles from where we're sitting.' Jess looked up into the DCI's face. 'Worth a try?'

'Do I really want to ruin another woman's day?' Warlow stood up.

'She's on Boscombe's list. I suspect her life isn't exactly rosy as it is.'

'Good point.' Warlow took his jacket from the back of the seat. 'Let's do it.'

CHAPTER THIRTY-FOUR

KATHERINE YOUNG OPENED THE DOOR, looked at the warrant card Jess held out, and nodded. 'I wondered how long it would be before you turned up.'

The house was a newish property on a road appropriately named Yr Allt, meaning the hill, overlooking Llangennech. It stood high up with views of the town below and far too much in the way of lawn for Warlow's liking. They'd driven in through wrought-iron gates and parked next to a new Volvo to the side of a double-fronted bungalow with a hipped porch and two bay windows.

It looked clean and tidy. As did Mrs Young. The photo hadn't done her justice. Warlow put her anywhere between fifty and sixty-five in jeans that showed off her figure. Well-proportioned sprang to mind, unlike the scarecrow sculpting that Anita Boscombe had favoured.

Jess responded to Mrs Young's intriguing greeting with a question. 'Were you expecting us?'

'I watch the news. It's about Malcolm Boscombe, isn't it?'

'It is.'

'Then you'd better come in.'

They sat in a room with a tan leather three-piece suite and that tantalising view. Jess made the introductions and, for once, Warlow turned down the offer of tea but took a glass of cold water. He wanted to know what Katherine Young was concerned about. She sat with a straight back on an armchair, while Warlow and Jess took the sofa. It was big enough for them not to be cramped up. In fact, the whole team could have sat on it.

Warlow kept his eyes on the woman in front of him, but he'd already clocked the room. He could smell new carpets and polished leather. It had freshness about it that spoke of recently spent money.

'Nice place you have here.' He glanced around.

'I've only been here a couple of years. When Meirion died, I sold the business and built this. We enjoyed walking up here.'

'Meirion was your husband?'

She nodded and smiled, unable to hide a rawness that still flickered. 'We'd bought the land. This would have been our retirement home.'

'It's lovely.' Jess said.

'It's not. I built it because it's what Meirion would have wanted. It's too garish. It screams new and that's not me. But I'll probably sell. Move west, to the coast.' Her smile showed lots of very white teeth in a face that still held the slightly pocked remnants of what must have been an aggressive teenage acne, well hidden by good make-up. Her dentist must have loved her.

Niceties over, Mrs Young got down to business. 'They said on the news that you had not ruled out foul play.'

There it was again. The two magic words that said everything and nothing.

'That's correct" Jess answered.

'Is there anything you can tell us about that, Mrs Young?' Warlow asked.

The woman's eyebrows went up. 'No. But let's just say I'm not surprised. First of all, can I ask what brought you to me?'

Jess answered. 'We found Boscombe's laptop. Your name and a photo appeared on it. We also know you paid money into Boscombe's account. In all three tranches of £600, is that correct?'

'It is.' She sat a little straighter. 'Is it only a photograph you found?'

'Yes.'

'I see.' She reached for her sweating glass and drank.

'Are we going to find anything else, Mrs Young?' Warlow sat forward. The leather creaked beneath him.

She put down the glass. This time, her smile was bitter. 'I have a condition. An irritable bowel. I know, delightful conversation maker. Really, it's ulcerative colitis. I've managed it for years, but I get flare-ups. No one knows what the triggers are, but it got worse after Meirion died. He was at a game. Scarlets against Munster out there in Ireland. The last time I saw him alive was when his friends picked him up to catch the ferry to Rosslare.' She shook her head. 'I haven't been able to bear watching a game since.'

She sucked in a breath. 'Afterwards, I was alone. I was unwell. I needed big doses of steroids to calm things down. My joints were bad. My eyes flared up. Let's just say I was down and desperate. Not much to do other than spend time online. I found Alternis.'

'So you contacted Malcolm Boscombe?' Jess had her notebook out again.

'I did. Of course, I read all about him. I knew he'd been struck off. And don't ask me why I went through with contacting him after knowing that. But his spin on it was that he was an innovator. The establishment didn't like his approach to surgery, and they wanted him out. It's all out there. Interviews he gave. Testimonials. It's very convincing. And talking to him helped. I did it online to start with. He understood and seemed very knowledgeable. Recommended some things, some of his products. I suspect they work because of the placebo effect and the fact that here was this educated man who actually listened to you. So when he suggested meeting up, I said yes.' Regret made Katherine Young's lips razor thin.

'Was this at the Easystay Hotel?' Warlow kept his gaze even.

Mrs Young nodded. 'He said it would be easier to talk face to face. He could examine me if needed.' She covered her eyes and shook her head. 'I've thought about that long and hard. But I convinced myself it would be the same as visiting any other doctor. I went. He was charming. Well dressed, a good listener. I let him examine me. To feel my stomach. He wasn't suggesting a colonoscopy or anything like that. It was easy. I felt at ease. He suggested a glass of wine and...' She shook her head again. 'I'm not someone who considers herself vulnerable, Mr Warlow. Never. But I can only explain what happened in those terms. I gave in. A part of me had gone there wondering if it ever came to it, if I would.'

'Was it only the once?' Warlow asked in a soft voice.

'Yes. Just the once. But then he sent me another... appointment.'

'How soon after?'

'A couple of months. With it came a little slip of paper that said failure to attend would incur a charge. I laughed at that. I didn't go. The more I thought about what had happened...the more stupid I felt. Naïve. Used even.'

Jess had stopped writing. Now she was only listening.

Mrs Young sipped water from her glass. 'The date came and went. And then I got an email. An invoice for a missed appointment for further consultation. I ignored that too. And then, on my phone, I got a WhatsApp message. From a number I didn't know. A little video clip, fifteen seconds long. Me and Malcolm. Only, his face was pixilated out. But there was no doubt what we were doing in that hotel room.'

'Was there a message with it?'

Mrs Young nodded. 'Pay your bills.'

'Do you still have it? The WhatsApp message?' Warlow knew the answer, but he had to ask.

'No. I have children and grandchildren. When I saw that clip I felt sick. I got rid of it and I paid the bill. Six hundred pounds and I've paid two more since.' She took another sip.

Warlow noticed her hand was trembling.

'That's why you're here, isn't it?' Mrs Young asked. 'You've found the videos?'

Warlow shook his head. 'We haven't. We found your name and an image of you in a file. We think Boscombe may have been blackmailing other women too.'

Mrs Young's shoulders sagged. 'Oh, God.'

Warlow stood up. 'I'm sorry to have to put you through this, Mrs Young.'

'It's Kate.'

'Kate, I'm sorry. Boscombe has a lot to answer for. We may need you to make a statement. But for now, we'll do what we can to be discreet.'

'Thank you.' She stood up. 'Five years ago, if you'd seen me, you would have thought me the last person to turn out to be a silly, lonely old woman.'

'I don't think that now, Kate. In fact, I can't think of many people who would have been so candid. That takes guts.' Warlow looked into her eyes.

She stared back at him, searching for the lie. When she found none, she nodded. 'Thank you.'

'We'll be in touch,' Jess said. 'Try not to worry.'

In the car, as they drove out, Warlow took out his phone. But before he dialled, he turned to Jess. 'This is the first case I've dealt with where so many people had a reason for Boscombe to disappear.'

Jess nodded. 'We've got a ton of motive. What we now need is opportunity.'

She was right. Everyone they'd checked out so far was accounted for. They had a lot more information, but little in the way of a lead. He called up his contacts, pressed the button, and called Gil.

'I'm picking my car up from Llanelli nick and we're on the way back.'

'Anything useful?'

'If you like muck, then yes. A lorry load.'

'Anything we can do?'

'Tell Rhys to get that bloody kettle on.'

CHAPTER THIRTY-FIVE

WARLOW ATE his Tesco sandwich in the car and by the time he got back to the Incident Room, it was mid-afternoon and the Job Centre and the Gallery were pleasingly full. Gil had a mug of tea ready, and the biscuit display out on the table, well away from Rhys's long reach.

A clutch of CID and indexers clicked at keyboards at the back of the room, and so the team gathered at the front for a pow-wow. Jess kicked things off.

'We called in on Anita Boscombe. She'd already called Alan Corrigan. So the four of us had a nice get-together.'

'And?' Gil asked.

'And yes, Boscombe tried to make their lives a misery. He'd been stalking his wife and had photographs of the still-married Alan Corrigan and her cooing to one another in cafes and out for long romantic walks.'

'Was he asking for money?' Rhys chipped in from his desk.

Jess shook her head. 'I'd say more emotional blackmail. Threatening to tell Corrigan's wife if he didn't provide a reference. Threatening to tell his own kids that Anita Boscombe was canoodling with a married man.'

'So there's a motive there,' Rhys suggested.

'We've got motive coming out of our rears, Rhys.' Warlow got to his feet. 'Boscombe had things set up at the Easystay. We've spoken to two women that visited him there. One was his old secretary. She certainly should have known better. Boscombe, for want of a better word, seduced her, and taped what they'd done together. He used that to manipulate her into telling him what was happening at work, specifically in relation to Corrigan.'

Jess pinned another Post-it Note under Paula Roberts' name on the board. It read, "Check Movements". 'She says she was involved in childcare all last weekend. That'll need verifying.'

Warlow continued. 'Then we called in on Kate Young. One of the women from the Golden Egg file. Same but different. This time Boscombe arranged to see her and examine her at the Easystay. She has a condition that he'd offered to treat. She walked into the spider's web and was caught. The bank records showed she paid three lots of money, but she only saw Boscombe once. The other payments were blackmail. She's a widow with children and grandchildren. Boscombe had her on tape too.'

Catrin shook her head. 'What the hell did they see in this bloke?'

They all followed the DS's gaze and looked at the images of Boscombe from his website and the other snaps they'd managed to collate. He was tallish, clean shaven, full lips, a sly smile. Looking at it now oozed unsavoury. To the uninitiated, though, he'd look capable and professional.

'Do we need to establish her movements, too, sir?' Rhys asked.

'We might need a statement. But not yet. She might yet be one of many.' Warlow scanned the Job Centre. At the timeline Catrin had established and the images of the body on the beach and the boat. 'What else have we got?'

Catrin stood forward. 'It's more what we haven't got. We've not found Boscombe's phone. It stopped signalling at 10.17 on Saturday morning. We're assuming that's when it went into the water. Last calls were the evening before and we have the phone at Moor Cottage all night. Switched off at 9pm. He made no calls between 1pm and 9pm. The phone was switched back on at 5am the next morning.'

Warlow listened. He knew most, if not all, of it, but hearing Catrin summarise it seemed to help fix it in his head. The last time anyone saw Boscombe alive had been recorded on the Laugharne car park CCTV. They'd all seen that. They'd tracked down another fisherman who arrived fifteen minutes after Boscombe. He confirmed seeing Boscombe's boat leaving as the dawn light crept in. Saw rather than heard because the electric outboard made little or no noise. He remembered only one person being in the boat.

Rhys stood up. Warlow heard Gil mutter the old joke of "That's the long and the short of it." Something he did whenever Catrin and Rhys were in proximity. Six foot two versus five foot four in heels was always comment worthy.

Rhys outlined the post-mortem report. Death from drowning. Water in the lungs confirmed that. The blows to the head may well have caused unconsciousness, though the fracture was not severe. Blood alcohol level was not high, but combined with the Ativan would undoubtedly have caused drowsiness. They'd been unable to find any source of Ativan in Moor Cottage or in Boscombe's car. The conclusion was that he'd obtained them on the black market.

Gil talked from the sitting position. A trawl of Boscombe's emails showed that he'd been pressing hard through a third party to recommence his surgical career. A British qualification was still the gold standard in the

Middle East. But it was clear that one of the stumbling blocks was the lack of references. This tied in well with Boscombe's attempted blackmail of Alan Corrigan.

He'd failed on two occasions to secure employment at a couple of prestigious hospitals in Dubai and the UAE. But recent correspondence had been with a hospital in Qatar.

'Do we think that hitting a road block with the Middle East was enough to make him suicidal?' Jess asked. 'Fiona Needham said he could sometimes be moody.'

Gil pushed his lower jaw forward. 'Possible. But *Iesu*, this bloke had skin like a pachyderm. Hard to believe that he let anything get to him.'

Rhys was still on his feet.

'Tell us what you make of the Golden Egg file, Rhys?' Jess asked.

'What it says on the tin. The names there are the ones who paid the most into Boscombe's bank account.'

'The ones most likely to have been blackmailed.' Jess agreed.

'Exactly. But there's nothing I can find that helps us there. No MPEG or Mp3 files.'

Gil cleared his throat.

Rhys held a hand up in apology. 'English. Sorry, sarge. I mean no video files or clips. But there is a video player. A VLC player. It's kind of universal software that plays any format. Looking at the history, it's obvious it's been used. There's a list of four clips. But the file name is the important thing.'

Catrin and Rhys had set up a small projector, and Rhys dimmed the lights and stuck a clean sheet of A1 paper over the Gallery. A blown-up image of a computer screen appeared, filled by an opened app. VLC media player stood out on the top. Beneath that a black area where presumably the video played. To the left was a menu. Catrin clicked on something, and Playlist lit up. The blackened area showed four files. She clicked on one and another box opened in front of the VLC player. This one read "media information". Another click and this time a string of letters and symbols appeared.

file:///Volumes/M-G327-1/Golden   Eggs 18/PL8.mpg

Rhys explained what they were seeing. 'As I say, the important thing here is the Volumes. It means that this file was played from another source.'

'As in?' Warlow asked.

'A different drive.' Catrin explained.

Rhys pointed to the number. 'We searched M-G327, and it looks like it might refer to a model of thumb or flash drive by a company called Espresso Drives. It refers to the memory size, not the model. The 327-1 means 1 terabyte of memory.'

Gil guffawed. 'Christ, I remember when these things came out, you were lucky to get 16 megabytes. How many megabytes in a terabyte?'

Rhys shrugged. 'A million.'

'Does that mean it's any bigger physically?' Warlow asked.

Rhys shook his head. 'No. Not at all.'

'So we're looking for a flash drive?' Jess asked.

Rhys nodded. 'Yes. Probably no bigger than a couple of inches or even smaller.'

He walked to the wall and the lights came back up.

'Nothing was found at Moor Cottage?' Jess looked at the images of the shambolic house.

'No,' Rhys said. 'I've been through the search findings.' He held up his own small thumb drive attached to his car keys. It was a couple of inches long and silver, shaped like a key but with four tiny golden bars at one end, the USB interface set in black. 'Nothing like this on the manifest.'

'Or this.' Catrin held up a small black oblong and

pushed a button. The silver USB interface extended before she retracted it again.

So they were looking for something that had a hundred different iterations. Still, it was something.

'What was wrong with floppy discs and CD-ROMS?' Gil said.

'Or cave paintings and abacuses,' Rhys muttered, without looking at his sergeant.

'Thanks Rhys, Catrin.' Warlow nodded at the younger officers. 'Good work. So what have we got left to do?'

'Man the phones. Check alibis. That's the most important thing now.' Gil pushed himself out of his seat. 'Good old-fashioned on the blower work.'

Warlow nodded. 'And get some Uniforms over to Kidwelly. Some of the houses overlook the river. See if anyone saw the boat on Saturday or Sunday. I'll be in the office talking to Povey. She's going to be delighted when I ask her to take another look at Boscombe's car for a bloody two-inch-long stick.'

No sooner had he got to the SIO's room than Jess joined him, looking agitated.

'Evan, the school has rung. Molly's had a fall playing soccer at school. Banged her tooth. They think it's okay, but she's at the dentist. I said I'd pick her up.'

'Of course. We're treading water here. Gil's right. It's sit on a chair and use the phones time. I'll let you know as soon as something happens. Don't hold your breath.'

'Frustrating, isn't it?'

'It is when I've got this terrible bloody irritation that's trying to tell me I'm missing something.'

'We all get that. It'll come to surface.'

'Hmm. It better had by Friday morning.' Thoughts of the threatened TV crew drew a long Warlow sigh. 'Give Molly my best.'

CHAPTER THIRTY-SIX

MOLLY FINALLY RANG Jess as her Golf sped along the dual carriageway past the Showground in Johnston.

'Molly?'

'Hi, Mum.'

'Are you okay?'

'Fine. I'm in the car with Gwennan and her mum.'

'Okay. Let me pull in and we can talk properly on video. I'll ring you back.'

Jess took the slip road right towards Meidrim and pulled in near a bus stop. She had the phone in a cradle on the dash and pressed the video icon on WhatsApp. Molly's face swam into view, a little shaky because of the car's movement, but smiling brightly.

'Are you okay, Mol?'

'Yeah, Mum. I don't even know why they rang you from the school.'

'What about your tooth?'

Molly pointed a finger at a slightly bruised upper lip, lifted it up and showed her teeth. 'Teeth are fine. I banged my lip and my gum bled a bit.'

'What did the dentist say?'

'Exactly that. Nothing to worry about, he took an X-ray. Everything is fine.'

'Good. So you're alright?'

'I'm fine, Mum. Oh…' The phone swivelled towards a girl sitting next to Molly. 'This is Gwennan.'

A girl with dark hair held back in a band, looked up from a phone, waved, and sang out a 'Hi.'

The phone shifted again to the back of a head and a half-turned face next to a hand that waved.

'That was Gwennan's mum. She's driving.' Molly's face swam back into the frame.

'Did they take you to the dentist?'

'Yeah. And they waited. Well, Gwennan waited while her mum did some shopping. Win win.'

'Make sure you thank them for me, Mol.'

'No, I thought I'd hurl abuse and tell them what an uncaring mother you were for abandoning me and not being there when I fell on the soccer pitch.'

Despite herself, Jess smiled. Molly being her acerbic self was always a good sign. No permanent damage, obviously.

'It was only five-a-side, anyway. And we won.' Molly added the afterthought. Off camera, Gwennan let out a little whoop.

'Okay, so where are you now? I'll come and pick you up.' Jess fired up the Golf.

'No need, Mum. Gwennan's mum is taking me home. I'm going to be there in like, ten minutes.'

Jess tutted. 'And there's me thinking you'd need nursing. You know chicken soup, a blanket.'

'New phone?' Molly threw in the suggestion in a neutral, matter-of-fact tone.

Gwennan giggled.

'Nice try, but you'd have to do something really serious for me to stretch to that level of sympathy.'

Molly sighed. 'In that case, I'm going to have a hot chocolate and get stuck into my science homework. My usual glamorous lifestyle.'

'I'm coming home, anyway.' And then, as was the way of these things, a thought struck Jess. 'Mol, when you left Manchester, what did Camilla give you as a leaving present?'

'Some stuff. A mug, a hat, some chocs.'

'Didn't she give you a box set of something?'

'Mum, how random is this? I've suffered major facial trauma and all you want to talk about is leaving pressies.'

'It's a simple question, Mol.'

Molly sighed again. Her default response. 'Yeah, there was a box set. *Pretty Little Liars.* Season One.'

Next to her, Gwennan said, 'Really?'

'I know.' Molly sent her a look. 'But me and Camilla watched that together when we were twelve. Five times. It was our thing.'

'I don't remember seeing any DVDs.' Jess frowned.

'That's because she burnt them onto a USB stick. Mum, what century are you from?' Molly delivered this with as much derision as she could muster.

When Jess didn't say anything else, Molly elaborated. 'It's on my desk, Mum. It looks like a lipstick.'

'I thought that was a lipstick.'

Exasperated, Molly swung the phone towards Gwennan for her to see Jess. 'This is my mum the' – she made inverted commas with her fingers so that Jess could see – 'detective inspector.'

Gwennan gave an exaggerated smile.

'Molly, this is important.'

Molly's face reappeared. 'What? That you're having a mental breakdown about novelty flash drives?'

'What else can they be?'

'Anything you like. A bar of chocolate, a football, a pack of chewing gum. How long have you got?'

'Good question. Right. Since you're well, I'll carry on working for a bit. Won't be long. I'll be back in an hour.'

'Don't rush. Honestly, Mum. I'm fine.'

Molly hung up, leaving Jess to sit, thinking. She googled novelty flash drives. Molly was right. They came in all shapes and sizes. If Molly hadn't said that the lipstick sitting on her dresser was in fact a flash drive, she'd never have known. Even when you took the top off, it looked like a lipstick. The USB port must have been in the base.

Hide in plain sight was the phrase that kept going around and around in her head. They'd searched Moor Cottage and taken away a load of content. But not everything.

She was twenty minutes away from Amroth. It was virtually on the way. Jess put the Golf in gear and set off.

The school runs had finished, but the roads were busy. It took a while to get out of the junction and back on to the A40. After that, it was a clear run to Amroth, and the satnav took her the rest of the way along the quiet lanes to Moor Cottage. As luck would have it, she had to pull in to let a Forensic Services van pass half a mile from her destination.

She flashed the driver, wound down her window, and showed her a warrant card.

'DI Allanby,' Jess explained.

The driver, a woman Jess had seen at more than one crime scene, smiled. 'I know who you are, ma'am. We're clearing off the site. Collecting up our markers.'

'Don't suppose I could have the keys?'

The driver handed over a sealed bag. 'We have several sets.'

'Did you get a message about a flash drive?'

'We did ma'am. We're looking through the tech we've already taken away.'

'Thought I'd have a quick look at the house again.'

The technician raised her eyebrows in sympathy. 'Best of luck.'

'I'll hand these back to the office manager at HQ.' Jess let the van pass and pulled away.

Blue and white police tape fluttered across the wonky gate as she drove in and parked up.

A fresh breeze blew in from over the marshes, making the branches of the trees bow and bob. The rain could not be far off. Jess slid on some gloves and walked through the scruffy yard. Nothing had been taken away from the outside and the piles of refuse bags, though probably searched, were still stacked next to the broken pallets. This place was going to need a couple of skips to get it tidied up. But it was inside Jess needed to be. She sorted through the keys, found the one she needed, and unlocked the door.

Though it was still light, the gloomy interior combined with its musty smell made it seem darker than it was. Jess flicked on the light. The search team had moved a few things around, but all in all the place looked as shabby as it had before. Still, downstairs was not where she wanted to be. Jess took the stairs up to the first floor and the one decently appointed room where Boscombe had set up his laptop and camera for his online meetings.

Both of those items were with forensics, but the desk remained. Behind it on the wall was a bookcase, his certificates – within view of the camera – and a flotsam of paperweights, the odd decorative mug, and other accoutrements. It was to the bookcase that Jess gave her attention. She ran her finger over the book spines. She recognised nothing in the dry, academic titles. Some were old surgical textbooks, others more modern tomes. If someone asked her to categorise the little library, she'd probably come up with "Wellness" as a broad heading. Boscombe had taken his new role seriously. Jess picked out a dozen books and riffled through the pages before putting them back. Then she examined all the stacked boxes of IT equipment on the bottom shelf. All the usual suspects, a box for a phone, digital camera, earbuds, chargers, etc. Half of them were empty. The other half contained only what they should have.

Boscombe was old school. A Phillips radio CD cassette player stood on the top shelf. Beneath it in a box, a selection of CDs and some cassette tapes labelled with predominantly classical music. The CDs were a mixture of compilations, the odd audio book, and some technical medical transcripts from past conferences. She turned her attention to the certificates hanging on the wall.

His initial medical degree from Southampton University. A more ornately decorated one from the Royal College of Surgeons. She took them down. Looked behind them. Found nothing.

Then it was the bedroom's turn. A clock, a cufflink cabinet, a sock drawer. She examined them all and found nothing. The same thing applied to the bathroom.

After twenty minutes, Jess sat on the edge of the bed and looked around. Povey's team had already looked at all of this. Who was she trying to kid?

She wandered back into the adjacent study and stood in the doorway, letting her eyes drift across the bookcase again. The portable sound unit was plugged in, but with the power off. She walked across, pressed a switch on the socket, and the unit lit up. Radio 4 began telling her how much doom and gloom was coming her way. She opened the CD drawer. Empty.

She pressed the eject button on the cassette deck and the drawer snapped open to reveal a black cassette sitting inside. Carefully, Jess removed it and read the handwritten label.

"*G Eggs*"

A little jolt of electricity flickered somewhere inside her. Jess walked over to the window and examined the tape. It looked exactly like the others she'd seen except that when she shook it, it didn't rattle. And, instead of magnetic tape running across the open edge, there was a space with a small lever. She pushed it and a silver snout poked out.

The flattened end of a USB connector.

'Got you,' Jess said.

She slid the cassette into a plastic evidence bag and then into her pocket, and made her way downstairs. It was as she reached the bottom of the stairs that she heard the noise. A clang. Like something heavy had fallen over. Outside, the wind was still gusting. But the noise had definitely come from somewhere to the rear.

Jess stepped quietly through the murky corridor to the mudroom and opened the back door to peer outside. Nothing moved except the weeds and the grass on the overgrown lawn. Her eyes strayed to the workshop at the end of the garden. Was it one of the corrugated sheets that had moved in the breeze? But they were thin and tinny. That wasn't the noise she'd heard.

Something moved, and she caught her breath. The door to the shed swung gently open and swung back again, caught by a gust but too heavy to respond other than to move a few inches. Jess stood rooted to the spot, hidden in the shadow of the mudroom, waiting to see if anyone emerged. But then the door moved again, open and then shut with a bang as the breeze caught it.

The breeze. At least that was cause enough for the movement. But not an answer for why the door was open. Had the techs forgotten to close it?

Tutting, she stepped out on the path and hurried

across to the workshop, grabbing the door as the wind caught it once more before it could slam shut. There was one moment when her mind tried to add the wooden frame of the door shutting with the clanging noise that she heard and came up short. For no reason other than a need to reassure herself, Jess yelled, 'Hello? Anyone there?'

No one answered. She'd half stepped back to close the door when something struck her in the back, with a force that drove all the air out of her lungs and sent her tumbling forwards off balance. Both hands shot out to break her fall. Her left hand met the workshop floor first and took the brunt of her weight. She heard the snap and felt the pain shoot up her arm, which folded beneath her. Jess rolled with the momentum, elbow first, then shoulder, then back, knowing that something had given.

Something bad.

She looked back just as a wave of nausea washed over her and saw a blur of movement beyond the door before it swung inwards and slammed shut.

She lay there, trying to breathe, looking down at her wrist and the step in the bone that had not been there two minutes before, squeezing her eyes shut and willing herself not to throw up.

'Shit.' She hissed out the word as a long expletive.

After several slow breaths, she lifted her left arm and tried to sit up. She fell back again as a cold sweat broke over her. She knew then she'd fractured her wrist.

'Shit.' Again. Suddenly, it was her favourite word. This time, Jess sat up very slowly, keeping her left arm on the ground. She undid her coat and, still sitting, moved her injured arm back and the coat down until her left elbow sat in the armhole of the coat sleeve. Not perfect and looked ridiculous, but it gave some support.

She got to her feet, leant against a bench for a while,

and searched for her phone. Not in her pocket, nor on the floor.

'Nooo.' Jess groaned. She must have dropped it outside.

Weak afternoon light filtered in through a skylight. Jess staggered over to the light switch and pressed. Nothing. Someone must have turned the power off.

Footsteps. There was someone outside. Jess walked to the door, wincing with each step, and her wrist jarred. She tried the handle. The door didn't budge. She banged on the door with her good arm. Every time it struck a new pain surged through her left hand in its makeshift sling. 'I'm a police officer. Let me out. This doesn't need to get any worse.'

The footsteps receded.

'Let me out now!'

Only the wind answered her.

'Shit.'

Jess shivered. Probably shock. No other reason for it to be so cold. She turned to look into the workshop and saw the little pool of steam around a fallen-over cylinder towards the rear benches.

This was the noise she'd heard.

A falling, cylinder-shaped Dewar flask that was now slowly spilling something onto the floor.

Jess turned and banged on the door again and shouted even louder.

But no one answered. Because no one was there to listen.

CHAPTER THIRTY-SEVEN

WARLOW LOOKED UP HALF a dozen of the womens' names that appeared on the Golden Egg list they'd found on Boscombe's laptop. Not all of them were on social media, but those he found ranged in age from forty-five to seventy. The two standout things they had in common were that they'd been in relationships that had ended and had significant medical problems. Two were widowed, the others divorced. But their feeds looked peppered with references to a variety of illnesses: Crohn's Disease. Endometriosis. Oesophagitis.

He'd needed to look most of them up but managed to resist ringing Tom. It didn't really matter what they were. What did was that these womens' health problems bracketed them together. Warlow had no doubt Boscombe targeted them as vulnerable marks.

Boscombe the Butcher.

A little after six, Warlow walked out into the Incident Room to find the team still there. He sent Catrin and Rhys home.

'Get some rest. We'll have a breakfast briefing at eight.

I'm buying. Text me your order. Anything you like from Norma's.'

'*Arglwydd Mawr*, Premium Bonds come up, Evan? Or have you had a stroke?' Gil looked up from his screen.

Warlow feigned a scowl. 'It's called team building. Text me your orders.'

'I know already.' Rhys got to his feet; screen already clicked off. 'Mine's an egg and bacon on sourdough with brown sauce.'

'Just the one?' Warlow asked. 'What about a slice of red velvet cake to top it off?'

'Now you're talking, sir. I…' Rhys caught the others looking and stopped. He didn't blush for once. 'Good one, sir.'

'Catrin?'

'Thank you, sir. I'll let you know.'

Warlow paused before continuing. 'I've been looking at the Golden Egg victims. Because that's what they all are. We'll need to contact them. More for reassurance than anything. A promise that we'll be discreet.'

Rhys put an arm through the sleeve of his coat but stopped as a realisation struck him. 'They'd all have motive though, if we're right about Boscombe filming them.'

'Agreed,' Warlow said. 'So we be discreet and subtle. Mull it over. We'll talk through a strategy tomorrow morning.'

When the young officers left, Warlow ambled back to the office for his own coat. Gil, however, remained at his desk.

'What's keeping you occupied?' Warlow asked when he re-emerged.

'Emails from Two-Shoes and KFC.'

Warlow scowled again. This time there was no pretence. 'What does Caldwell want?'

'He's trying to arrange a meet and greet for the TV crew. We're all invited.'

Warlow didn't speak. He preferred to fume in silence. After two counts of ten, he found his voice. 'I thought we'd get this case sorted out by now. Then there'd be nothing for the buggers to film. We've missed something, Gil. I can feel it.'

'It'll come to you when you least expect it. Sometimes I find routines help. Doing something I don't need to think about.'

'Like answering emails from KFC and Two-Shoes, you mean?'

'No, that's a painful necessity that takes all my concentration not to reply with scorn and blasphemy. I was suggesting something more mundane. Brushing my teeth. Walking the dog. Sitting on the toilet.'

Warlow winced. 'Magical images, Gil. All except for the last one. What's your order for breakfast?'

'Cheese and marmite breakfast bap.'

'Blimey, you didn't have to think much about that, sergeant.'

'Some things do not need thinking about. They choose themselves since it's impossible to improve on perfection.' Gil's eyes glazed over in anticipation.

'Right.' Warlow left Gil to it, turned off his computer and headed out.

A cloud-free bar of pale light on the western horizon threw long shadows in the car park as he pulled out. Warlow did a mental checklist of groceries he should probably call for. Cadi didn't need anything. He bought most of her food online. Frozen raw preparations she seemed to thrive on. But the milk in his fridge was coming up to five days old and he needed eggs. The Morrisons just off the Pensarn roundabout would be the closest big store. But then he could get eggs and milk in the petrol station, and the Jeep needed filling up anyway.

Decision made, Warlow pulled off the roundabout and turned into the station just as his phone rang. He pressed a button on the steering wheel to accept the call.

'Molly. How are you? I heard you had a fall.'

'Oh My God. You make me sound like my gran. I'm fine.'

She wasn't. He could tell from her voice. He pulled in to park up near the car wash on the petrol station forecourt in a spot not in anyone's way.

'Jess told me you hurt yourself.'

'It's only a bruise.'

'That's good. Face plant was it?'

'A trip. We got a penalty.'

Warlow waited. Her answers were too straight. Something was up. 'You okay, Molly?'

She sighed. 'This is going to sound stupid, but Mum told me that if she was ever later than she said she would be I should contact someone.'

'What do you mean later?'

'She rang me and said she'd be an hour. It's now an hour and a half and I can't get hold of her. Her phone goes to messaging after six rings.'

'She left the office a while ago,' Warlow pointed out.

'That's when she phoned me. On her way to pick me up, but I already had a lift.'

Molly wasn't panicking, but he could hear the anxiety plucking at her voice. 'Did she say where she was going?'

'No. We had this weird conversation about novelty USB sticks. Mum can be so random when she's on a case. I had a lift home, so she knew where I was. She said she wanted to do something before coming home. It's not like her not to have texted or rung.'

A little warning light went on in Warlow's head. Molly was right. Jess wouldn't stay off radar voluntarily.

'Maybe wherever she is there's no signal. We have lots of dead spots in West Wales. In fact we specialise in them. You know you're in one when you see groups of tourists wandering around, panic stricken, staring at the sky. What they're really doing is holding their phones up in the hope that they'll snag a bar so that vital selfie they just took gets to Instagram before the world ends.' Warlow's vague attempt at reassuring humour sounded hollow even to his own ears.

'So, you don't know where she went?'

He saw no point in lying. 'No. But I'm sure I can find out. Don't worry, Molly. Let me make some calls and I'll get back to you.'

'Thanks, Evan. See you.'

She signed off.

Said goodbye before even asking about Cadi.

A first. As good an indication as any how worried she was.

He rang Jess. Let it ring until it asked him to leave a message and then ended the call. After that, it was a list. First Gil, then Catrin, then Rhys. Jess had said nothing to any of them about where she might have gone. Warlow played it through in his head. Novelty USB sticks were what they'd been talking about before Jess left. It would be on her mind. Had the discussion with her daughter merely been an extension of working through that, or had something struck her? Something she'd wanted to check out.

Warlow was only ten minutes from HQ.

He toyed with returning and had his hand on the gearstick when his phone rang again. Povey.

'Alison, what have you got?'

'I presume you want to be updated whenever we find something. I realise you don't have another life so…'

Warlow snorted.

'It's about the boat. It had an electric outboard. Looks like the battery ran flat.'

'Relevance?'

'Not sure, but it means that it kept running. It means it wasn't switched off when Boscombe went into the water, if we assume that's what happened. The boat would not have been stationary. The throttle was not idling. With an engine like this, it would've kept going until the battery ran out.'

'Hmm. More Marie Celeste.'

'Exactly. Sorry to add to the mystery. Did DI Allanby find what she was after?'

Warlow started. 'What?'

Povey's words took on a faintly indignant air. 'She ran into my lot leaving Boscombe's place. Wanted keys. I'm surprised because we've gone over the place pretty thoroughly, Evan. Was she looking for something in particular?'

'Boscombe's place?'

'Yes. This afternoon.'

'Alison, I need to ring you back.' Something in his voice alerted Povey.

'You okay, Evan?'

But Warlow was already accelerating the car out of the petrol station. 'I'll get back to you.'

———

JESS WALKED the length of the workshop for the tenth time. Her wrist hurt and the pain made her feel a little sick. The light was fading, but she needed to see what had made the clanging noise she'd heard. The cylinders were stored under a bench at the back of the shed. It was gloomier there, but she could make out the squat containers with ridges on their sides. One had a solid oval attachment to the regulator and a lead going off to an electrical wall plug. From the other end of this oval attachment, a rubber tubular arm led off and hung in the air, a thin whisper of steam drifting up from its end.

A smaller grey container, a third of the size of the bigger cylinder, but big enough to hold ten litres, lay on its side, its stopper missing. From this smaller cylinder something trickled out, instantly turning the water vapour in the air above into a grey mist that smoked and rolled slowly across the floor.

Fiona Needham had said they used nitrogen to package up the products. Sometimes to freeze-dry the wild samphire they sold before extracting the moisture. Jess didn't know much about hard science, but she knew what liquid nitrogen did if you touched it: freeze the water molecules in anything instantly.

A sizeable pool of the stuff had gathered on the floor and the closer she got, the colder the air around her legs became. She turned and walked back towards the door. The liquid sucked all the heat from the surrounding air. Best to stay away.

She hugged her wrist to her chest, gazing around as she did so. The cold was getting colder.

She could remember no landline in the lab when they'd first visited it. But Molly would figure out something was wrong when she didn't come home. Only a matter of time until someone worked it out.

She winced. But not with pain. At the realisation she'd told no one where she was going.

Still, as long as she stayed away from the nitrogen and kept warm, someone would come looking.

She quashed all negative thoughts and turned her mind to analysis. There'd been a spate of thefts of medical gasses in the area hospitals over the last year. People stealing nitrous oxide to use as a drug and sold as hippy crack in tiny whippet vials. A large medicinal pressurised gas cylinder was worth a lot of money to someone who got hold of one.

But the gas in the cylinders at the back of this workshop wasn't nitrous oxide. It was nitrogen, a very different animal. But knowing the mindset and level of intelligence of the criminals she came across, especially those involved in drug crime, it was entirely possible they'd make that simple mistake.

And criminals were nothing if they weren't opportunistic.

Had she stumbled on a thief in the middle of a B and E?

Jess found a chair and sat down to wait for help. She found some bubble wrap and draped it over her legs and around her coat. She was no scientist, but she knew she ought to keep as warm as she possibly could. And nitrogen made up most of the atmosphere we breathed, didn't it? So it wasn't as if the bloody thing was cyanide.

The trouble with science, though, was that there was always something else to know. Like an onion ring flavoured mint, under the sugar coating of familiarity there often lurked a very unpleasant surprise.

So Jess knew that nitrogen was cold and you risked losing a finger if you were stupid enough to poke one into it. But minus 200 degrees in liquid form was more than cold. The sizeable pool on the floor at the back of the workshop kept growing, white vapour rolling forward from it over the floor. Jess moved as far away as possible and banged on the door once again.

CHAPTER THIRTY-EIGHT

WARLOW FLOORED the accelerator as he shot along the outside lane of the A40. He'd punched the details into the satnav because the route he'd taken to Moor Cottage the last time had been from the coast. This time he was looking for speed.

It was fully dark now. A thin drizzle spattered the windscreen. Not enough to have the wipers on full blast, but enough so that it turned oncoming headlights into smeared starbursts until he flicked them clear. He took the Red Roses bypass, all the while wondering what circumstances might have made Jess not answer her phone. She was far too organised to have let the battery run down.

Had she lost it?

Dropped it in a toilet?

He shook his head. Not Jess.

He called up her number from his contacts and pressed the button. Once again, the call went to the messenger service after six rings. He did that three times until he got to the turning off the A477 on the quieter lanes that led to the cottage. He was minutes away now and driving too fast. Twice he had to pull in to let a car pass with a squeal of brakes, but at last drove through the rotten gateposts and past the fluttering police tape.

'You have arrived at your destination.' The Jeep's calm satnav voice announced. But Warlow didn't feel calm as he slowed to a crawl, eyes peeled for anything unusual until he stopped. Jess's car stood outside the barn. Warlow got out, found a torch and walked to the Golf.

Locked.

He crossed to the cottage's front door, knocked, found it open.

'Jess?' He called out. 'Are you here?'

Lights glowed in the kitchen and living room. Warlow flicked more switches on as he walked through, checking every room on the ground floor before running upstairs, calling Jess's name, and getting no reply.

It was when he came back down into the passageway that he felt the breeze and saw that the back door stood ajar. He pulled it open and stared into the unkempt garden and the dark corrugated tin workshop beyond.

He turned back to look into the house.

'Where are you, Jess?' Warlow muttered. He tried her number again. Nothing, no answer. Only ringing until the voice message kicked in, telling him she wasn't available and for him to leave a message. She might even have had the phone on silent. In which case, him listening out for her ringtone would be futile. He stabbed at the red button on his phone and tried again. Illogical, he knew but desperation brooked no logic. He listened, phone to one ear, listening and hearing only what a caller would hear, pulling the phone away to stand and listen in case he heard…Something.

He stopped breathing. Was there something?

Standing in the back doorway, he heard a faint noise under the wind and spitting drizzle. He swivelled and looked out again. A buzz. The vibration of a phone on silent. He flicked off the torch and peered into the blackness outside. Something glowed on the floor in the grass just in front of the workshop. Warlow hurried along the pathway until he reached the point at which he discerned a light in the grass. On went the torch again. Jess's phone lay face down. Its lights almost totally obscured other than a rectangle around the edges.

He knelt and picked it up. The phone was intact. A little damp from the drizzle, but intact and charged. The door to the workshop stood only feet away. Warlow turned around through three-sixty degrees and called out. 'Jess? Jess?'

No answer.

He stepped across to the shut workshop door.

Shut with the hasp closed...he peered closer in the stark torchlight. No padlock...but the hasp had been secured by a stick wedged through the staple.

Would Povey's team have left it like this?

He doubted that. Warlow looked at the door. Something moved at his feet, oozing out beneath the door. A tiny wisp of what looked like steam.

'Jess?' he called, as he slid the stick out and yanked the hasp free. He pulled open the door and a billow of water vapour followed and snaked around his feet before disappearing in the breeze. He lit up the workshop with the torch. His beam picked out more low-lying, coiling steam and illuminated a dark and shadowy interior of shelving, benches...and a slumped, seated figure covered in bubble wrap, a head leaning against a wall, mouth open, unmoving.

'Jess!' Warlow stepped in and felt the cold encasing his legs. He grasped the DI, shook her. She did not respond. 'Jess! Jess!'

Warlow picked her up and dragged her out of the workshop and back across the garden to the house. 'No, no, no.' Warlow mumbled, as he laid her on her back in the passage from the mudroom. Under the stark corridor light, she looked sheet white. Her lips an alarming battle-ship grey. Something odd about her coat struck him. The way it was done up. But he noticed this only fleetingly as his mind did cartwheels, pulse thrumming in his ears. He knelt in close, tried to listen for a breath. Heard nothing.

'Christ, Jess, come on.'

He shook her again.

Nothing.

He pressed two buttons on his phone with fumbling shaking fingers as he thumbed the SOS, shouting out the address when the services answered. The operator told him to stay calm. He ignored her and tilted Jess's jaw back, pinched her nose and blew air into her lungs. Once, twice, three times, he blew.

He placed his hands on her chest, midline. What was the bloody song? The Bee Gees. *Staying Alive*. He dragged it into his mind then pressed hard and fast. He counted to thirty, breathed into her mouth again twice.

Then he reached for her hand for a pulse. Her left arm was conveniently up on her chest. Something scrunched under his fingers and then horribly, wonderfully, Jess Allanby moaned.

'Jess, Jess, are you okay?'

Her eyelids fluttered, she moaned again. Her lips turned purple, then a pale pink as she sucked in air, gasped, sucked in more.

Warlow looked dumbly at her wrist and saw the step where there should not be one. Where he'd squeezed on the fracture. It would have been painful.

Painful enough to trigger a response.

Jess moaned again, half conscious. But at least she was breathing. He stayed with her, reassuring her, wrap-ping her in as many coats as he could find in the mud room, tucking one under her as insulation from the cold floor. Tempting as going back into the workshop was, Warlow dared not move from her side until the cavalry came.

Jess kept saying how cold she was and that everything had started to get dark. Warlow didn't mind that. He needed her to talk, to stay warm and conscious now that she was back. The shivering started soon after that, but her words started to make a little more sense, too. By the time the ambulance came, Warlow had managed to piece together the fact that she'd been pushed and that someone must have locked her in.

While the paramedics took over, he spoke to Molly, explained what was happening and sent Catrin to get her. Gil he sent to the hospital to await the ambulance.

Forty-five minutes after he'd pulled up outside Moor Cottage and parked behind Jess's Golf, she was in hospital and the forensic vans were parked all around the Jeep, like a wagon train waiting for an attack.

It didn't feel like only three-quarters of an hour had gone by to Warlow as he stood outside the workshop. It felt like a bloody lifetime.

Povey had returned, watching firemen in breathing apparatus carrying out cylinders.

'They've spooned up what's left of the spilled nitrogen,' she said, dressed once more in her blue suit, booted and gloved, her and her techs waiting to go into the workshop that was, once again, a crime scene. But this was a different Povey. No jokes this evening. There never was when it was one of their own.

'What do you know about nitrogen, Evan?' They'd set up arc lights in the garden. The place now looked more like a film set than a scruffy cottage and outbuildings.

'Not much,' Warlow muttered. 'I know that divers can get nitrogen narcosis when they dive. Too much nitrogen and not enough oxygen sends them a bit doolally doesn't it?'

Povey waved to the last of the firemen, unrecognisable in his gear. 'You assume correctly.' She turned back to Warlow. 'Bloody dangerous stuff. I've been to a couple of inert gas deaths. One a helium suicide, the other a factory accident where they'd purged a processing tank with nitrogen. It's lethal.'

'Why? I thought we breathed air that had a ton of nitrogen in it already.' Warlow frowned.

'Well done. You remember your school science and you're right. Air is 78% nitrogen, 20% oxygen. But change those numbers and it's a killer. The nitrogen spill in that room will have changed the percentages drastically. Still, it's not the nitrogen as such, it's the lack of oxygen that causes the problem.'

Warlow stared into the workshop's interior. It looked innocuous. Difficult to imagine it as a gas chamber.

Povey pointed to the back of the workshop. 'The spilled cylinder was only a ten litre Dewar. But the main tank was also switched on, leaking nitrogen at a steady rate. My guess is that someone was filling the Dewar from the main tank and maybe Jess disturbed them. The nitrogen boiled off and expanded. It's not a small shed, but it's a confined space. Slowly but surely, the oxygen level would have fallen as the nitrogen expanded. It's good at that, too.'

Warlow's expression hardened.

Povey took the lack of objection as a signal to keep talking. 'It takes only a slight change. You need 20% oxygen to function. Anything less, say 17%, you start to lose cognitive abilities. 10% your lips turn blue. At 8% it's a matter of time. If you're exposed for eight minutes, it's a 100% fatality. Anything less than 5% it just takes three breaths.'

'Jesus, it must have been awful for her. Slowly choking.'

Povey shook her head. 'That's the mistake everyone makes. Why there are so many accidents. Jess would have been unaware that there was anything wrong. In normal asphyxiation, drowning, or strangulation, victims breathe in one last gasp of oxygenated air and carbon dioxide builds up. It's the high CO_2 that stimulates panic and the fight for air. In low oxygen situations, the normal process of carbon dioxide formation is already failing because there's too little oxygen to metabolise. There's no build-up of CO_2 to stimulate breathing.'

Warlow thought about it. Forced himself to ask. 'What was the percentage of oxygen in here?'

'You'd opened the door. So it's difficult to—'

'Best guess?'

'Thankfully, Allanby had placed herself near the door. Halfway between the tanks and the door it was around 8%. Another couple of minutes in this room and she would have died. It's lucky she was sitting up. If she'd fallen to the floor where the nitrogen was at a higher concentration...'

Warlow nodded and tried not to think about how close he'd been to not having heard Jess's phone buzzing. If the wind had gusted at that moment. If the rain had been harder and clattered against the corrugated roof...

He buried these thoughts, reached into his pocket and took out the evidence bag containing the cassette that wasn't a cassette and held it out to Povey.

'Jess gave me this before they took her away. Can you get this copied and back to me by tonight?'

'I will.' Povey gave him a look that bordered on tender. 'You look rough, Evan. Go home and get some rest. I'll be in touch.'

She was probably right. But it wasn't going to happen.

'Someone did this to one of ours, Alison. Like my sons always tell me. Yolo, Dad. You can sleep when you're dead.'

CHAPTER THIRTY-NINE

JESS WAS in a cubicle in A&E. At least they'd found somewhere discreet to keep her. Somewhere they usually kept recovering overdose patients, the charge nurse explained to Warlow as he led the way.

There were Uniforms in the waiting room. A police presence, as the press always liked to call it. Not that they were expecting any trouble, but a police officer had been hurt and that merited some special attention.

Jess lay propped up on a trolley as Warlow entered, a pink plaster cast on her forearm. She wasn't the only person in the curtained-off space. As soon as Warlow stepped in, he heard a chair scrape and Molly stood up, took two steps, and threw her arms around him.

'Whoa, what's all this?' he whispered, his voice gruff from shouting for Jess earlier.

Molly let out one convulsive sob, but her head didn't move from his chest. Warlow let his eyes drift over the girl's head to Jess, who was a much healthier pink colour than the last time he'd seen her, and who seemed to be fighting back her own tears.

'Thank you,' Molly whispered and gave Warlow an

extra squeeze. She sniffed once, pulled back, blinked, and recovered her almost-seventeen-year-old poise. The one she used as armour against a harsh world. 'The extra squeeze was from Mum. For saving her life. Obviously, she can't do it because of her broken wrist.'

Warlow scowled. 'I don't know about—'

'I spoke to Povey,' Jess said. 'And Molly's been googling nitrogen asphyxiation. You've got nowhere to run to.'

Warlow looked into two sets of defiant, almost identical eyes and gave up. 'Then I won't. Did you see anything?'

Jess shook her head. 'I was facing into the room when I was hit from behind. I dropped my bloody phone. Can you believe that?'

'You are a bit clumsy, Mum.' Molly muttered.

Warlow ignored her and spoke again to Jess. 'I know you've given Catrin a statement and she'll have it all up on HOLMES within the hour, but you think the noise you heard was the cylinder tipping over?'

Jess nodded. 'That's what I'm assuming.'

Warlow didn't see another chair, so he stood, feeling like a bit of an interloper. 'There's a path through the copse behind the workshop. It comes out on a lane that leads to a farm. Someone could have parked there and walked in.'

'Presumably they waited until the forensic team left.' Jess sighed. 'I got there at exactly the wrong time.'

'Povey's got the cassette that isn't a cassette.' Warlow stepped forward as a nurse entered and checked Jess's blood pressure. 'I see they've fixed your arm.'

Jess waved the pink cast. 'Molly's choice of colour I hasten to add.'

The nurse threw Jess a smile. 'We're waiting for the check X-ray to come back. Then we'll let you go.'

Warlow didn't try to hide his surprise. 'They're not keeping you in?'

'No point,' Molly answered. 'Either you die from nitrogen induced oxygen depletion or you don't. If you don't, you survive. Simple as that. The doctor said we should look out for permanent damage. Things like clumsiness, forgetfulness, unexplained loss of concentration. I said—'

'You can imagine what she said,' Jess intervened.

Warlow grinned. 'So you're being discharged? Okay, then I'll run you home.'

'No, Evan. That's—'

'Not even a discussion. Povey wants to keep your car for another hour or two. We can get the Uniforms to run it over to you tomorrow. How long until you can drive?'

'A month at least the doctor said.' Molly sounded dubious.

Jess shook her head. 'I've been enough trouble for one night, Evan. Forget taking us home. We can get a taxi. You haven't even eaten yet.'

'I'll survive. But was that a tea dispenser I saw in reception?'

'Ooh, I could do a cup of tea some damage, too.' Molly agreed.

Warlow fished change out of his pocket and handed it over. 'Mine's white and one. Jess?'

'No, I've been plying myself with tepid water. I'll burst if I have any more.'

Molly left the cubicle. Warlow pulled the curtain back, watched and waited until she was well out of earshot before turning back to Jess. 'How is she holding up?'

'See for yourself. On the outside, an old boot. Inside, she's had a big scare. The hug is a first. You're in danger of becoming a Molly favourite.'

Warlow ignored that. 'And how about you? How are you holding up?'

'I was fine until Molly read out the stats about how

deadly nitrogen could be. I remember only thinking how dark everything got. The weirdest thing was the not caring. I felt…well, okay about it. About myself. The crappy workroom. How amazing the patterns the corrugated roof made…I know what it is now, Then I…' Her mouth trembled. 'I don't think I was very far away from not seeing Molly ever again.'

Warlow crossed the space and took her right hand in his. 'We'll find who did this, Jess.'

She leant into him and he held her head and waited for the trembling to stop. It had by the time Molly came back with the tea.

Warlow spoke with Gil and Catrin in the waiting room and sent them both home after they'd looked in one last time on Jess.

The check X-ray was fine. They put her in a sling, gave her some strong painkillers, and let her go home.

Molly sat in the back of the Jeep, zoning out with earbuds in. Jess sat in the front with Warlow. He had the radio on low. Something neutral, a barely audible background noise. He wanted it that way, so that if Jess wanted to speak, she could. They went fifteen miles before she did.

'I think whoever was in the workshop panicked. They must have seen or heard me and hidden.'

'That's no excuse for doing what they did, and you know it.'

Jess sighed. 'I do, but I don't see it as a set-up.'

'So if you'd died, it would have been manslaughter, not murder?' It sounded harsh, but needed to be said. He kept his voice low, one eye in the rear-view to check on Molly's reaction in case she heard. She hadn't.

'It's ripples in a pond, isn't it?' Jess turned to look out at the dark night through the window. 'Boscombe is the stone and everything radiates out from him.'

'I'd say more tsunami than ripple, but I know what you mean. Want me to call somewhere for some food?'

'I don't think I could eat anything now, and Molly gorged on crisps and chocolate at the hospital. Hot chocolate and bed for me.'

He dropped them off, walked them in, and made sure all was well. On the way back to Ffau'r Blaidd, he phoned the Dawes.

'Sorry it's so late.'

'Still at work?' Maggie Dawes answered.

'Kind of. Would it be okay if Cadi stayed the night with you?'

'You know there's no need to ask.'

'Thanks.'

Ten minutes later, Warlow opened the door of his cottage and flicked on the light. He shrugged off his coat and drank a pint of cool, soft tap water. He'd read somewhere that an entire generation of people were growing up in Britain who refused to drink tap water because the government put chemicals in it. And not only fluoride; there were, apparently, other "things" that affected a range of functions from sterility to the way you thought. This was a generation that believed in mind control, were ashamed of their country's heritage, demanded everyone apologised for sins past, sins for which they had no responsibility, and dismissed anyone who questioned this as a reactionary idiot.

Aware that he was generalising, and at risk of looking in the mirror and finding a gammon, Warlow usually stayed away from all of this. Politics were games other people played. But the tap water issue really got to him. Millions, if not billions, of people on the planet would consider being able to walk into any house or building in the country, turn a faucet and get potable drinking water, a genuine miracle. What the hell was wrong with people?

He knew what this was, of course. Someone and something to rant against. He was angry with himself and someone unknown who had almost killed one of his colleagues. While they were at large, he needed to rail at some other topic.

Tap water would do just fine.

Standing at the sink, he eased off his shoes without untying the shoelaces. It felt good to flex and extend his toes in his socks. Then he picked up the shoes and undid the laces because he'd only have to do it in the morning.

He yawned and realised how dog tired he was.

He smiled. Very apt and wishful thinking on his part. Whereas Cadi could fall asleep in an instant, Warlow, despite his physical exhaustion, might still struggle.

He needed to eat something, but it was getting late. He opened the fridge and decided this was no time to faff around with preparation. A tin of tomato soup from the cupboard, two slices of buttered toast and a wedge of Black Bomber extra mature from the Snowdonia Cheese Company made a meal in four minutes flat.

He sat at the table, eating and wondering how such simple food could taste so good. When his phone buzzed, he contemplated not answering, but one glance at the caller ID changed his mind instantly.

'Evan, you're still up then?' Povey's voice sounded wide awake.

'Don't you have a home to go to?' Warlow picked some toast crumbs off the plate with the ball of his index finger and nibbled on them.

'What time did you get to yours?'

'Ten minutes ago.'

'Pot, kettle, black.'

'What have you got?'

'Not much. But there are fresh shoe prints on the dirt path leading from the back of the workshop to the farm lane. Someone left in a hurry is my guess. How's Allanby?'

'At home with her daughter.' Warlow felt a smile play at the corner of his mouth. This was the real reason Povey was ringing.

'No ill effects then. That's good to hear.'

'It is.'

'She dodged a bullet there.'

Warlow said nothing, He'd thought the same thing ever since she'd left in the ambulance.

'Once we get a pattern for the shoe print, I'll let you know. It isn't big though. A seven, I'd say.'

'Kids then?' Warlow guessed.

'Possibly. I'll get back to you as soon as I can.' There was a pause before Povey continued. 'I hear you had to resuscitate Allanby.'

'A couple of breaths. That's all she needed.'

'You're a real Prince Charming, Evan.'

'I'd keep that observation to yourself if I were you.'

She was chortling as he finished the call.

Her words stayed with him as he lay in bed that night. Jess had indeed dodged a bullet. An invisible, coiling one maybe, but still lethal.

It wasn't difficult to put yourself in harm's way in this job. It didn't happen often, thank God. But criminals were desperate people with no conscience. You had to keep reminding yourself of that fact if you were going to survive. Yet it wasn't only Jess who had a near miss tonight. Warlow would never have forgiven himself if she'd died. Of course, he would not have been held directly responsible. Not by anyone in authority. Jess had acted on her own, responding to an instinctive urge to check out a theory. But Jess was on his team. And the team was his responsibility.

His gut roiled over at the thought: an internal investigation and a coroner's report. And he'd have had to tell

Molly and explain it all to her absentee father. Then he'd have handed in his resignation and walked away. And yet, Jess had not been reckless. After all, she was walking into a property that was part of an investigation, if not an actual crime scene.

And she'd found what might be highly significant evidence.

Yet Warlow was convinced he was missing something. With all that they'd uncovered about Boscombe and his arrogant, manipulative, coercive behaviour, it was easy to miss the small things. The little thread that you pulled which unravelled the whole shebang.

More than ever, he needed to find that thread and pull it before someone else ended up getting hurt.

He held on to that thought as he lay waiting for sleep, nursing it, cherishing it because it meant he didn't have to contemplate the other thing that ate at him. The fact that he'd been forced into being so very intimate with Jess.

Mouth to mouth. Lips to lips.

He kept telling himself he'd had no choice.

But there would have to be a reckoning.

He owed it to them both.

CHAPTER FORTY

The following morning, Warlow stuck to his plan. Awake at six with no prospect of more sleep, he'd showered, shaved, and set off early. He'd promised the team a breakfast meeting, and that's what they were getting. He phoned through his order to Norma's, pulled in and picked up the four paper packets carefully wrapped and placed in a cardboard box.

Four orders instead of five.

Yes, well, he would use that.

He was back on the road by 7.45 am.

The team were all there as he walked into the Incident Room. But it was a subdued team. Anxiety hung like a low mist over everyone. Warlow carried the box in and called to Rhys.

'Help me get this stuff distributed, DC Harries.'

Rhys levered away from the desk. 'No problem, sir.'

The food smelt wonderful. The coffee even better. They sat at desks with napkins spread out. Catrin had opted for some kind of bran muffin. Warlow stayed simple with the breakfast bap: bacon and scrambled egg inside a soft wholemeal bun with a tomato ketchup chaser. It tasted bloody marvellous.

Warlow's phone chirped. He read the message out loud between chews. 'DI Allanby sending her regards. She says she's fine and not to forget to get her car back to her.'

Catrin chewed a mouthful of muffin and washed it down with a swallow of her flat white. 'I'll get on to that, sir.' She frowned. 'She isn't trying to get back to work, is she?'

'What are the rules on driving with a broken wrist?' Rhys asked between chews of his enormous sandwich.

Gil had already demolished half his marmite and cheese bap. 'Varies. No hard and fast rule. A cast limits mobility. Gear changing hand, too. Can't drive unless you're in full control of your vehicle.' He nodded at Catrin. 'DS Richards will confirm that.'

Catrin narrowed her eyes. 'I'm not Traffic.'

'But you know a man who is.' Rhys winked lecherously.

'I'll trust her judgement not to turn up here for the next few days,' Warlow said.

'Did you manage to speak to her about it last night, sir?' Rhys was trying to remove a scrap of fallen bacon off his lapel with the corner of a napkin.

Warlow added. 'I—'

'That'll stain.' Catrin observed.

'Don't say that.' Rhys looked stricken. 'It's only just been cleaned.'

Gil stopped eating and sent them both a scathing look before slowly turning his eyes back towards Warlow. 'You were saying, sir?'

Warlow put his food down and walked to the Job Centre, pointing to the image of Moor Cottage.

'Jess's theory is that someone was watching the forensic team. Waiting for them to leave. She arrived shortly after they left and probably surprised whoever it was. They pushed her in and ran for it after half locking the door with a stick.'

'I read up about nitrogen asphyxiation,' Rhys began.

Gil nodded. 'We all have, Rhys. We all know how this could have ended.'

Warlow added, 'But it didn't. Jess has a broken wrist and that's all. So, what I want to find out is how and why this happened. Did the thieves break the lock? If so, where's the padlock? Povey's going to come back to us today with her prelim. She thinks she has a take on how whoever it was got to the cottage unseen along a path to a farm lane. Let's look at what leads we have on medical gas thefts. Someone wanted what was in those cylinders. Perhaps they got it wrong and thought they were getting something else. Who knows? We owe Jess that.'

Everyone nodded.

'Gil, I want a separate team on Jess's case. Use DS Leyland. Get him to keep in touch with the forensic team at the cottage and me. If they find anything, I want to know. But I don't want the rest of you distracted from Boscombe.'

Gil picked up the phone on his desk and made a call.

Warlow turned to the images of Boscombe. 'I know how you'll be feeling about DI Allanby. But will finding out who locked Jess in get us any closer to sorting out this bugger, I wonder.'

Something flashed up on Catrin's screen. She turned and read the message. 'Sir, that was an update from digital forensics. They've uploaded the contents of the USB file labelled "G Eggs" and sent us a secure link.'

'Genius finding that in a cassette player.' Rhys smiled and shook his head.

'It was. So let's make the most of it for DI Allanby's sake.' Warlow wheeled back around. 'Five minutes to finish our breakfast and then an hour digging in to whatever we've got. Back here at half nine.'

Everyone nodded.

Warlow took what was left of his coffee through to the SIO room, settled himself, and found the link to "G Eggs". Nineteen names. Not the same number as was on the laptop file, but close. Young K was there. Warlow clicked on it and a video started. An edited file, five minutes long. No sound. It showed Katherine Young entering the room and sitting on a chair, Boscombe sitting opposite her. A minute of chat. Cut to Boscombe leaning in, the good, earnest listener. A bottle of wine opened. A jerky edit to Boscombe and Katherine on their feet. No longer talking because their mouths were otherwise occupied. Another jerky edit. Boscombe standing half naked, Katherine on her knees in her underwear, the edit zooming in on a blurry and unnecessary close-up.

Warlow stopped it there and clicked it off. He sat back and pondered before opening another two files. Not exactly the same, but more or less. He saw no sign of coercion. Boscombe was not forcing himself on unwilling victims here. That somehow made it worse for the women. They'd participated and that, Warlow was certain, would have added to the humiliation of having these images sent to friends or family.

Not exactly revenge porn. More *I-should-have-known-better* porn.

The coercion followed on naturally. Keeping the files a secret in exchange for money.

Golden Eggs indeed.

He went back over the report of Boscombe's post-mortem. Two blows to the head. Death by drowning. Alcohol and benzodiazepines in his blood.

All these people with a reason for Boscombe to die. But what wasn't he seeing here?

He walked out of the office to find Catrin pinning up more information on the Job Centre. Warlow stood next to Gil's desk, arms folded. 'What have you got?'

'Not much. Uniforms have a report from house to house in Kidwelly. You were right about someone having a view over the estuary. A resident says they saw the boat late on Saturday afternoon beached on the sandbank. They didn't see it actually beaching, but it wasn't there two hours before.'

'Empty?'

'No sign of any occupant or any other boat near it. No one disembarking onto another boat. Or trying to wade out.'

Gil looked up at Warlow. 'That gives us some help with the timeline. But that's about all.'

Rhys had his eyes on his screen, writing something on a pad. He swivelled in his chair to address the team. 'Reports on the medical gas thefts. No one has been arrested, but the thinking is that it was an organised gang maybe operating out of the West Midlands. They worked down from Shrewsbury to Gloucester, Worcester and then us. A small workshop isn't really their style. They target hospitals and clinics.' He wrinkled his nose in disappointment.

'Okay, put it up on the board.' Gil ordered.

Rhys got up and found a space next to where Catrin had posted his handwritten sheet. He had to lean down and when he stood up, once again he towered over the DS.

Next to him, Warlow heard Gil habitually mutter, 'That'll be the long and the short of it then.'

Warlow frowned. 'What did you say?'

Gil sat up straighter, hands up in apology. 'Is that a bit too heightist for you? It's a silly joke I know but—'

Warlow was staring at his two younger officers. The thread. He could almost feel it within his grasp.

The long and the short of it.

'Does anyone we know in this building own a Mazda CX-30?' Warlow barked out the question.

Catrin turned her head up in thought. Rhys tilted his down. Gil kept staring at Warlow as if he'd turned purple. Rhys answered first. 'I think Superintendent Goodey has one, sir. A grey one.'

Gil confirmed it. 'Yes, she does. There's a sticker in the back saying "Now We're Sucking Diesel".'

Rhys looked confused.

Catrin mouthed, 'Line of Duty' at him.

Warlow, however, was on a roll. 'Right. I want everyone down in the car park. Gil, bring your phone. We're going to make a film.'

'Is this something to do with the TV crew?' Rhys actually scratched his head.

Warlow grabbed his coat and marched out. Rhys and Catrin didn't move until Gil got up and said, 'Come on, you heard the man.'

'We did, but—' Catrin began.

Warlow put his head back through the door, his eyes full of a dangerous energy. 'Not a bloody request.'

Everyone moved sharply after that.

CHAPTER FORTY-ONE

THEY FOUND Goodey's Mazda in a designated parking spot. The weather was dry, but grey. A typical late winter's day. No rain, but it didn't look that far off, judging by the thickness of the clouds.

Warlow walked to the car and then counted forty steps back.

'It's not the Hokey Cokey, is it?' Gil watched the DCI with amused interest.

Warlow turned to him. 'You're going to film this.'

'For Tok-Tik, is it?' Gil asked.

'It's TikTok, sarge,' Rhys said.

Catrin growled and sang out, 'He knows that. He's jerking your chain, Rhys.'

Gil frowned. 'What's going on here, Evan? '

'Bear with.' He turned to Rhys and Catrin. 'I want you two to walk in front of Superintendent Goodey's car, squat down and then, on my signal, get up, walk around to the boot, face the car, and then face me. I'll be standing here with Gil.'

'Are we meant to say something, sir?' Rhys looked perplexed.

'You can sing a medley from *Mamma Mia* if you like.' Catrin grinned. 'I hear 'Dancing Queen' is your go-to karaoke track.'

Rhys reddened.

Warlow shouted. 'In your own time.'

The two officers walked self-consciously towards the car, Catrin took left, Rhys right. When they reached the bonnet, they turned back to face Warlow. 'Ready?' yelled the DCI.

Gil had the phone up in front of his face. 'Say the word.'

Warlow signalled with a downward pat for Catrin and Rhys to squat down and said to Gil, 'Now.' He counted to three and then called out, 'Stand up and walk to the back of the car.'

They did as instructed, glancing at each other, self-consciously, Catrin having to lift her chin to eyeball Rhys across the car's roof. When they got to the rear, they stood a couple of feet apart, turned towards the car, and then back towards Warlow.

'Stop now,' Warlow instructed Gil.

'We've got an audience.' Gil jerked his head up to the buildings' windows where some people were gazing down. One or two rude gestures appeared but quickly disappeared with one glare from Warlow.

'Thursday Film Club, if anyone asks,' Warlow mumbled. 'Come on. Back upstairs.'

He led them back inside and to the Incident Room but didn't give them time to get comfortable. By now it was well past mid-morning. 'Rhys, call up the CCTV footage of Boscombe from Laugharne car park.'

They clustered around the DC's desk while he found the clips.

'Gil, sit next to Rhys. Set up that video you just made.'

Gil grabbed a chair and set the phone up in front of him, teeing up the video.

'Rhys, run the Laugharne CCTV.'

They watched in silence as a grainy, black-and-white Boscombe arrived in Laugharne, parked his car, got out, removed the tackle from the boot, closed it and walked away.

'Run it back to where he gets out of the car and closes the driver's side door.'

Rhys did as asked.

'Freeze it.'

The clip stopped with Boscombe about to turn to walk back towards the back of the car.

'Gil, you're up.'

They watched Rhys and Catrin in the clip. Warlow made Gil freeze it at the point where they were both standing opposite the front doors in the same position as Boscombe was on the desktop screen.

'Great, Evan. Very artistic. What is it we're supposed to be looking at?' Gil's eyes swung pendulum-like from the desktop to the phone and back again several times.

'How tall was Boscombe? Rhys, you were at the PM.'

'Six one. I remember.'

'Okay, that's an inch less than you, right?'

'An inch and a bit. Yes, sir.'

'We've taken the video at about the same distance as the CCTV camera in Laugharne was from Boscombe's car. I've already looked up the height of a Mazda CX-30. Just over five feet.' He glanced at his notebook. 'That's 1.52 metres in new money. You're a head taller than the car. But look again. The person who parked that car in Laugharne is nothing like as tall as you. In fact, if you compare them, they're more like Catrin's height. A little taller, perhaps, but not far off.'

They all stared at the screen. It was barn door obvious

now that it had been pointed out. Warlow said it anyway. 'Whoever parked that car and took out the boat wasn't Boscombe.'

'Oh my God.' Catrin's mouth dropped open.

'Sir, that's genius.' Rhys kept staring at the images.

'We've got DS Jones to thank for that. His repetitive, irritating "the long and the short of it" joke. Why the hell it's taken me all this time to work it out, I do not know.' Warlow shook his head.

'So, what do you think's going on here, sir?' Gil was on his feet. A seasoned copper, even he was shaken by this new revelation as he ran a hand through his thinning hair.

'I think Boscombe might well have been already dead. Someone drove his car to Laugharne, took Boscombe's boat, maybe with him already in it, dumped the body, and let the boat drift.'

'Bloody hell.' Rhys said.

'So we're back to the sailors. People who can handle a boat. Someone less than six foot obviously,' Gil said.

Catrin was back at her desk. 'Shouldn't be too difficult to check again on Pryce. I can't remember how tall he is, but we have his physical description on record.'

'What about Boscombe's colleagues, umm…Corrigan and the secretary?' Muttering, Gil went back to his desk, too.

'We have nothing on the Golden Egg suspects though,' Rhys said. 'No stats.'

'No, so the best thing you can do is get the kettle on DC Harries.' Gil smiled at the young officer.

For once, he did not look bothered. He sauntered off, muttering 'genius' to himself.

Warlow wandered out into the corridor and saw DS Leyland – the bearded and heavy-set officer he'd seconded to look into Jess's attack – signalling to him.

'Glad I caught you, sir. Alison Povey has posted her

findings. She was wondering if you had another number for' – he glanced down at his notebook – 'uh, Mrs Fiona Needham? Apparently, they need her fingerprints to eliminate her from what they've found at Moor Cottage. Hers are all over the place since she worked there and all. Povey can't get hold of her at home.'

Warlow nodded. 'I'm sure we've got her mobile number somewhere. I'll get Catrin to let you have it.'

'Thank you, sir. We'll send some Uniforms around and knock on the door.'

From behind him, Warlow heard his name called. 'Evan, got a minute?'

He turned, preoccupied enough with Leyland not to have recognised the voice. When he saw it was Caldwell beckoning to him, he almost turned away again. But there were other people in the corridor and no way of pretending he hadn't heard. Instead, he stood where he was and watched Caldwell saunter down the corridor, a smirk hovering over his lips.

'What the hell was that little performance in the car park, Evan? We're taking bets it's for the TV people. You written a sketch, have you? A take on "four candles"? Someone else said you might be thinking about keying Goodey's car.'

'What do you want, Kelvin?'

Caldwell let the smirk linger a little longer before answering. 'I thought it might be good if you did a little piece to camera first thing tomorrow. Introduce yourself. Wear something snazzy. Big us up.'

Warlow looked at his shoe and imagined it flying up to connect with Caldwell's face. His response emerged as an unsuppressed groan. 'Big us up? Christ, man, listen to yourself.'

Caldwell ploughed on; his expression suddenly earnest. 'It's only that we didn't want them zeroing in on the negatives. On Jess Allanby's near death experience, for example. On top of Rhys Harries getting stabbed last year and then threatened with a fake gun.' He tutted and gave a little shake of his head. 'That's Jonah territory is that. You don't want the TV lot lumbering you with that label, right?'

The thing about Caldwell was that you couldn't tell if he was taking the mick or not most of the time. Tragically, it was easy to believe that he was being genuine. Never mind the insult. Never mind that he sounded like a total pillock. Was a total pillock.

Warlow smiled. 'I don't think so, Kelvin. I have no intention of doing a piece to camera tomorrow or any other day. I'll leave all that to the prima donnas and the chronically bloody useless. That puts you in with two chances right there.'

Caldwell smiled again. It made him look like he'd swallowed a spider. 'Looking forward to seeing you beaming back at me from my wide-screen plasma, Evan. It'll be a treat.' He let his eyes flick up to the DCI's head. 'Probably need to get that bruise touched up, though. If it gets any bigger you'll be needing a wheelbarrow.'

The lump on Warlow's head had reduced from the size of Everest to a little short of Kilimanjaro on inspection in the mirror that morning. The sutures were healing nicely. But he knew it stood out like a sore thumb – or a sore haematoma on the head, as Tom would have correctly said.

He turned away before his irritation got the better of him. Caldwell was a distraction and one that he could do without right now.

But the DI couldn't let it lie. 'I could always ask them to film you lot doing a team building exercise in the car park. That would be entertaining.'

Warlow stopped and turned back, retraced his steps, leant in and whispered, 'Tell me, Kelvin, were you born this way, or is becoming a total twat something you've grown into?'

Warlow was the shorter of the two men, but from the way Caldwell had pressed himself against the wall, it made no difference. There were other people in the corridor. They'd all gone quiet and were looking. Waiting for what came next.

'Hang on,' Warlow said loudly, his face three inches away from KFC's. He reached up and pretended to remove something from the DI's hair and drop it on the floor. 'Piece of straw.' Warlow grinned for the audience and spoke loud enough for everyone to hear. But only the others in the corridor heard what he muttered as he walked away. 'No prizes for guessing where that came from.'

CHAPTER FORTY-TWO

By the time Warlow got back into the Incident Room, tea was up. Catrin had posted a rough table on the board and next to the names she'd written heights. Top of the list was Boscombe at six foot one. Using Rhys as a yardstick for the CCTV footage had not been that far off the mark as a foot taller than the car. Now they were looking for someone around five six. Rhys had done some maths and by his reckoning, based on a comparison of the CCTV images and Gil's video of him and Catrin, the fake Boscombe had an extra inch or two on Catrin.

Both Corrigan at five foot ten and Pryce at five nine were too tall. Now they were trawling through the Golden Egg file, trying to find what they could.

Warlow sipped his tea and watched them working. But Rhys sat back, his face with the remnants of his black eye now faded to a sickly yellow, looking troubled.

'Something bothering you, Rhys?'

The DC stretched out his long legs. 'Yes, sir. There is.'

'Well?' Warlow put his mug down and folded his arms.

'I can't make it add up, sir. Not with the suspects we have. Corrigan and Mrs Boscombe and everyone on the

Golden Eggs' list were being blackmailed. But how would getting rid of Boscombe help?'

Catrin looked across from her screen. 'Pretty obvious, isn't it? The blackmail ends when the blackmailer dies.'

'Yes,' Rhys agreed with a slow nod. 'But then we get involved and stir up the pot, and all the stuff that was being kept secret comes out into the open. That's shooting yourself in the foot, that is.'

Gil had a ballpoint between his teeth. He took it out and agreed. 'Fair point.'

'Keep going, Rhys.' Warlow encouraged the DC.

'We've assumed this – the blackmail – is the obvious motive. There's only one other person with a different motive. That's Pryce. He hated Boscombe because of what he did to his grandmother.'

Catrin raised her eyebrows. 'Killed her on an operating table, you mean?'

Rhys shrugged. 'Butchered her. His words. But Pryce has an alibi.'

Warlow followed Rhys's train of thought. 'So who else might want to get rid of him for a different reason?'

'What about the other victim's relatives? The other cases of manslaughter left on file?' Catrin was interested now.

'They all checked out.' Gil stood up, arched his neck and massaged the big muscles there with his hands.

Catrin took up the baton. 'Perhaps when we contact Fiona Needham to get her prints for Povey we should ask her again about Boscombe's patients. Did anyone call him out for pulling the wool over their eyes about their gastro-intestinal health? That sort of thing.'

By way of emphasis, Gil's gut gurgled obligingly.

'Bloody hell, sarge, should we move back behind some sandbags?' Rhys looked alarmed.

'Hunger.' Gil explained. 'You're quite safe.'

Warlow snorted at the exchange. He was about to mention the fact that he'd seen Gil eat a big marmite and cheese bap less than two hours ago when he glanced across at Catrin. The DS looked frozen in place, sat forward on her chair, staring ahead with the whites of her eyes showing all around her irises.

'Catrin?' Warlow prompted.

She swallowed and gasped in air. 'Sir, I think Rhys might be right. We've been looking in all the wrong places.'

They all turned to stare at her.

'The Ativan, sir. I knew I'd seen it somewhere, but I couldn't think where. I'd seen it and dismissed it because it was with a whole load of other drugs on a bathroom shelf.'

'Whose?' Rhys demanded.

'Edith Moreton's. Fiona Needham's mother.'

'Her mother? Isn't she in hospital?' Gil asked.

'Terminally ill.' Warlow muttered, feeling his brows bunch together, mind racing. Feeling them shift apart as the mental thread revealed itself at last. He pulled and saw it unravel everything in front of his eyes. The CCTV, the boat, Jess, everything. 'What ward?' Warlow barked.

Catrin thumbed through her notebook. 'Seven,' Catrin said.

'Ring them. Make sure she's there.' He turned on his heel and barged back out of the room. He found DS Leyland in an office. The man looked startled as the DCI strode over to him.

'Did you send Uniforms to Needham's house?'

'Yes. They're on their way.'

He pointed a finger at Leyland. 'Get hold of them. Tell them to stay in the car. They're not to go in.'

'Okay, I'll try.'

Warlow leant in. 'Don't try. *Do it.* They are not to go in.'

He ran back to the Incident Room, stood in the doorway and glared at Catrin, who was still on the phone.

'Thanks...yes...okay.' She looked up, confusion wrinkling her brow. 'Edith Moreton isn't on the ward. Her daughter came first thing this morning to take her home. The ward Sister didn't sound too happy. She wanted to keep her in for another day at least.'

Warlow squeezed his eyes shut, but then forced them open wide. 'Gil, make sure Leyland does what I've asked him to do. Rhys, Catrin. Car. Now.'

He turned and hurried away, hearing the garbled sounds of his officers scrambling to keep up with him.

Rhys was right. Blackmail was one thing. But a patient's relative with a grudge was something else altogether. Pryce had shown them that. They were looking for someone who hated Boscombe enough to kill him and cared nothing for the consequences.

But consequences there would be. That was the one thing Warlow was certain of as he hurried out to the Jeep.

CHAPTER FORTY-THREE

WARLOW TOOK the Jeep and followed Rhys and Catrin in the Focus. She was the one who knew the way to Needham's address in Llanmiloe. A parked incident response vehicle stood on the pavement outside the property on Woodland Close as he pulled up at 12.25pm.

Rhys and Catrin were already out and talking to the uniformed officers. A red Citroen sat on the driveway that Warlow recognised as Needham's. He walked up the path towards the bungalow and Catrin joined him a moment later.

'Both front and rear doors locked, sir. No response to knocking. They can hear the telephone ringing but no one is picking up.'

Warlow turned to Catrin. 'You've been inside. What's the layout?'

'Front door leads to a small hallway. Kitchen on the right. Living room beyond that. Two bedrooms on the other side. Bathroom at the rear.'

'Anything strike you about the place when you were here?'

Catrin thought. 'Needham was decorating her mother's bedroom ready for her to come back. Plastic sheeting on the floor to protect the carpet, yellow tape over the window frames, sheets on the bed.'

Rhys joined them at a trot, breathing hard after a once around the house reconnoitre.

'Anything?' Warlow asked.

'No, sir. No sign of anyone or anything.'

Catrin looked around. 'Where could they be? I mean the car's here, and Edith Moreton is hardly likely to have gone for a stroll.'

Warlow glanced up at the sky. Blue patches were fighting with big cotton wool balls of cloud. The breeze was fresh and cool. You could walk in this, but you'd need to dress for it. Catrin was right. Not convalescent stroll weather by any means.

'Jackson, that's one of the Uniforms, did say one thing, sir.' Rhys said. 'He's had a peek in through the windows, those he could see through. He didn't clock anyone but he said that the windows at the back feel cold. Colder than normal.'

The icy shudder that churned Warlow's insides had nothing to do with the weather.

'Which window?' Warlow demanded.

Rhys called over to Jackson who indicated left.

Catrin saw it, too. 'That's Edith Moreton's bedroom.'

Warlow led the way around the side of the bungalow to the bedroom window. Curtains drawn, the window shut tight. Pale yellow tape was visible around the inside of the glass. He stared at it, the ice churning a little more.

'These are UPVC windows,' Rhys observed. 'They don't need painting inside or out. Why would you have tape on the windows?'

Warlow reached out and touched the glass. Cold verging on icy. He retraced his steps. Another bedroom, this one with the curtains open, a bed visible inside. He touched the glass. Cold, but nowhere near as cold as Edith Morton's.

'Shit,' he muttered.

'Sir,' Catrin began. 'What do you think—'

But Warlow was already moving. He ran past the officers to the rear. The back door was a simpler affair than the front. Composite and half glazed. Rhys and Catrin followed, looking totally bemused.

Warlow tried the door. Locked. He banged on the window. No answer.

'Get the Uniforms. We need to break down this door. Rhys, hunt around. They may have left a key somewhere under a pot or in the eaves.'

Jackson was a big lad. He brought a crowbar with him. The other Uniform was a female PC called Llewellyn. Catrin spoke to her and sent her off to radio-in for help. Warlow stood for ten seconds of concentrated thought before running back to the Jeep, rummaging in the boot and coming back with a tyre iron. Within a minute he was at the door with Jackson, on his knees, trying to wedge open a gap below where the Uniform was working.

Both men were grunting with effort until, with a crack, the frame gave and the door shuddered open. Jackson took a step over the threshold, but Warlow yanked him back. 'No!'

Jackson looked at the DCI in astonishment. 'Just wanted to make sure—'

'I know you did. But it's not safe. Stand back in the garden. You too, sergeant.' Catrin took some steps back. Warlow grabbed her arm. 'Moreton's bedroom. Last one on the left, so nearest to us on the right, yes?'

Catrin nodded. Warlow turned back towards the property, took three deep breaths and walked in. There was no smell, but he felt the cold around his legs instantly as he crossed the threshold. The door to Moreton's bedroom was shut. One glance told him most of the others in the bungalow were open. Still holding his breath, Warlow put his hand on the handle and almost let go.

Cold. Icy cold.

He pushed down, opened the door. It did not open smoothly. Something at floor level snagged its travel. He looked down. A heavy blanket. He pushed harder. The door moved and water vapour billowed out. But above his knees the view was unobstructed and showed two bodies. Moreton on her bed. Needham on the floor, head on a pillow. He knew there was no point trying to resuscitate either of them.

Far too late for that.

To the left of the door, a metal cylinder lay on its side. Water vapour steamed from its neck.

Nitrogen in a gas chamber. And if he took one breath in that room, he'd die too.

Warlow turned away and, still holding his breath, hurried back out to join his colleagues before he exhaled and took in a lungful of air. 'Two dead,' he said. 'We need Povey and the fire service. Tell them there's more liquid nitrogen to clear up.'

The Uniforms got to it. Catrin had her phone out, but hesitated. 'Both dead? But who could have done this?'

'The answers are in that bedroom, sergeant. When it's clear and we can go, in, I think we'll find that Fiona Needham wears size seven shoes and is about an inch or two taller than you are.'

Rhys gawped. 'She killed Boscombe?'

'And her mother, and herself.' Warlow sucked in clean air. 'Murder and suicide. Let's hope there's a note.'

———

It took the better part of two hours to render the scene safe for Warlow to enter the bedroom. The crew that cleaned up the nitrogen gave Warlow nods and the odd salute as they entered the bungalow. One had his hands up, pretending to shiver. There might even have been smiles under all that protective gear.

There were dead people inside, but Warlow was still a target of black humour.

'They're calling you Mr Freeze,' Rhys explained.

Warlow found a smile from somewhere and returned the nods. They were good lads.

Mostly, he passed the time pacing up and down the length of the garden or taking calls from Gil and Jess. He'd sent Rhys and Catrin to interview the neighbours. They didn't learn much. Both returned with reports of how shocked everyone was to see the police presence. Needham had been private, keeping herself to herself. But no one thought her strange.

'Always smiling,' said one.

'Looked after her poor mother,' said another.

After that, Warlow sent the two younger detectives back to the office since he had no idea how long the clear-up would take. He maintained the vigil alone. But eventually, Povey stuck her blue-suit hooded head out of the back door and called to him.

'Clogs on, Evan. It's peep show time.'

Warlow did as asked and walked into the bedroom behind Povey in his plastic overshoes. The windows were open, and everyone wore masks. The bodies had not been moved. Fiona Needham lay where he'd seen her earlier, dressed in jeans and a sweatshirt, curled into the foetal position.

Edith Moreton was in bed. Tucked up with a blanket under her chin. Mouth open in death, almost as if she was about to sing.

In both cases, and in the room itself, there was no sign of struggle or violence. But Needham had done a good job of rendering the place airtight.

Povey nodded towards the tipped over container to the side of the door. 'A ten litre Dewar flask. There was about half a litre left inside.' Next to the bed on the floor, a small triangular clear plastic tent lay on its side. Warlow squatted down to peer at it.

'Yeah,' Povey nodded. 'That's my guess too. She waited for her mother to be asleep and put the tent over her upper body. It's a propagator. Used to bring plants on and to guard against frost, about 1.5 metres square volume. There's a steel bowl on the bed. Empty now, but I suspect Needham poured some nitrogen into that. It would have filled up the tent quickly. If her mother breathed that in, it wouldn't have taken long.'

Warlow got up, turned again to look at Fiona Needham. 'Then she seals the bottom of the door and empties the whole flask and lays down.'

Povey looked from mother to daughter impassively. 'There's an ongoing debate in the states about using nitrogen for executions. Some say it's the most humane way. No one has to give a lethal injection. You simply purge a chamber with the gas. Or release it into a room like this. It's quick.'

'How quick?' Warlow sent Povey a sharp glance.

Povey shrugged. 'In accidents, people exposed to high levels in an enclosed space die quickly. A matter of seconds. Two or three breaths. Sometimes co-workers who rush in to rescue them die too. Not long is the answer.'

Warlow looked at the woman on the bed. Mainly because he didn't want to look at Povey. Didn't want her to see his expression as he realised how close Jess had been to looking like Needham. Curled up on the floor, dead.

But Povey read his thoughts. 'It's supposed to be painless. There's no suffocation reflex. Before passing out people feel light-headed, dizzy or maybe even euphoric, and vision may dim. The Air Force have done the most work on it.'

'Jess must've disturbed her last night at Moor Cottage. Collecting more nitrogen.'

Povey nodded and pointed to the dead woman's feet. 'Needham was a size seven.'

A tech appeared in the doorway and signalled to Povey. She followed him out, leaving Warlow alone. He stood in that room of death wondering what he could have done to prevent this. Needham had fooled them all. Underneath that staid and steady exterior, something dark and tortured must have writhed in pain.

Povey came back and looked in. 'Evan, you'd better see this. There's a letter in the kitchen and it's addressed to you.'

CHAPTER FORTY-FOUR

IT WAS ALMOST four before Warlow called the team together in the SIO's room. He'd convened there with Gil, Catrin, and Rhys because he wanted to include Jess. And though the Internet connection wasn't stellar, he'd rather have her face on a desktop than a tiny image on his phone.

There was fresh tea in his mug and the HUMAN TISSUE FOR TRANSPLANT box had been raided. Warlow sat at his desk, Gil drew a seat up next to him, the framework creaking a protest as the big DS sat down. Catrin and Rhys stood at the back. The long and the short of it indeed.

Warlow chose to address Jess, because she was the only one not in the room. He had his phone out in front of him, reading glasses on. He'd briefed her on the crime scene and told her about the letter. But its contents were still to be revealed to the rest of the team.

'Povey's still got it, obviously. They're going to give it the once over, make sure there's no trace of anyone else there. But I'm convinced it's all Needham's work. I took photos of the letter and the easiest thing to do would be to read it out to you now.'

A tiny delay showed in Jess's nod. No one else spoke.

Warlow picked up his phone, scrolled to the images and pinched the first one open to reveal Needham's tidy handwriting. With his lilting accent, he read out what she'd written to him.

DEAR DCI WARLOW,

I am writing this after bringing my mother home from the hospital for the last time. I'm going to give her a mid-morning lunch of roast pork with potatoes because that's her favourite. She will not eat much of it, but after that, I'll be getting rid of all her pain, and mine too. If you're reading this you will already know what I mean.

I hope that DI Allanby is okay. I wasn't expecting her to be at Moor Cottage last night. I waited until the technicians left because I needed another few litres of nitrogen to be sure. Seeing movement in the cottage spooked me and I knocked a flask over. Hopefully she will have phoned for help—'

WARLOW STOPPED and looked up at Jess. The DI wore a ragged expression. 'She wasn't to know I dropped it.'

Was that forgiveness of sorts, Warlow wondered? He turned back to his phone.

MY MOTHER, Edith, is what people call a sensitive person. Highly strung after the polio got her. When I was three, she gave birth to my brother Leo. He was not a well baby. Poor mite had a heart defect. He died undergoing surgery when he was fourteen months old. My mother never recovered. She lost her faith in medicine then. She became agora-phobic and a hypochondriac. My father and I had a difficult time coping. I escaped, for want of a better word, and got married, leaving my poor dad to do what he could. When he passed my mother was alone. She did not do well. But it was only after my husband died, I reverted to being my mother's carer. That has not been easy. When she found Malcolm Boscombe and Alternis, she changed. You have to understand that since my brother died, life has been a burden for my mother. An existence without joy. Often, she would say to me what a relief it would be to die.

When Malcolm began to talk to her, she listened. We even managed a trip to her old town in Essex, to the beach where she played as a child, on his recommendation.

I could see how much my mother believed in Malcolm. He had a gift for that. I also saw how easy it was for him to manipulate those that did, too. I saw how he was with women. I let myself be manipulated a few times. I knew that I, and they, were nothing more than intermissions. I was a convenient body to be used. I did not pursue a relationship. I did everything I could to put him off. But I needed a job and the money. So, I lay down rules and mostly he abided by them.

But then Mum became ill. The indigestion that preoccupied her, that Malcolm had treated with herbs and reassurances, turned out to be something else. Something much worse. When she was admitted for obstruction and had the surgery, they told me that her symptoms should have been dealt with much earlier. She should have been referred. They might have been able to do something then.

When I told Malcolm this, he said that he could not be expected to take every hypochondriac he came across seriously. He wasn't a doctor after all.

But that wasn't true. Being a doctor again was what he craved. It was then, for the first time, I saw who he really was. Why all the things that had happened to him had happened. He didn't care. He didn't care for anyone except himself. I couldn't stop thinking about how many more people he would lie to. Had lied to.

When I asked him to speak to my mother in hospital, he said no. What he actually said was that there was no point picking rotten fruit because it would only get more rotten.

That was when I decided to do it.

With Mum in hospital, I told Malcolm she'd decided to leave him something in her will on condition that we scattered my dad's ashes, which she'd kept, in the estuary. She said that would make her happy.

We needed to inspect the samphire beds anyway, so I took a hamper and champagne that I'd already treated with some of Mum's sleeping pills. I told Malcolm it would be to toast my dad.

I drove to a quiet spot that was not overlooked. An access lane no one used. We walked seventy yards out to the water on the flats. I opened the champagne. It was an expensive one, and Malcolm drank two glasses within ten minutes. I scattered my father's ashes, though they were not really his ashes, and gave Malcolm more to drink. I kept him there. It was a nice day. A sunny day and almost warm in the sunlight. I'd made sandwiches and a salad with croutons to disguise the crunched-up Ativan in the mix. It didn't take much to keep him occupied. I won't go into details, but he wasn't difficult to entertain and I knew from experience what he liked.

He drank another three glasses. An hour after we got there he passed out. The tide was going out but there were pools scattered over the ground. I dragged him to one, a muddy hollow no more than nine inches deep. When I tried to hold his head under, he fought. Not much, but enough. That was when I hit him with some driftwood. Twice. He didn't fight after that.

I stepped on his head, and he drowned in those nine inches of water.

I had ropes. I tied them around him and tied the other end to two buoys and hooked them around the remains of a sunken jetty. I took his phone, covered him in kelp and left him to go and visit Mum in hospital. I went back to Moor Cottage and left his phone there.

The following morning, I drove to the cottage before dawn, dressed in some of Malcolm's fishing gear. It was way too big for me, but it did the job. I drove his car to Laugharne. I took his boat out and found the jetty and the buoys. I towed his body out into the deep water, undid the ropes and let him go and threw his phone in after him. I took the boat back to the jetty, got out and sent it back into the estuary before walking out from the flats the four miles back to Moor Cottage. I saw no one the whole time. Then I drove home.

Perhaps you know all this. I suspect you and DI Allanby are clever people. I don't think I'm clever, but I needed time to sort my mother out. To give her peace. She would not do well with the treatments they're suggesting. With her gone, I have no reason to stay.

I'm writing this because I don't want anyone else blamed. Malcolm was a monster. I don't feel any regret. I'm going to sleep knowing he will not be able to do what he did to my mother to anyone else.

I'm going to meet my Nigel.
Fiona Needham.

NO ONE SPOKE for several long seconds. Eventually, it was Warlow who broke the silence.

'Right, let's get back to it. I'm taking this up to Two-Shoes. Let her know we've cracked it.'

'She's not going to like it,' Gil said.

'Ah well, tough…excrement.' Warlow pushed back from the desk.

From behind, Rhys asked a question. 'What do we do about the other things we found, sir? The Golden Eggs list and the videos on the cassette that isn't a cassette?'

Warlow's face stayed grave. 'Catrin and I will speak to the women on that list. I see no need for any of that to be used as evidence. It isn't relevant anymore.'

'I'll help with that.' Jess's voice came through the desktop speaker and made them all turn around to look.

'They'll be relieved.' Gil nodded.

'But he was breaking the law by blackmailing those women.' Rhys looked a tad indignant.

Warlow nodded. 'Fair point. But if we drag their names through the mud, as Boscombe threatened to do, and splash it all over the newspapers—'

'Or the TV, even,' Catrin interjected.

'Or the TV,' Warlow agreed. 'What does that make us?'

Rhys pondered the question and struggled to answer it.

'Not compassionate.' Warlow pinned the young DC with a glare.

Jess had the last word. 'There's more to this job than a collar, Rhys. But you're a quick learner. We have a confession here. There will be no trial, just a coroner's report. The Golden Eggs can stay in their basket for that.'

They all filed out leaving Warlow with Jess on screen. 'Can I call in tomorrow on the way to work? Something I need to run past you.'

Jess held up her left arm with its pink cast. 'I'm not going anywhere.' She paused before asking, 'Nigel was her husband, right?'

Warlow nodded and sighed. 'Now for Two-Shoes.'

Jess grimaced.

But Warlow found a smile from somewhere. 'Don't worry. I think I might even be looking forward to it.'

CHAPTER FORTY-FIVE

DCI Evan Warlow sat in his car on a street around the corner from Jess and Molly Allanby's rental property in Cold Blow. The dashboard clock showed 8.50am. She'd be up. Molly was on her way to school. He'd told Jess he'd be there before nine. But here he was, sitting in his car, both hands on the steering wheel with rivulets of cold sweat running down the inside of his shirt.

A psychiatrist interviewing him now would have a bloody field day.

'You've arrested murderers, is that correct?'

An affirmative nod.

'Chased killers and robbers. Interviewed kidnappers. Fought with thugs?'

Nod

'Then why is it you tremble outside this woman's house?'

Warlow squeezed his eyes shut and his fingers whitened as they gripped the steering wheel. He rested his forehead on his knuckles, told the imaginary psychiatrist to go and do something anatomically impossible, then fired up the ignition and drove the two hundred yards to park in front of Jess's house.

Someone had brought her Golf back. It needed a good clean. Some wag had written, "Under this I'm a smart car" on the boot. Warlow did not discount the possibility that it had been Molly.

He got out, walked to the front door, and rang the bell. Jess, in jeans and a blue shirt, opened the door and greeted him with a smile.

'Come in. Coffee is on.'

Warlow glanced at the cast on her arm. 'How is it?'

'A pain. As in, it gets in the way all the time. Not in an ow-that-hurts way.'

He followed Jess into the kitchen. Two coffee cups sat waiting on the table.

'You've had breakfast, I take it?' she asked.

'Had mine with Cadi at six thirty.'

'How is she?'

'Consistent. Reliable. No subtext.'

Jess turned from where she was fetching milk from the fridge and frowned. 'That's an interesting description.'

Warlow waited while Jess poured the coffee from a cafetiere and said, 'In comparison with most humans, I know it's true. And I include myself in the generalisation.'

She paused in her pouring. 'Oh dear, Evan. It's not Two-Shoes and KFC that have put you in this mood, is it?'

Warlow shook his head and breathed in long and deep. 'Not them. This is all me…I need to tell you something, Jess. I'm a coward for having waited this long. But since the episode in Moor Cottage, I have no choice.'

Jess did a double take. 'Did I say something I shouldn't have when I was delirious from nitrogen narcosis?' She tried to keep it light, but when Warlow didn't respond, a nervous laugh escaped her lips. 'You're worrying me, Evan.'

He picked up his cup. It was small, the coffee within it dark and thick. It trembled visibly in his hand, and so he put it back down before taking a sip. 'You've asked me a dozen times why I retired.'

'Yes, and you never answered me.'

'No, I haven't.' He looked up at her. 'But I'm going to now.'

'You don't have to if you don't—'

'I do. I must. When I pulled you out of the workshop, you weren't breathing. I didn't know what to do. My training took over. I did the only thing I could. I gave you mouth-to-mouth and CPR.'

'I've got the bruises to prove it.' She massaged her sternum, still smiling. 'I know I've said thank you a hundred times, but—'

'Please, Jess. I'm not here looking for thanks. Hear me out.'

A half smile faltered in the DI's lips. 'Okay.'

'Once, when Catrin Richards was a freshly minted DC, I went with her to interview a junkie.'

He remembered it with crystal clarity. Cerys McLean was a low life who hassled people for money outside the Odeon and Nando's in Llanelli town centre so she could get a hit of whatever poison she was injecting. She spent most nights in an abandoned house near the canal with her "partner" Adrian Long, who burgled to feed his own habit. But good old Adrian left an eighty-year-old needing fifty stitches after a B and E went south. He'd gone AWOL once he'd re-entered the atmosphere from whatever drug-induced orbit he'd been in during that violent assault and realised he was now very much on the police radar. Caldwell had the case, one of his first. But he'd wanted to "blood" the new DC on his team and suggested rookie Catrin Richards head down to the East Gate Shopping Centre to find McLean and ask her what she knew of Long's whereabouts. But at the very last minute Caldwell cried off with a forgotten "urgent" meeting.

'He passed on the case to Mel Lewis. But, Mel, as we know, had other fish to fry. That left DC Richards to go it alone.'

Warlow met the DC on the way to her car by chance. She'd been helping him with a fraud case over the previous month, and they'd struck up a rapport. Their meeting had been pure chance. She on her way out to McLean, he on the way back from a day out in the autopsy suite in Cardiff.

Warlow picked up on how terrified Catrin appeared at the thought of going it alone and volunteered to go with her. They found McLean outside Joe's Ice Cream Parlour in Llanelli's East Gate wearing a Rambo headband, a #Youtoo T-shirt and calling people anatomical names if they didn't put money in her Costa cup. Unfortunately, and as per, cooperation was not on her agenda that day. As soon as the DC approached, she began shouting and swearing, protesting police harassment. There were a couple of Uniforms nearby and they quickly joined in the fun.

Warlow was not a big man, but the DC was smaller and therefore McLean's natural target for when she finally lunged out. She missed with a flailing punch, allowing Warlow to step in and grab her arm and shoulder. He remembered feeling something sharp in his palm, but adrenaline shoved it deep down into the bottom drawer of his awareness under the more immediate unpleasantness of *eau de unwashed* McLean and struggling junky. The Uniforms quickly took over and got her, squirming and swearing, to the ground. They didn't arrest her, there was no point. Instead, they moved her away from the crowd that had gathered to witness the entertainment. And all the while McLean denied all knowledge of anyone called Adrian Long.

It wasn't Warlow's case. The DC was unharmed. So,

he used extra sanitizer on his hands, noted a few scuffs on his knuckles just like in the old days, and put the whole thing out of his mind. He dragged Caldwell, whom he outranked, over the coals. Told him in no uncertain terms judiciously peppered with obscenities, never to let the DC go anywhere alone again and more or less forgot all about it.

Only when McLean OD'd in the squat she shared with Long six months later, did her proclivity for secreting needles in her clothes at her elbows and shoulders and headband become known to him. Even then he hadn't given it a second thought. Not even when someone had muttered, 'Lucky no one got Ebola from the bitch.'

Warlow recounted all of this in Jess's kitchen as if he was watching it play out in front of him. He came back to himself and blinked. 'A year later I went to give blood. As you know, they screen you. My tests flagged something up. Bottom line? McLean gave me hepatitis C and, as a bonus, I end up being HIV positive as well. Birthday and Christmas rolled into one.'

Jess said nothing but her big eyes were now larger than ever.

But Warlow hadn't finished. 'I'm here to say I'm sorry. I should've said something. I should've done something. Used some kind of barrier between my mouth and yours, but there was no time. I'm sorry, Jess.' Warlow couldn't keep his gaze up. He dropped it to the cup.

'You're HIV positive?' Jess repeated the phrase as if to make sure she'd heard it correctly.

'Yes. The hepatitis has gone. But I have the virus. I'm on meds and the viral load is low. But it's still there.'

'And you're telling me because you think you might have given it to me?' Jess lifted her phone off the table and started typing.

For a moment, Warlow wondered if she was calling it

in. Going to have him arrested for assault. All he could do was explain his own jumbled thoughts on the matter. 'I know there was no exchange of fluids. But there's always a chance. I've spoken to the consultant who looks after me. She'd be happy to see you—'

Jess frowned. She had an odd expression as she kept looking from his face to her phone. 'I know someone in Manchester with a positive viral titre. From a long time ago. They got it from contaminated blood after transfusion. He's married. Got kids.'

Warlow's pulse hammered at his temples. 'Jess, the whole team should have known. I told myself it wasn't a problem, so long as I remained careful. But the shit was always going to hit the fan at some point.'

'And that's why you walked away from the job? Because you got HIV from the junkie?'

'I couldn't stand the thought that I'd be a danger to my colleagues. And now look what's happened.'

Jess's frown deepened. 'What has happened?'

Warlow stared at the DI. 'Don't you understand? There's always going to be a risk.'

She turned the phone towards him, open on a website. An NHS page entitled Common Health Questions. The bold headline was. "Can You Catch HIV from Kissing?" 'Shall I read you what it says?' She didn't wait for his answer. 'Evidence shows that the HIV virus is spread through the exchange of bodily fluids such as blood, semen, and vaginal fluids, but not saliva. Although HIV can be detected in saliva, it can't be passed to other people through kissing because a combination of antibodies and enzymes found naturally in saliva prevent HIV infecting new cells.' She looked up at him, eyebrows arched.

'I know what it says, Jess. I've been up every night scouring the net looking for reassurance. But then there's this, too.' He pointed to the healing cut on his head.

'That's different. I bled and people offered to help. To wipe it up. What if—'

'I'll get a test if it'll make you feel better. It'll be negative. For God's sake, Evan, we didn't have unprotected sex. You breathed six lungfuls of air into me, that's all.'

Warlow stood up. 'There's no good way of looking at this, Jess. I'm a liability.'

'Oh, I'm aware of that.' It was a quick comeback. Warlow was astonished to see the smile playing over her lips. When he didn't reciprocate, Jess added. 'Evan, be sensible. HIV is the last thing I frigging want. But you saved my life.'

Warlow sighed. He hadn't known what to expect from Jess. Horror, disgust even. But not this...defiance. 'I had to tell you,' He breathed deeply. 'Should have told you weeks ago.'

'Well, I'm glad you did.' Her eyes fell to his untouched coffee. 'Don't you like this blend. Guatemalan, apparently. Fruity with a touch of chocolate. At least that's what it said on the packet...'

Warlow shook his head. 'Why are you being so bloody calm about this?'

'You're worked up enough for both of us, don't you think?'

He looked up at the ceiling but found no solace there. 'It's all I've been thinking about for weeks. Months even. Ever since I found out I had it.'

Jess nodded. 'And all I've been thinking about is how dead I would have been if you hadn't turned up. Whatever comes next I can cope. And, if you do not want to say anything to the rest of the team, you don't have to. Who else knows?'

'Only Buchannan.'

Jess nodded. 'I won't tell anyone. It's up to you.'

Warlow snorted. 'My dirty little secret.'

'Ours now.' She grinned.

Warlow shook his head. 'I thought you'd be livid.'

'You thought wrong. Let's live with that and drink our coffee.' She lifted her cup. Warlow did the same. He sipped. It tasted wonderful. His heart was still running fast, but not pounding as it had been.

'How did Two-Shoes take it when you said you'd closed the case?'

Warlow rolled his eyes. 'Exactly as you'd expect. She pretended she was pleased. Lucky she was holding a ball-point and not a pencil because she'd have snapped the bugger in half. You could see it pissed her off. No case for the TV crew to follow. You injured. The team otherwise engaged and me away.'

'Away?'

'Oh, didn't I tell you? I spoke to Buchannan. There's a case they're struggling with up in the far reaches. North of Welshpool. I said I'd help.'

'Just you?'

He nodded. 'To start with. I might take Rhys to do a recce. Then I'll call everyone else up if needed.'

'I could work from home,' Jess offered.

Warlow finished his coffee, and for the first time in days, smiled. 'No, you're on sick leave. But I'll keep you in the loop.'

He picked up his keys and walked to the door, opened it, felt the Pembrokeshire breeze ruffle his hair.

Jess followed him. At the door, she said, 'Thanks for coming, Evan. For being honest. You look a lot better now than you did when you arrived.' Her grey eyes danced.

'I feel better.'

Jess leant in and kissed him on the cheek. 'There you go; double jeopardy.'

Warlow grimaced. 'What'll the neighbours think?'

Jess shrugged. 'They can lump it. It's not every day you get to thank the man who saved your life.'

Warlow gave her arm a squeeze and headed out into the day, relieved and ready for what the fickle world had to throw at him next.

THE END

FREE BOOK FOR YOU

Visit my website and join up to the Rhys Dylan VIP Reader's Club and get a FREE novella, *The Wolf Hunts Alone*, by visiting:

www.rhysdylan.com

You will also be the first to hear about new releases via the few but fun emails I'll send you. This includes a no spam promise from me and you can unsubscribe at any time.

ACKNOWLEDGMENTS

As with all writing endeavours, the existence of this novel depends upon me, the author, and a small army of 'others' who turn an idea into a reality. My wife, Eleri, who gives me the space to indulge my imagination and picks out my stupid mistakes. Sian Phillips (not the actress), Tim Barber and of course, Martin Davies. Thank you all for your help. Special mention goes to Ela, the dog, who drags me away from the writing cave and the computer for walks, rain or shine. Actually, she's a bit of a princess so the rain is a no-no. Good dog!

But my biggest thanks goes to you, lovely reader, for being there and actually reading this. It's great to have you along and I do appreciate you spending your time in joining me on this roller-caster ride with Evan and the rest of the team.

CAN YOU HELP?

With that in mind, and if you enjoyed it, I do have a favour to ask. Could you spare a moment to leave a review? A few words will do, but it's really the only way to help others like you discover the books. Probably the best way to help authors you like. Just visit my page on Amazon and leave a few words.

AUTHOR'S NOTE

Ice Cold Malice is a story that comes from my other life and the way that even doctors sometimes lose sight of what makes them who they are. Unfortunately, I have come across the odd Boscombe in my career. Or as near as damn it. They leave a mark, or is that a stain, on your mind. Best to get it all down on paper, I find. But then there is the chance to set it all on the wonderful Carmarthenshire coastline. That bit, at least, is all true, including the amazing Ginst Point. And as for Laugharne, you've got to go there to appreciate it.

Why the Black Beacons?

Spread over 500 square miles, the Brecon Beacons mountain range sits like a giant doorstop at the heads of the South Wales valleys. To the North and West, they nestle in the crook of the ancient kingdoms of Powys and Dyfed, stretching from the eastern borderlands to the wild western coast. Many of the mountain peaks in the range have names. Others are simply referred to as black. It is in this timeless landscape that the books are set.

I'm lucky enough to live in this neck of the woods

having moved here in the 1980s. It's an amazing part of the world, full of warm and wonderful people, wild coastlines, golden and craggy mountains. But like everywhere, even this little haven is not immune from the woes of the world. Those of you who've read The Wolf Hunts Alone will know exactly what I mean. And who knows what and who Warlow is going to come up against next! So once again, thank you for sparing your precious time on this new endeavour. I hope I'll get the chance to show you more of this part of the world and that it'll give you the urge to visit.

Not everyone here is a murderer. Not everyone…Cue tense music!

All the best, and see you all soon, Rhys.

READY FOR MORE?

DCI Evan Warlow and the team are back in…

SUFFER THE DEAD
Nothing bad ever happens in the countryside… right?

When a farmer and his son go missing whilst chasing rustlers, DCI Evan Warlow and his team are called in to investigate. Everything points to a botched raid by heartless thieves, but with no bodies, and little or no clues, the team quickly start chasing their tails.

The close knit community reels from the shock, but not everyone they come across is being entirely honest and it quickly transpires that under their prim and proper facades, everyone has secrets they are desperate to keep.

But even Warlow isn't prepared for the monstrous truth

when, like a rabid sheepdog, it finally sits up and bites him on the leg.

He's too busy trying not to get killed himself.

READ ON FOR A SAMPLE

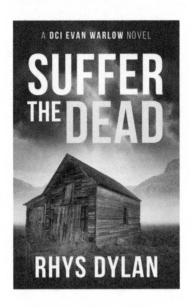

SUFFER THE DEAD

Police Community Support Officer Hana Prosser rarely drove this way to work. Still, these were not normal times. And though today's route was a detour from her usual commute, this was no early morning jaunt to Aldi.

Today she was on the clock five minutes after leaving home. She smiled. Conscientiousness could be a curse. No change there, then. And with that thought, the smile died. It was not the first time she'd driven these byways. This was her backyard. And the last time she'd been up here it had been to investigate a killing.

Her father, whose land she now skirted as she headed up towards the isolated Hermon Chapel on a rarely used lane, blamed the tourists. The price of milk, most of farming's woes, sheep on the road; he blamed tourists for more or less everything. Well, bloody tourists and their dogs. But then he had a special place in his farmer's black book for tourists and their dogs. His opinion was that the increase in sheep attacks – the 'killing' she'd previously investigated had been of three sheep – directly resulted from naïve people clamouring to own cuddly canines that quickly turned into raving beasts at the drop of an ewe's hat. The majority, in his not so humble opinion, had no clue about dog etiquette in the countryside.

And a dog could do a lot of lethal damage in a very short time faced with a flock of bleating sheep.

Despite all the signs her father, the other local farmers, and the local council had put up reminding people to keep their dogs on a leash, there'd been some nasty, atrocious incidents. Sheep terrified and mutilated, lambs slaughtered, dogs destroyed. No one wanted to see that, least of all Hana, who loved dogs and had a soft spot for sheep, stupid as they were.

Having been brought up on a farm with a flock of 700 scattered over 150 acres in this quiet corner of Powys close to the border with England, she knew all about the horrors that resulted from a dog attack. And now, as part of one of Dyfed-Powys Police Service's Rural Crime Teams, she also had to investigate these things.

But dogs were not the reason she was winding her way along the edge of the Berwyn Mountains in north-east Wales this cool morning. A call from an old school-friend first thing that morning had alerted her. The woman, mid-twenties like Hana and living in a house near St Cadwaladr's Church, heard the gunshots a little after 1am, she'd said. Probably nothing, but she thought someone ought to know.

Hana might have noted it down and written it off had she not taken a call from her sergeant in Rural Crime based in Newtown an hour ago. He'd rung to say he'd received a call from a fraught farmer's wife whose husband and son had gone out late the night before but had not returned.

'Gone out late means sniffing about for rustlers,' Sergeant 'Tomo' Thomas had muttered in the call Hana'd taken at 7.15am as she set up breakfast. Iestyn, her teacher husband, had still been in the shower, but Hana, disturbed already by her friend's earlier call, was in uniform and sipping her second coffee as she listened to Tomo's gripes. 'You know what these buggers are like. Probably met up with another lot and gone over for a quick whisky in a barn. They'll turn up in a minute, I daresay.'

She told him then about the gunshots.

Tomo didn't give it much thought. 'Yeah, well. Probably them taking a pot shot at a stray dog or a fox. Most of that lot are equal opportunity cullers.'

Hana pondered the "that lot" and wondered if Sergeant Thomas ever considered he might be putting his size eleven foot in it by referencing "that lot" in discussions with her since she was from "that lot" stock. She doubted it as Tomo was not known for his emotional intelligence. But he knew the patch and the sort of things the locals got up to having grown long in the tooth patrolling it. In that way, he was wise enough.

'Since you're up there, might as well check it all out. Any idea where the shots came from?' he'd asked.

Hana did have a rough idea. She knew how sounds travelled across the valleys and given where her friend lived, she'd worked out a rough area that might fit the bill. She'd started to explain but realised Tomo's attention span would not last the distance, so she'd shortened the answer to something simple. 'I'll pop up there now before I come to you.'

Tomo grunted his approval.

They were working out of Welshpool this week and her journey to work took about half an hour on a good day. Otherwise, the base was Newtown station. Only thirty miles but on these roads a good hour's journey if traffic, or the weather, was bad. Far more likely to be the latter than the former now that the bypass had opened, thank God.

The Rural team were carrying out traffic stops on forestry roads, targeting illegal use of off-road motorcycles as well as investigating two cases of animal theft in the surrounding areas. Rustling remained a real problem with gangs targeting lambs especially, as well as some premium cattle. But it was a big patch to cover, and they were thinly spread. Even so, the experiment with establishing a Rural Crime team a couple of years before seemed to pay off for the Dyfed-Powys service and it delighted Hana to be a part of it.

As soon as Tomo rang off, she'd stuck her head into the bathroom and kissed a naked Iestyn on the cheek with a playful grin before setting off. She'd toyed with asking her dad to come with her, for the company and because of his familiarity with the land, but he'd be busy with feeding now. Besides, this was police business.

She climbed north out of Llanrhaeadr towards the border with Gwynedd and, after a couple of miles, took a lane that did not appear on any Google map. She stopped at a gate and parked the car, frowning on seeing the gate unlatched and open. There were no sheep nearby but there were on the hillside not half a mile away. This gate should have been closed.

Looking south, she spied a cluster of houses where the friend who'd alerted her to the noise of the supposed shotgun lived. A cluster of five perched on the hillside, pale regular shapes in the broad sweep of the valley. Behind the houses the land rose again and Hana had concluded that with a north-easterly wind, noise would have carried from this direction.

She stood on the high ground, breathed in the air and looked out across the landscape. God's own country, as her dad would often describe this little corner of Powys. God's forsaken country as Sergeant Thomas preferred to describe it. Few tourists came this way even though she was not that far from Pistyll Rhaeadr, a 270-foot waterfall that attracted visitors from across the border and beyond.

But not this grey morning. A mist hung low, mercifully not low enough to obscure her friend's house, but blurring the line between hilltops and sky. These hills were flat-topped, but on a day like today, it would not be difficult to imagine they reached up into the clouds, like the bottom of a giant's staircase.

As her eyes swept across and down to where the land fell away, another open gate led to a small feed-shed. From where she stood, she couldn't make out if there were any vehicles parked behind it though it would be the only logical reason to leave the gates open.

Hana's Skoda had four-wheel-drive; even so the suspension bounced and squeaked as it navigated the rutted lane down towards the sheds. When she got to the bottom of the hill, she pulled up next to the crumbling walls of some old sheep pens and got out.

Spring had arrived, and the hedgerows were filling out. But the sun sulked in its blanket of grey and the chill wind spoke more of the end of winter than the beginnings of summer.

She could still see the tops of the houses on the other side of the valley. Noise would definitely carry up from here well enough.

Hana walked towards the building. The Randals, whose land this was, put a new steel roof on the sheds last year, but the wooden walls had gaps and cracks that allowed Hana a murky inside view when she put her eye up to them.

Empty.

But what she saw through the cracks was the shape of a vehicle on the other side of the building.

A vague apprehension gnawed at her insides. Hana walked around to find a Land Rover Defender with two of its doors open but no sign of driver or passenger. She scanned the number plate. Definitely the Randals. She called out their names.

'Hello? Aeron? Jo?'

No one answered. All she heard was the moaning of the wind rising and falling through the gaps in the feed-shed walls.

Even though she was warm in her thick coat, she shivered.

Slowly, and for some reason trying to make as little noise as possible, Hana crept around to the shed doors. They were big and heavy and one of them stood open to reveal the shadow-filled dark space beyond. Spilled silage from the plastic-coated bales stacked at the rear littered the floor. Nothing unusual in that. She took all of this in within seconds before her darting glance focused on the other, closed half of the doors.

The half with two dark-red smears spattered over the bleached wood. One at about chest height that had run down towards the floor. The other, higher by a foot or two. This one with something lighter at the centre of the darker smudge.

Something still glistening…

Available Now

Made in the USA
Middletown, DE
27 July 2024